S0-DVG-776

Big Book of Everything for Kindergarten

Introduction

Instructional Fair's *Big Book of Everything for Kindergarten* has been designed to provide kindergarten teachers with an enormous amount of activities to supplement their programs in eight major subject areas (music, art, cooking, language arts, math, science, social studies, physical fitness and human development).

The guided discovery activities in this book are designed to be enjoyable yet challenging for students at this level. The goal is to have the children learn through exploration and play and the activities are aimed at whole body experience. It is through these activities that each child's mental, physical and social capacities are challenged.

The activities also provide opportunities for individualized, small and large group participation.

Each of the eight chapters in this book begins with a short introduction of the subject and a discussion of the activities represented in the chapter. Each chapter also has several concluding pages of bulletin board ideas.

Each activity includes:

- **Objective(s)**—the general learning goal of the activity

- **Materials** – a list of everything needed for the activity

- **Directions**—exact instructions for conducting activities

Also included as part of many activities are extensions. These are ideas for additional activities which complement the activity presented.

It is recommended that you read through the introduction of each chapter first, then search through the activities in each chapter to give yourself an overview of the materials and activities available to you and the children. The chapters are not ordered thematically. If your curriculum is organized around themes or units, you may wish to select activities from several chapters that relate to particular themes.

A great way to keep parents involved in the children's activities is to send home the children's work on a regular basis. Frequently changing the bulletin boards using the suggestions in this book will also help keep parents informed.

Finally, it is hoped that this book can complement your existing program by supplying you with new ideas and a springboard for developing ideas of your own.

Music Activities

This chapter is dedicated to teaching children about musical instruments, their classification, sounds and styles. It also serves to teach children about music and movement. Whereas the physical education chapter in this book focuses most of its attention on the physical movements, this chapter mainly deals with the understanding and utilization of musical instruments and the sounds they make.

Many of the activities in this chapter involve the children making their own instruments. The goal is to have the children become confident in their musical skills by removing the intimidation and fear of expensive and often awkward instruments.

As in other areas, the music activities presented in this chapter require active, hands-on involvement. Every one of the body senses will be used in almost all the activities. This ensures a meaningful experience for all who participate.

Oatmeal Box Drums

Objective: To create a percussion instrument for rhythm and skill development

Materials: yarn, glue, construction paper, scissors, empty oatmeal boxes, music player, music, chopsticks

Directions: Have each child bring an empty oatmeal box from home. Explain that they are going to make a musical instrument using the box. Have them decorate everything but the top and bottom of the carton using yarn, construction paper and any other scraps. When the cartons are decorated and have dried, give each child a set of chopsticks. Play some music and ask the children to beat their drums in time with the music.

Cardboard Kazoo

Objective: To make a musical wind instrument

Materials: one paper towel tube per student, rubber bands, wax paper, hole punch, kazoo

Directions: Tell the children that they are going to make a wind instrument of their own. Show the children a kazoo. Tell them that that the instrument they are going to make resembles a kazoo. Have them follow the directions below for assembly.

1. Have the children punch a hole in one end of their cardboard tube.

2. Show the children how to attach the wax paper to the end of the tube opposite the hole.

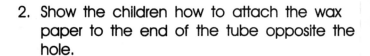

3. Let the children use a rubber band to wrap around the wax paper and tube to keep the wax paper in place.

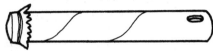

4. Have them hum into the open end of the tube.

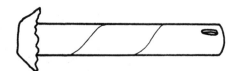

4

Wooden String Instruments

Objective: To make a string instrument

Materials: one 12" x 3" strip of plywood per child, rubber bands of varying widths, hammer, nails, acrylic paint, paintbrushes, sandpaper, string instruments (if possible)

Directions: Have a hardware store cut a twelve by three inch strip of plywood for each child. Tell the children that they are going to make a string instrument. Discuss some string instruments the children are familiar with and show them some if they are available. Let the children paint their strips of wood using acrylic paint. When the paint is dry, give each child a small piece of sandpaper to use to sand his/her strip. Help the children hammer three nails in a row on each side of the strip. Have the children loop three different widths of rubber bands around the nails. (See assembly illustrations below.) Have the children explore the different sound each rubber band makes when it is pulled, stroked or picked.

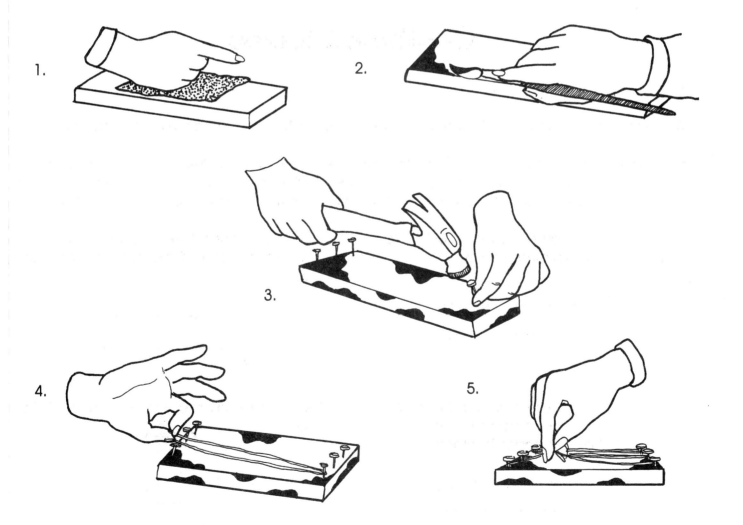

Tree Gong

Objective: To make gong sound instruments

Materials: string, flower pots, hub caps, kitchen metal cooking pot, wooden spoon, chopsticks, empty coffee cans, small hand broom

Directions: Tie a series of things that the children can gong to a tree. Tie some of the things mentioned above from string. Get the children to experiment with different striking tools (wooden spoon, chopsticks, small hand broom, etc.) and different size gongs. Discuss the differences.

Box Guitars

Objective: To make a guitar

Materials: scissors, one shoe box with lid per child, 5 rubber bands of varying thicknesses per child, paint, paintbrushes

Directions: Have the children bring an old shoe box from home. Help the children cut a four inch circle in the top of a shoe box lid. Let the children paint their guitar box using tempera paints. When the paint is dry, have the children stretch five rubber bands around the box and hole opening. Let the children strum a tune. Experiment with the high and low sounds of varying thicknesses of rubber bands.

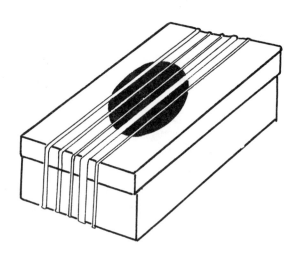

Plectrum

Objective: To make a plectrum to use on a string instrument

Materials: laminating paper, posterboard, scissors, plectrum pattern below, markers

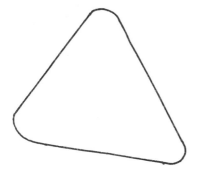

Directions: Refer back to making the box guitar (page 6). Give each child a copy of the plectrum pattern. Have the children guess its purpose in relation to string instruments. Let the children color their cutouts and help them to laminate the plectrums. Let students experiment with them on their children's box guitars.

Homemade Panpipe

Objective: To make a wind instrument that resembles a panpipe

Materials: straws, scissors, masking tape, a panpipe if available, sewing needle

Directions: Talk about wind instruments with the children. Show them a real panpipe if you have one available or see if you can find some pictures of one to show the children. Tell the children that you are going to help them make their own panpipe. For each child, cut straws in the following lengths: 6 1/2", 6", 5 1/2", 4 1/2", 4",3 1/2", 3"

Give each child a set of the straws. Have the children arrange their straws from longest to shortest. They should place them in a row with the bottoms even. Help each child tape his/her straws together to form a panpipe. (See illustration.) Next, using a sewing needle, prick a hole in the bottom end of each of the straws. Have the children blow through the straws as if they were playing a panpipe.

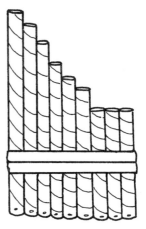

Maracas

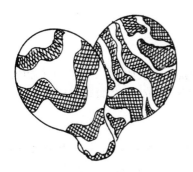

Objective: To make a maraca

Materials: old light bulbs, one-inch pre-cut strips of newspaper, paper towels, wheat paste, water, mixing bowls, acrylic paint, paintbrushes, shellac

Directions: Bring a maraca to class and tell the children that they will each be making a maraca. Have each child bring an old light bulb to school. Prepare a work table for this project. On the table, set out the following: pre-cut, one inch, strips of newspaper, paper towels and several mixing bowls filled with wheat paste thinned to the consistency of cream. (Be sure to have the children wear smocks for this activity.) Follow the directions below.

1. Have the children dip strips of newspaper into the paste and cover their old light bulb so that none of the bulb is visible.

2. Next, they should wrap a final layer of paper towel around the bulb and smooth all the lumps out of the paper. The bulb should be saturated with paste.

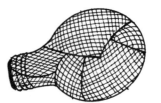

3. Once the paper dries and hardens, have the children break the bulb inside by hitting it gently on a table.

4. Let the children paint their new maracas with bright colors of acrylic paint and spray with shellac when they are dry. Encourage the children to use their maracas in a dance.

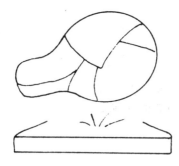

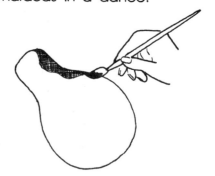

African Rain Sticks

Objective: To make a rain stick

Materials: uncooked rice, empty wrapping paper tubes, waxed paper, rubber bands, 3" pre-cut squares of tissue paper, water, glue, bowls, large paintbrushes, large sandwich toothpicks

Directions: Have each child bring a wrapping paper tube from home. Tell the children that they are going to be making an African rain stick instrument using the tube. On a work table, set out diluted white glue in bowls and large paintbrushes. Have the children follow the directions below.

1. Have the children paint squares of tissue paper onto their wrapping paper tubes using diluted white glue. They should cover the entire tube overlapping the tissue paper till none of the tube is showing.

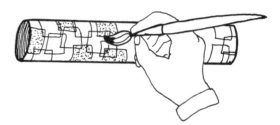

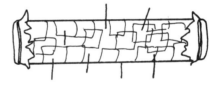

2. Once dry, have the children use rubber bands to cover the open ends of the tube with wax paper squares.

3. Help the children poke seven or eight large sandwich toothpicks into their tube at various points.

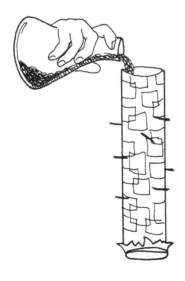

4. Tell the children to remove the wax paper from one end of the tube. Help the children pour rice into the tube.

5. Once the rice is in the tube, cover the end of the tube and let the children experiment with the sounds of the rice pouring over the toothpicks while it runs from one end of the tube to the other.

Sound Shakers

Objectives: To make a set of sound shakers and to discriminate between varying volumes of sound

Materials: colored markers, empty toilet paper tubes, wax paper, posterboard, rubber bands, rice, pebbles, sand, dry macaroni noodles

Directions: Make sets of four sound shakers by following the steps below.

1. Use wax paper and rubber bands to cover one end of an empty toilet paper tube.

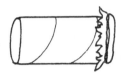

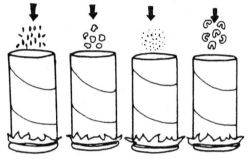

3. Cover the tops of the shakers using wax paper and rubber bands.

2. Fill each shaker with a different product: rice, sand, pebbles, dry macaroni noodles.

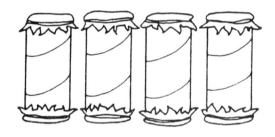

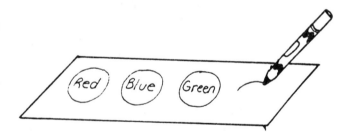

4. Draw four, 2" circles on a strip of posterboard. Each circle should be one of the following colors: blue, green, red, yellow.

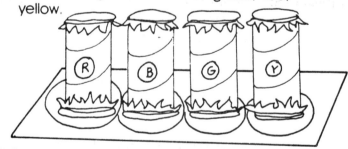

5. The order of the colored circles on the posterboard should be the children's guide to matching loudest to softest shakers. Sit the shakers on the posterboard circles from loudest to softest. Color a tiny dot on each toilet paper roll to match the appropriate color of circle it is sitting on. Make the activity available for the children's use. Tell them they can check their work by matching the colors, but encourage them not to look at the colors first.

Water Sounds

Objective: To explore the different sounds made by bottles containing varying amounts of water

Materials: 4 glass bottles, pitcher of water, funnel, wooden chopsticks

Directions: Fill a large pitcher of water. Using a funnel, have the children help you fill four bottles with water. Each bottle should be filled to a different level than the others. Explain to the children that there are high and low sounds in music. Ask them to tell you which bottle, when tapped with wooden chopsticks, made either a high or low sound. Then, demonstrate how to blow across the top of the bottles. Ask the children which whistle sound was high or low. Give the children a chance to experiment with the bottles by themselves.

High/Low Singing

Objective: To discriminate between high and low sounds

Materials: piano or keyboard

Directions: Tell the children that you are going to play some high and some low notes on the piano. Ask the children to describe the feelings the music gives them. When the children hear high notes, tell them you would like them to jump up and act happy and excited. When they hear you play low notes, ask them to crouch down and make scary faces. This is an enjoyable exercise around Halloween time.

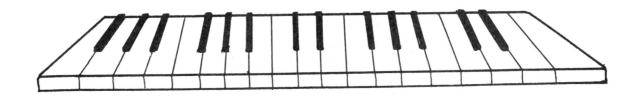

Dances With Dowels

Objectives: To make and use decorative flags for dancing

Materials: one 1/2" 2 foot long dowels per child, crepe paper streamers, masking tape, yellow or orange caution tape, lively music, music player

Directions: Tell the children that they are going to be making flags for dancing. Give each child a one-half inch wide dowel that is approximately two feet long. Let them tape four or five crepe paper streamers to one end of the dowel. The fluorescent colored caution tape makes an especially fun dowel wrap. Let the children wrap the dowel, taping the ends with masking tape. Play some lively music and encourage the children to dance moving their flags to the music. Be certain to remind the children repeatedly to exercise caution when swinging their flags.

Old MacDonald Had a Band

Objectives: To minimize the intimidation of performing in front of others and to practice playing new instruments in front of others

Materials: laminating paper, darkroom gloves, Velcro, markers, musical instruments, animal patterns (pgs. 13 and 14), crayons

Directions: Use the animal patterns to make character gloves for music time. To do this, cut out the patterns and color them. Laminate them and attach a side of Velcro to the center back of each animal. On the top of darkroom gloves, attach the opposite side of the Velcro. The children should place the glove on their hand and attach the desired animal to it. Begin music time by telling the children that they are going to be a part of Old MacDonald's Band. Distribute an instrument to each child. Ask the children to join you singing some songs and playing their instruments. Rotate the instruments between the children frequently.

Farm Animal Cutouts

Farm Animal Cutouts

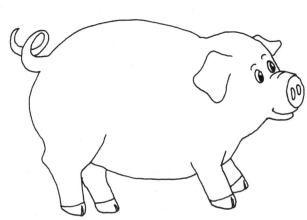

14

Musical Chair Fun

Objectives: To make music and to build listening skills

Materials: chairs, drum, blindfold

Directions: Tell the children that they are going to play musical chairs but in a new way. Instead of listening for pre-recorded music to stop, they are going to be waiting for one of their friends to stop beating on a drum. To play the game, place chairs (one chair short of the number of players in the group) back to back, in a row. Then, blindfold one child who is going to beat the drum. When the drummer stops beating the players must seek and sit in an empty chair. The child left without a seat must wait till the end of the game to join in again. Remove a chair each round till there is only one chair left. The winner is the child seated first when the beating of the drum stops.

• •

Balance to the Beat

Objective: To respond physically to different music tempos

Materials: masking tape, music with different tempos, balance beam

Directions: Using colored or masking tape, make a large oval track around the classroom. Move the furniture out of the way. Place a balance beam along one part of the line. Have the children skip, bounce, jump, clap, stomp their feet, walk, skate, etc. to the different tempos of music being supplied. When a child gets to the balance beam, he/she must walk along it and resume the activity taking place. If they feel confident of their balance skills, encourage them to try to carry out the skills while on the balance beam. Steve Millang and Greg Scelsa's song, *Listen and Move*, from the album entitled *We All Live Together*, is a great resource for this activity. The singers suggest the movement to make to match the tempo. Remind the children to stay on the masking tape line at all times. Discourage children from passing one another while moving around the oval. For added fun, give each child a flat, wicker paper plate holder to balance on his/her head. Happy balancing!

Suggested Music: *Learning Basic Skills Through Music* by Hap Palmer

Conducting An Orchestra

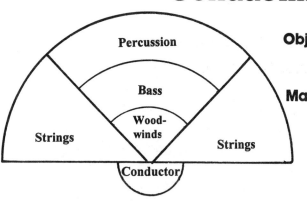

Objective: To recognize the significance of the role of the conductor of an orchestra

Materials: chairs, large open space, dowel, podium, music

Directions: Direct the children as they place their chairs in a semicircle, facing the front of the classroom. Put a podium at the front of the room. Explain to the children that this is like arranging the seating for an orchestra. Then, have the children take a seat. Discuss what instrument each child might be playing in the orchestra based on where he/she is sitting. Explain that you are going to pretend to be the conductor of the orchestra. Tell the children to follow your hand and dowel gestures while singing. If the conductor's guide (dowel) moves very quickly, so should the tempo of the song. If the conductor moves his/her guide very slowly, the musicians must also play much slower. Let the children pretend they are playing in an orchestra. Sing your favorite songs so that the children do not have to recall lyrics and so that they can focus on the conductor's actions.

Musical Match-Up

Objective: To match similar musical instruments according to their classification as wind, percussion, string and electronic

Materials: pictures of instruments or actual ones if available, copies of activity page 17, pencils

Directions: Discuss the similarities among the different classifications of instruments. Group pictures of instruments according to category. Give each child a copy of the activity, "Musical Match-Up."

Musical Match-Up

Draw a line to match the musical instruments that belong to the same musical category (i.e. wind, percussion, string, electronic).

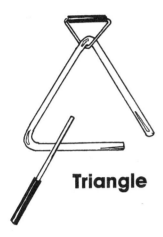

Triangle

Harp

Violin

Harmonica

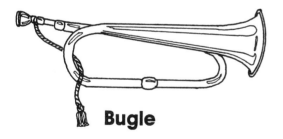

Bugle

Tambourine

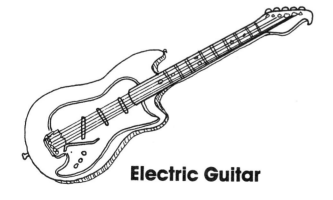

Electric Guitar

Synthesizer

Music Player Operation

Objective: To teach the children how to operate music players properly

Materials: radio, tape recorder, microphone, record player, compact disc player, cassette tapes, record albums, compact discs

Directions: Set the five music players mentioned above on a table. Demonstrate how to operate each one (i.e. how to turn each player on and off, insert the music cartridge into the correct spot, care for the players, etc.) Discuss with the children the function of each music player. Give the children the opportunity to manipulate them and be certain to provide close supervision.

Styles of Music

A, B, C...D...E...
F, G, H...I...J...
K, L, M...N...O...

Objective: To discover the many styles of music

Materials: examples of the following types of music: rap, jazz, rock, classical

Directions: Play the various music styles mentioned above. Let the children listen and give their opinions of what they are listening to. Break the class into small groups and let the children choose their favorite style of music to share with the whole class. (For example, the children could sing the "Alphabet Song" to different music.)

Extension: Consider looking at music from various cultures (i.e. Africa, Japan, Hawaii, Jamaica, etc.)

Nursing Home Field Trip

Objective: To visit a local nursing home and share some music

Materials: several complementary musical instruments (They could be the homemade instruments.), memorized songs, paper, markers

Directions: Locate a nursing home near the school and arrange to visit it to share some music. Help the children learn three or four songs. Add some instruments and some dance movements to the performance. Practice several times stressing to the children how important it is to feel confident about the performance before actually getting up in front of an audience. Talk about being nervous, manners and most of all the happiness they would be bringing to the elderly people. Have the children make cards for their elderly friends. Help them write messages in their cards. If the nursing home has its own music program, see if you can join them.

Civic Arts Center Field Trip

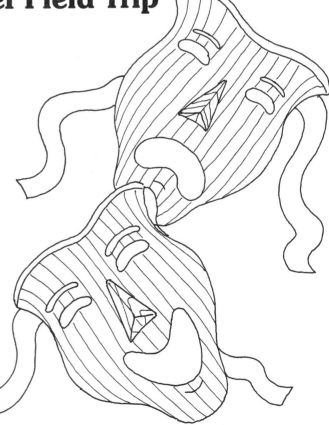

Objective: To plan a field trip to the local civic arts center

Materials: pre-paid tickets, adult volunteers

Directions: It seems as though performing arts centers are springing up across the country. The popularity of children's music concerts has also increased. Check your closest opportunity and see if there are any age-appropriate performances for the children. Look for descriptions of shows that discuss audience participation. This field trip should be arranged well in advance in order to get seating together and ample adult volunteers. The holidays are ideal times for planning this kind of trip.

Musical Notes

Objectives: To decorate the classroom and to introduce the concept of musical notes

Materials: individual classroom photographs of each child, black construction paper, note pattern, tape, stapler, light colored paper

Directions: Cover the bulletin board with light colored paper. Using a marker, draw a music bar across the bulletin board. Cut out the note pattern on page 22. Use the pattern to cut one note per child out of black construction paper. Staple the notes to the bulletin board. Tape a child's photograph to each note. Title the bulletin board, "Special Musical Notes." Introduce the children to the concept of notes in music but keep it simple.

Special Musical Notes

Favorite Finger Plays

Bulletin Board

Objectives: To decorate the classroom and provide a variety of finger plays

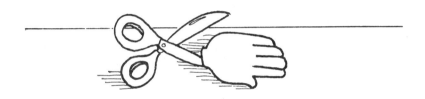

The Itsy Bitsy Spider

The Itsy Bitsy Spider
went up the water spout
Down came the rain
and washed the spider out.
Out came the sun
and dried up all the rain
And the Itsy Bitsy Spider
Went up the spout again.

Materials: construction paper, index cards, handprint pattern on page 22, finger plays, scissors

Directions: Give each child an index card to take home. Tell the children that the index cards need to have their favorite finger play printed on it. Obviously, this requires parent involvement. Once the children return their index cards, display them on a bulletin board. Cover a bulletin board with a solid color of paper. Use the handprint pattern as a guide to cut out handprints from construction paper. Staple the handprints on the bulletin board and pin one of the children's index cards on each hand. Each day, choose one child's favorite finger play to read. Let the child who brought the finger play lead the group if he/she feels confident.

Musical Note Pattern

Handprint Pattern

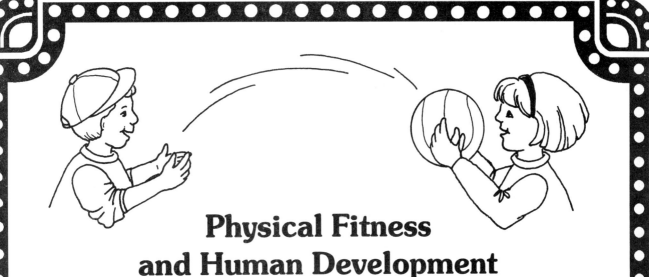

Physical Fitness and Human Development

The activities in this chapter focus on the development of motor skills, health fitness and nutritional knowledge, handicapped awareness and whole body awareness. In this chapter, learning is doing!

Motor skill development is an integral part of every activity in this chapter. There are, however, very specific activities designed to develop very specific skills. These motor skills include throwing, catching, balancing, running, striking, dodging, jumping, galloping, dribbling and kicking. The activity skills are presented in the order in which they should be introduced. Many motor skills are cumulative.

Handicap awareness activities in this chapter are aimed at having the children relate to the physical challenges of handicapped people. To relate to handicap challenges, the children assume the handicap in many of the activities. Seeing and feeling is easiest for believing.

Health fitness and nutritional knowledge are developed through games like Health Food Bingo and the making of a food pyramid. The activities teach the children that taking care of the body on the inside allows the whole body to function at its best.

Balloon Throw

Objective: To introduce children to the motion of throwing

Materials: chalk, inflated balloons

Directions: Have the children stand behind a chalk line. See how far each child can throw the inflated balloon. Mark the spot where the balloon touches the floor with the child's initials. Each child should aim to beat his/her own personal best throw.

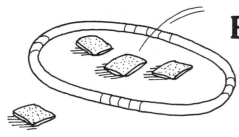

Beanbag Toss

Objectives: To practice the throwing motion and to develop some accuracy

Materials: beanbags, hula hoops

Directions: Place a hula hoop in the center of the room. Have the children form a large circle around it. Have the children take turns throwing a beanbag from the circle's edge to the center of the hula hoop. Encourage the children to cheer for each other as each child attempts to toss the beanbag into the hula hoop. See how many beanbags the whole class can get into the hula hoop in one rotation around the circle.

Bushel Basket Bodies

Objective: To develop the throwing motion

Materials: small to medium size rubber balls

Directions: Have children stand in two lines facing one another. Have them start by standing quite close. The children receiving the toss should form a bushel basket shape with their arms. The children tossing the balls should try to throw the balls into the bushel baskets. If the child throwing the ball manages to get the ball through the bushel basket, he/she and his/her partner should take a step apart. See which pair can toss the farthest if you decide to play for a winner.

Shadow Toss

Objectives: To practice throwing and to develop accuracy

Materials: 2 beanbags

Directions: Line children up in rows as though they are going to run a relay. The first child in each row stands facing the front of his/her line about 15 - 20 feet away. The next child in the line tosses a beanbag at his/her teammate's shadow. Once he/she has hit the shadow, the child must go to the end of the line and sit on the ground. The team with all its members sitting first is the winner.

The Challenging Toss

Objectives: To practice throwing and to build eye-hand coordination

Materials: hula hoop, small balls or beanbags

Directions: Have children line up in two rows facing one another. The children should be approximately 18 feet apart. Give each child in one row a ball or beanbag to use for tossing. Roll a hula hoop down the middle of the rows. The row with the children holding the objects should try to throw their objects through the hula hoop as it is moving. The children that were not tossing should count the number of objects that go through the hoop and then collect the objects. Alternate the rows of throwing and receiving teams.

Snowball Toss

Objective: To develop throwing skills

Materials: snow, plastic containers of various sizes

Directions: Have the children make a large pile of snowballs. Place containers in the snow and label them with a point value. The larger the container, the less the point value. Using your feet, stomp a throwing line in the snow. Have children take turns throwing the balls into the containers to score points. Have the children focus on the throw as opposed to the point value. Try underhand, overhand, high, low and blindfolded throws for new challenges.

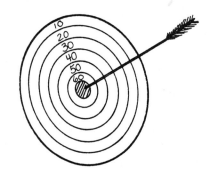

Target Toss

Objective: To develop accuracy in the skill of throwing

Materials: all different kinds of balls, hard cardboard, rope, a tree, scissors

Directions: Cut a 2 1/2-foot diameter circle out of hard cardboard. Cut a 2-foot diameter hole in the center of the circle. This is the target. Tie a rope around the circle and through the target. Attach the other end of the rope to a tree or post. Once the target is hung, have the children line up behind a designated throwing line. Using a variety of balls, have the children keep count of how many balls they throw that make it through the target. Give each child five throws.

Answer the Call, Catch the Ball!

Objective: To develop catching skills in a playful manner

Materials: chalk, basketball or similar size rubber ball

Directions: Divide the children into groups of 6 to 8 players. Using chalk, draw a medium size circle for each group. One player must stand in the center of the circle while the others stand around the edge of the circle. The child in the center must throw the ball straight up into the air. The ball must land in the circle. Before the ball lands, the thrower must call out the name of a player on his/her circle's edge. That player must catch the ball after it has bounced only one time. If the ball is caught after the first bounce, the catcher becomes the thrower, and the cycle begins again.

Color Catch

Objective: To build catching skills and other basic movement skills

Materials: colored labels (adhesive or homemade), basketball or similar size rubber ball

Directions: Give each child a colored label before starting this game. Spread children out along a wall or large open space. Give commands for a color (i.e. Reds, jump 2 steps to the left. Yellows, skip in a circle). Toss the ball towards the children and call out the color wanted to catch the ball.

Fruit and Veggie Catch

Objective: To practice catching and throwing skills

Materials: beanbag or small soft ball

Directions: Have one child stand in the middle of a circle of sitting children. The child standing should toss a beanbag or soft ball to a child sitting in the circle. The child receiving the toss must call out a fruit or vegetable name, not used in the game yet, before catching the ball/beanbag. If the child catches the ball/beanbag and names a fruit or vegetable in time, that player may choose to give the throwing object back or decide to be the tosser.

Tennis With a Twist

Objective: To practice catching skills using a tennis ball

Materials: flat concrete surface, chalk, tennis balls

Directions: Divide the class into pairs. Designate a play area for each pair. The play area should consist of a moderate size rectangle with a line drawn through the center. (See diagram.) One player serves the tennis ball. (This means that he/she throws the ball so that it bounces once on his/her side and once on the opponent's side.) The line acts as the net in tennis. If the receiving player catches the ball after a single bounce on both sides of the court, then he/she serves the ball. If the receiving player does not catch the ball, then the serving player gets a point. If the serving player does not make a good serve, he/she must lose the serve. Play the game until one person in the pair scores 10 points.

Parachute Catch

Objectives: To develop eye-hand coordination for catching and to practice large group cooperation skills

Materials: parachutes or large sheets, rubber balls

Directions: Divide the class into groups of about ten children. Give each group a parachute or large sheet. Have the children grab onto a portion of the parachute. Place a ball in the center of the parachute and on the count of three, have the children pull the parachute taut. The ball should go into the air. The children should try to catch the ball with the parachute as well. It might take some teamwork in order for the children to get to the place where the ball is landing. The higher the ball is projected into the air, the more precision is needed to catch the ball.

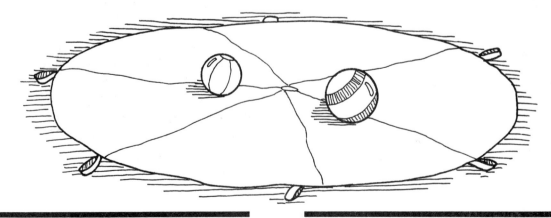

Animal Dance

Objective: To make create movements using full body action

Directions: Have the children dramatize the movements of various animals.   Have the children chant the verse below while they act out the movements.   Remove the underlined words and insert your own choice of animal.   Try bears, cats, mice, dogs, lions, giraffes and whales.

Elephant, elephant
I'd like to see,
You dance for me.

Music Movement

Objective: To introduce full body movement through music

Materials: music player, music

Directions: Clear a large area and have the children find their own space in that area. Encourage the children to listen to the music and find movements that fit the rhythm of the music.   Before trying this activity, you may want to find music that encourages movements like skating, hopping, running, crawling, rolling, etc.   If the children cannot discover their own creative movements to match the music, give some verbal association clues.   These clues might include the above mentioned actions.

Streamer Dances

Objective: To practice dance movements using homemade streamers

Materials: 2" wide party ribbon, newspaper, duct tape, music

Directions: Make streamers as follows:

1. Roll a section of newspaper into a pipe form and wrap it with duct tape.

2. Cut 10 strips of 2" wide party ribbon about 2' long and attach them to the end of the pipe using duct tape.

3. Wrap a long strip of ribbon over the duct tape pipe and tape the ends in place. Use a few extra pieces of tape for reinforcement if necessary.

4. Play music and have the children dance and use their streamers to enhance their dance.

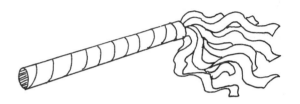

The Elephant Move

Objective: To give children the opportunity to use their entire bodies for movement and expression

Materials: "Learning Basic Skills Through Music" by Hap Palmer, music player, "The Elephant Song".

Directions: Have the children gather around at circle time and choose one child to be the leader. The other children must follow the leader's movements. Play "The Elephant Song" for the children. Explain to the children that as the story becomes more frightening for the old elephant, his pace picks up. The leader should follow the elephant's pace. Tell the children to listen very carefully to the story being told through the music.

The Music Freeze

Objective: To develop whole body movement

Materials: music player, music

Directions: Have the children find their own space in an open area. When the music starts, allow the children to move to the music. Be sure to use music that has different speeds and tempos. When the music stops, the children must do the same. Children love this game especially when it is played with fun music.

· ·

Cheer, Cheer, Cheer

Objective: To use full body movement to create a cheer

Directions: Have the children practice basic actions like jumping, twirling, leaping, bending and vaulting. Encourage the children to create a movement for a cheer for the class. Cheers could be action, appreciation, victory, comical, etc. Perform the cheer for the rest of the school at an assembly or special event time. Example: Mr. Smith's class is so cool, We're the greatest in our school!

Strike Ball

Objective: To develop accuracy in striking movements

Materials: a soft rubber ball, chalk

Directions: Draw a circle about two feet in diameter on the playing field. Have all the children sit in a large circle around the small chalk circle. Have one person stand in the center of the small chalk circle. That person is not allowed to step out of the circle. The other children use their fists to strike a soft rubber ball towards the person standing in the small circle. Wherever the ball heads, the person receiving the ball must strike the ball with the intent to hit the person in the center circle. Whoever strikes the ball and touches the person in the center gets to take a turn being the center person. Try to keep the game moving fast!

Putt Putt the Fun Way

Objective: To develop striking skills with accuracy

Materials: yardsticks, dry sponges, rubber bands, empty yogurt containers, Ping-Pong balls

Directions:
1. Help each child make his/her own golf club by attaching a sponge to the end of a yardstick using rubber bands.

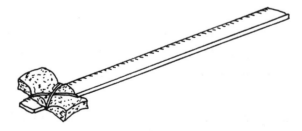

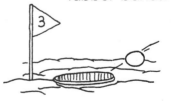

2. Set up a golf course by placing empty yogurt containers into the ground. Be sure the top of the containers are flush with the ground. Mark starting points for each hole and place obstacles (toys, boots, milk cartons etc.) on the course for added fun.

     32

Broom Ball

Objective: To develop the striking motion using a broom

Materials: brooms, large rubber balls, boxes or buckets

Directions: Provide each child with a broom. Divide the class into two teams. Each team must try to sweep the large rubber ball into the bucket or large box on the opposite side of the field. Use chalk or pylons to mark the field boundaries. The ball must not be contacted by hand or foot or the opposing team gets the ball. The team that sweeps the ball into its opponent's box/bucket the most is the winning team.

Poker Golf Ball

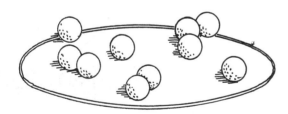

Objective: To develop striking skills with accuracy

Materials: golf balls, wooden spoons, chalk, markers

Directions: Using chalk, draw a circle about three feet in diameter on the concrete. Using markers, have each child decorate a golf ball and write his/her initials on it. Place ten golf balls in the center of the circle. From a designated starting point, the first player uses a wooden spoon to strike his/her personal golf ball towards the balls in the center of the circle. If the player knocks a white golf ball out of the circle, he/she may take his/her personal golf ball back to start and try again. When the player fails to knock a white golf ball from the circle (or if he/she has knocked all 10 balls from the circle), he/she loses his/her turn and the next player begins. The player who knocks the most golf balls from the center of the circle on his/her turn is the winner.

Ruler Run

Objective: To develop running skills

Materials: at least one ruler per player

Directions: Mark two lines on opposite sides of a playing field. Divide the class into two teams. Each team must form a row behind the same line on the playing field. On the opposite line of the playing field scatter rulers. On a signal, each player must run and carry back one ruler for his/her team's pile. Remind students to remain in their team row and to wait until their teammate returns before running to get the ruler. Have each child place his/her ruler in a pile by his/her row. Let the game last for approximately one minute. Then, stop and count which team has the most rulers in its pile when time is called. Replay.

• •

Weaving Run

Objective: To develop running skills

Directions: Divide the class into two equal teams. Each team should form a circle, leaving space between each player. Number the children in each circle consecutively. When the signal is given, Player No. 1 in each circle begins running and weaving in and out of the players in his/her circle. When Player No. 1 returns to his/her space and sits down, Player No. 2 repeats the weaving process. The game continues until the entire circle is sitting. The team with all the players sitting down first is the winner. Remind children to keep their hands in their laps and their feet crossed so that they do not get stepped on by the weavers.

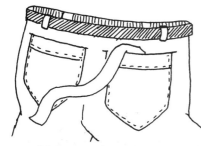

Tail Tag

Objective: To develop running skills

Materials: 2-inch wide ribbon

Directions: Give each child an 18" strip of ribbon. Have the children tuck the ribbon into the back of their pants or into a rear pocket. One child is designated "It." "It" must try to tag the players by removing their tails. Once a player has his/her tail removed, he/she must join "It" and catch the remaining players. A fun variation of this game might be to have the players pretend that they are animals with tails. Instead of running, they might act out the animal they have chosen to impersonate.

Name Tag

Objective: To develop running skills

Directions: Another variation of tag is to have the children contain themselves to a specific playing area. "It" runs after the players. To avoid being tagged, a player can drop to a sitting position and call out the name of a classmate in the group who has not yet been tagged. That player is safe as long as he/she has sat down and has called out a player's name before "It" has tagged him/her. The game becomes more challenging as the number of players left to be tagged decreases.

Squeeze Play

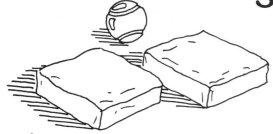

Objective: To practice running and baseball skills

Materials: a tennis ball or small softball, 2 cardboard bases

Directions: Set up two cardboard bases about eight to ten feet apart. Two players will be fielders and one player will be the runner. The runner will start out on one base. The two fielders will toss a tennis ball back and forth. The runner will try to steal a base while the fielders try to tag the runner with the tennis ball. Remind the runner that it is easiest to steal a base when the fielder closest to him/her has just thrown the ball.

Going Fishing

Objective: To develop galloping skills

Materials: music player, music

Directions: Have two players join hands and make an arch. These players form the net. Have the children gallop around in a circle to music, galloping under the arch as they come to it. These players are the fish. When the music stops, the net (arch) closes and anyone in it is caught. The player caught sits out of the circle until another player is caught and then they form an additional net. The game continues until all the players are nets and one fish is left.

• •

Horsing Around

Objective: To develop galloping skills

Directions: Have the children sit in a circle. Chose one person to be "It." As "It" gallops around the circle, he/she taps the head of a player and says, "Giddy up!" The seated player then rises and follows "It." They gallop around the circle until five players have been tapped by "It" and are following "It." Then, "It" stops and calls out, "Watering hole." All the children should run back to their places and sit down. The player seated first is "It" for the next round.

Galloping Ponies

Objective: To make and utilize a play pony to develop galloping skills

Materials: paper lunch bags, newspaper, construction paper, yarn, markers, empty fabric rolls, tape, glue, scissors

Directions:

1. Have the children fill a brown paper lunch bag with crumpled newspaper

2. Next, they decorate their bag with the above mentioned items to make a pony. Remind them to make a mane and ears.

3. Tape the base of the bag to one end of an empty fabric roll.

4. Have the children use the ponies to play galloping games

Blind Dribbling

Objective: To develop simple basketball dribbling skills

Materials: basketballs

Directions: Have the children practice the skill of dribbling. Explain how the bouncing must be continuous. After they have developed some confidence in their new skill, try blindfolding a few children. This movement helps the children feel the rhythmic motion of the skill. Remind children to use one hand to dribble once they feel confident with the bouncing skill.

Bounce Scoop

Objectives: To practice catching and bouncing and to develop eye-hand coordination

Materials: plastic milk cartons, scissors, small rubber balls

Directions: Cut plastic milk cartons in half. Give each child a half of a milk carton and a small rubber ball. Have the children practice bouncing the rubber ball with one hand and using the scoop to catch the ball with the other hand. Call out a number. The children should let their ball bounce the number of times that was called. Then, the players must use their scoop to catch the ball.

Four-Square

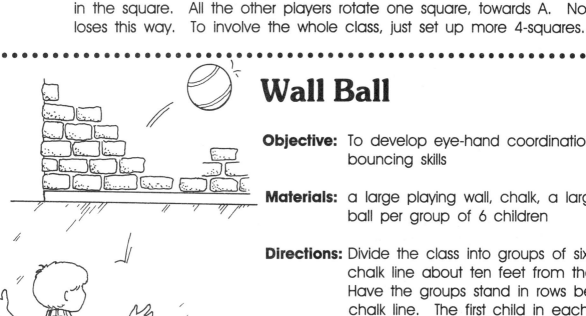

Objective: To develop bouncing and eye-hand coordination skills

Materials: large, flat playing surface, chalk, large rubber ball

Directions: Draw a large square on a flat playing surface. Divide the square into four equal parts. Give each square a letter from A-D. (See illustration.) Assign a player to each square. Give a large rubber ball to Player A. Using the palm of his/her hand, Player A should bounce the ball in his/her square and bat the ball into an opponent's square. The recipient of the ball must bat the ball with his/her hand into a square other than his/her own. The object of the game is to keep the ball bouncing between squares. When one player misses, or when the ball is hit but does not land completely in a square, that player moves to the D position in the square. All the other players rotate one square, towards A. No one ever loses this way. To involve the whole class, just set up more 4-squares.

Wall Ball

Objective: To develop eye-hand coordination and bouncing skills

Materials: a large playing wall, chalk, a large rubber ball per group of 6 children

Directions: Divide the class into groups of six. Draw a chalk line about ten feet from the wall. Have the groups stand in rows behind the chalk line. The first child in each row tosses the ball up against the wall. While the first child moves to the back of the line, the second child moves to the front of the line and bounces the coming ball towards the wall. He/she must focus on bouncing the ball hard so that the third child can continue the process. After each child on the team has bounced the ball in sequence without stopping or catching the ball, the team must sit down. The first team to sit is the winner.

Fill for Fun

Objective: To learn to dodge

Materials: a beach ball, 2 large plastic mixing bowls, enough golf balls to fill one plastic mixing bowl, chalk

Directions: This game is best played in front of a large wall. Have all but one child (the "hitter") line up with their backs against the wall. These children are called the "fillers." Fifteen feet in front of the children, place a large plastic mixing bowl containing golf balls. Beside that mixing bowl, place another empty bowl. About 20 feet from the wall, draw a chalk line for the hitter to stand behind.

The object of the game is to have the children try to fill the empty mixing bowl with the golf balls from the full mixing bowl. The challenge is to dodge the beach ball being thrown by the hitter. The hitter eliminates fillers by hitting them with the beach ball. If the fillers fill the bowl before all the fillers are eliminated, the hitter becomes a filler, and the last player to add to the bowl becomes the new hitter. The hitter can maintain his/her position if he/she eliminates all the fillers before the bowl is full. Remind the hitter to only throw from behind the 20-foot line.

Team Dodge Ball

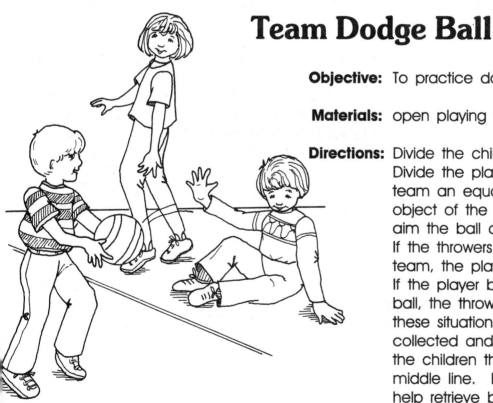

Objective: To practice dodging skills

Materials: open playing field, soft rubber balls

Directions: Divide the children into two equal teams. Divide the playing field in half. Give each team an equal number of balls. The object of the game is for the players to aim the ball at those on the other team. If the throwers touch a player on the other team, the player who was hit is eliminated. If the player being thrown at catches the ball, the thrower is eliminated. If neither of these situations happens, the balls are collected and the play resumes. Remind the children that they may never cross the middle line. Have the eliminated players help retrieve balls.

Leaves Kick

Objective: To develop kicking skills

Materials: a rake, leaves

Directions: Rake a large pile of leaves together. See who can kick up the biggest mess. Then, have leaf pile clean-up. Make a game out of a task!

Kick the Carton

Objective: To practice kicking skills

Materials: an empty milk carton

Directions: Choose one player to be the "kicker." The kicker kicks the carton, covers his/her eyes and sings "The Grand O'l Duke of York." The idea is to give the other players a chance to hide. At the end of the song, the kicker calls "Ready or not, here I come." The kicker looks for the hiding children. When the kicker finds someone, he/she calls the hider's name. The hider and the kicker then race for the carton and kick it over. If the kicker kicks the carton first, the hider must stand beside the can while the kicker searches for the other children. If the hider kicks the carton first, the game begins again. The hiders can try to come out of hiding at any time, but they must kick the carton over before the kicker.

The Grand O'l Duke of York,
He had ten thousand men.
He marched them up to the top of the hill
And he marched them down again.
And when you're up, you're up
And when you're down, you're down
And when you're only half way up,
You're neither up nor down."

Kick Ball

Objective: To develop kicking skills while reinforcing baseball rules

Materials: a baseball field, a large rubber ball

Directions: Kick ball is played much like baseball. The difference is that the pitcher rolls a large rubber ball to home plate and the batter kicks the ball instead of hitting it with a bat. All the rules of baseball apply. However, the fielders do not need gloves and the kicker cannot strike out.

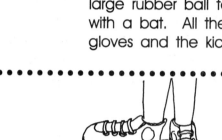

Kick Pick-Up

Objective: To develop kicking and receiving skills

Materials: soccer ball, smooth wall, chalk

Directions: Draw a line on the ground, fifteen feet from a wall. Divide the children into two equal teams and have each team line up behind the line and facing the wall. The first player from each team must kick the ball at the wall. As the ball returns, the next player in each line must receive the ball. That team member must then continue the activity by kicking the ball against the wall for the next player. After each player receives and kicks the ball, he/she must sit down at the end of his/her line. That team whose members are all seated first is declared the winner.

Soccer Swerving

Objective: To develop ball control using one's feet

Materials: pylons, soccer balls

Directions: Set up an obstacle course using pylons. Have the children line up and take turns running through the obstacle course keeping control of the ball with their feet. Remind children to use all sides of their feet for kicking and to make short kicks for control. Once the children feel confident with their ball control, try a few relay races.

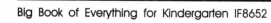

Tightrope Tricks

Objective: To develop balancing skills

Materials: garden hose, broomstick, stacks of blocks, buckets of water, piles of books

Directions: Place a garden hose in a straight line along the grass. Tell the children to use their imagination and line up to walk across the "tightrope" that is thousands of feet above the ground. Have them imagine that the rope is strung between two bridges high above alligator-infested waters. For variation, the children may try balancing a bucket of water, a stack of blocks, a broomstick or a pile of books as they cross the tightrope. For an even more challenging tightrope, make curves in the garden hose. Be creative!

Water Relays

Objective: To develop balancing skills

Materials: chalk, unbreakable bowls, water

Directions: Divide the class into 3-4 groups. Have each group line up in rows. About 20 feet in front of the rows of children, draw a chalk line. The first child in each line must carry an unbreakable bowl half full with water across the chalk line and back to his/her row. Then, he/she must give the bowl to a teammate who must continue the process. The first team to have each member successfully carry the bowl of water across the line and back is the winner. If this is too difficult for the children, make the winner the team that has the most water remaining in its bowl.

Egg Relay

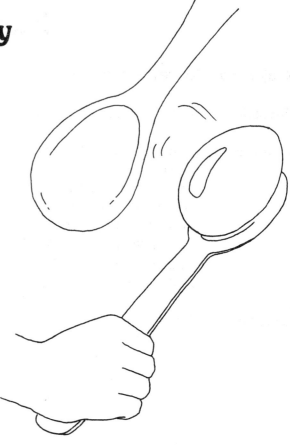

Objective: To develop balancing skills

Materials: spoons, real or plastic eggs, chalk

Directions: Divide children into two equal teams. Draw two lines approximately ten yards apart. Place half of each team on either side of each line in rows. Give the first person in each row on one side of a line a plastic spoon with an egg on it. When given the starting signal, the children must carefully carry their egg on the spoon to their waiting teammate on the other side of the line. The players must pass the spoon and the egg. The receiving players must then carry the egg on the spoon back to the next player at the first line. This cycle continues until all the players have carried the egg across the field. The first team to finish the relay is the winner. If an egg is dropped, the child should pick it up and continue the race. A new egg should be supplied if real eggs are used.

Obstacle Course Balance

Objective: To develop balancing skills

Materials: hula hoops, floor mats, wicker paper plate holders, large rubber balls, chairs

Directions: Set up an obstacle course using the items listed above or other things you might already have in the classroom. Have the children take turns balancing a wicker paper plate holder on their head while attempting to go through the obstacle course. Be sure to arrange the obstacle course so that the children are forced to squat, stand, dodge and lift their legs high.

Bunny Bounce

Objective: To develop balance

Materials: balance beam, enlarged copies of the bunny hat (below)

Directions: There are so many activities that can be done on a balance beam. For this activity, have the children wear bunny hats. Enlarge and copy the pattern below to make the hats. The focus on the hat often distracts from the fear of the balance beam. Have the children start by pretending they are Peter Rabbit tiptoeing into Mr. McGregor's garden. On their next trip across the beam, have them pretend they are hopping around the garden. For the third trip, have the children pretend that Mr. McGregor has spied them and that they must run across the beam to get away from danger.

Extension: Find some music to play while the children are crossing the balance beam. Try to match the music to the mood Peter Rabbit might be experiencing.

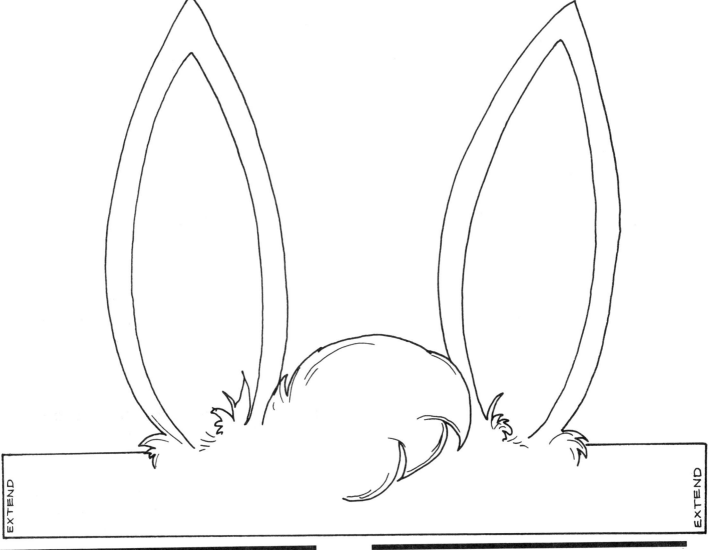

EXTEND

EXTEND

Somersault Specialties

Objective: To teach introductory gymnastics skills in a non-threatening way

Materials: floor mat, soft plush teddy bear

Directions: Place the stuffed animal on the floor mat. Have the children place their head on the teddy bear's tummy. Tell the children to pretend they are giving the teddy bear a tickle with their head. Then, instruct the children to tuck their chin to their chest and roll over the bear. Be sure to have a person helping the children to execute the move.

Wheelbarrow Balance

Objective: To develop strength and balance for early gymnastics movements

Materials: a beanbag character, floor mats

Directions: Have children form a line at one end of the floor mat. Help each child through the exercise. Have a child assume a crawling position. Next, place a beanbag character on the child's back, then ask another child to lift the child's legs while he/she uses his/her arms to move across the floor mat. Finally, instruct the child to give the beanbag character a safe ride to the other side of the floor mat.

Playground Gymnastics

Objective: To develop strength in the upper arms for gymnastic movements

Materials: a low monkey bar

Directions: Have the children line up and take turns hanging by the back of their knees from the low monkey bar. To do this, have the children grab the monkey bar with two hands. Instruct them to bring their feet up over the bar, inside their arms. When they feel comfortable, suggest that they let go of the bar with their hands. Reverse the order of movements to descend from the bar. Always be able to spot for a child. This activity demands careful supervision.

High Bars

Objective: To develop gymnastics skills and upper body strength

Materials: high playground monkey bars

Directions: Have the children line up in front of the high monkey bars. Give each child the opportunity to cross the monkey bars rung by rung. Be certain to support any child who needs assistance. Some children may be able to cross the monkey bars by skipping a rung while others may have difficulty simply holding themselves by their arms. Encourage personal growth and development.

47

Jump Rope Games

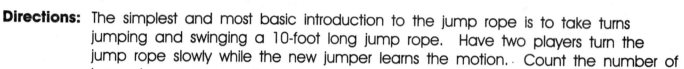

Objectives: To develop jumping skills and to build muscular and cardiovascular strength

Materials: jump rope, flat jumping surface

Directions: The simplest and most basic introduction to the jump rope is to take turns jumping and swinging a 10-foot long jump rope. Have two players turn the jump rope slowly while the new jumper learns the motion. Count the number of jumps in sequence until the jumper gets caught in the rope.

Double Dutch

Objectives: To develop jumping skills and to build muscular and cardiovascular strength

Materials: 2 jump ropes, flat jumping surface

Directions: This activity involves turning two ropes in opposite directions towards the middle. Each person has to jump over both ropes. This activity takes a lot more coordination than a single jump rope.

High, Low, Medium, Slow

Objectives: To develop jumping skills and to build muscular and cardiovascular strength

Materials: jump rope and flat jumping surface

Directions: This activity is done with one long jump rope and two players who turn the rope. The jumper enters the rope and the group chants, "High, low, medium, slow, rocky, jolly, peppers." As the words indicate, the tempo of the jumping increases. At "peppers," the swingers turn the rope very quickly and the audience counts till the jumper gets caught in the rope or chooses to stop from fatigue.

Partner Jumping

Objectives: To develop jumping skills and to build muscular and cardiovascular strength

Materials: jump rope and flat jumping surface

Directions: This jumping involves partners and a short jump rope. One person begins turning and jumping using his/her own rope. Then, the jumper chants, "Someone is under the bed. Whoever can it be? I can't reach the light switch so _____ (fills in the blank with the partner's name) come to me." Once the partner jumps in the rope, the jumpers begin counting together. The stroke of the rope on the ground should guide counting.

Snake Jump

Objectives: To develop jumping skills and to build muscular and cardiovascular strength

Materials: jump rope and flat jumping surface

Directions: Have the children line up on one side of the play area. Choose two players to swish the rope. The swingers should move the rope vigorously back and forth. The swingers should hiss like snakes while the jumpers attempt to jump over the wiggling rope.
The objective is
to not touch the rope.

49

Memory Images

Objective: To illustrate the importance of good eyesight and taking care of eyes

Materials: 10 small objects, large serving tray, towel

Directions: Have the children sit in a circle. Place a serving tray containing 10 small objects on the floor in the middle of the children's circle. Tell them to use their eyes to remember what is on the tray. Cover the tray with a towel after 30 seconds. Have the children take turns recalling what is on the covered tray. Discuss how important vision is for this game.

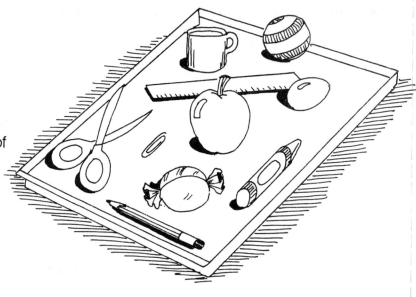

Mirror Images

Objective: To recognize body movements and the control one has over the movements

Directions: Divide the children into pairs. Discuss how a mirror functions. Let the children decide who will be the "mirror" in the pair first. Have the children be mirror images of one another. The mirror must make the exact movements of his/her partner. It is helpful to remind the children that their movements should be slower than normal.

Catch the Bell

Objective: To develop and demonstrate dependency of auditory skills

Materials: a small bell, blindfolds, a large play space free of large obstacles

Directions: Blindfold all the children except for one child. Fasten a small bell around that one child's neck. The child should move around the playing space freely while the blindfolded children try to catch him/her by listening for the bell. When a player catches the child with the bell, the two exchange places.

Simon Says

Objective: To develop body and spatial awareness

Materials: hula hoops, instrumental music

Directions: Provide each child with a hula hoop. Have each child sit in the center of his/her hula hoop to begin the game. Discuss how this is each child's individual space. Play a regular game of Simon Says, but use the hula hoop for added enjoyment. Try things like"
Simon Says...jump in your hoop.
           ...pull the hoop over your head.
           ...hold your hoop with your foot/hand/finger/arm/leg.
           ...rest the hoop on your neck."

Food Guide Pyramid Maze

Help the jogger make it to the top of the Food Guide Pyramid Maze.

Health Food Grab Bag

Objective: To reinforce the value of the food groups as depicted on the Food Guide Pyramid

Materials: empty containers and plastic replicas of foods and cartons, large grab bag

Directions: Divide children into two teams and have them sit in two circles. Allow a player from each team to come to the front and choose an item from the Health Food Grab Bag. The teammates can help the child to tell which food group on the Food Guide Pyramid the object belongs to and what function, if any, it performs in our body. For example, if the child picks a milk carton, he/she must say that it belongs to the milk, yogurt and cheese group and that it helps build strong teeth and bones. The team gets one point for the correct food group and one for the function it is able to identify.

Teeth Tenderness

Objective: To teach the importance of dental hygiene

Materials: dental floss, paper, crayons or markers, tape

Directions: Try to arrange for a guest speaker to come and speak to the children about dental hygiene. Give each child a piece of paper on which to draw his/her face. Remind the children to include their teeth in their drawing. Give each child a piece of dental floss to tape to the teeth in his/her picture. Also encourage them to draw toothpaste and a toothbrush. On the back of the picture, have the children draw things that are good for their teeth (i.e. apples, milk, cheese, etc.). Display pictures on a bulletin board for further reinforcement.

Health Food Bingo

Objective: To reinforce the food groups as depicted on the Food Guide Pyramid Maze

Materials: hat, unpopped popcorn kernels, copies of the bingo gameboards on pages 55 and 56, copies of the game squares below

Directions: Enlarge and copy the bingo cards on pages 55 and 56. Cut out the game squares below along the dotted lines. Place the game squares in a hat. Have one person select squares from the hat. For each bingo card square which matches a square selected from the hat, have the children place a kernel on the matched square. Repeat the process until someone gets three kernels in a row on his/her card. Have children rotate cards after a "Bingo." It is recommended that no more than eight children play at one time to avoid simultaneous "Bingo" winners. Reinforce activity by giving each child a copy of the Food Guide Pyramid Maze on page 52.

Health Food Bingo

Health Food Bingo

3-Legged Race

Objective: To discover how difficult it would be to not have complete control of your own body

Materials: scarves

Directions: Divide the class into pairs. Using a scarf, tie the left leg of one player to the right leg of his/her partner. Have the children discover how difficult it can be when you do not have complete control of your body. Have the pairs line up for a race in a large grassy field. Designate a turn-around place. When the pairs return and sit down to rest, discuss the inconveniences of having their legs tied together.

Blind Tag

Objective: To discover the difficulties of being blind

Materials: a blindfold

Directions: Choose one person to be "It." "It" must be blindfolded. He/she must try to tag the other players through the use of his/her ears. The other players should try to give clues by making sounds around "It." If someone is tagged, he/she must become "It." Be sure to give many children the opportunity to be "It." After the game, discuss with the children what it felt like to be "It." What was the most difficult part? What would it be like to be blind in our world today? Get the children thinking about ways to make life easier for blind people.

Wheelchair Races

Objective: To learn to appreciate the technology of modern wheelchairs yet recognize the difficulties of having to spend a lifetime in a wheelchair

Materials: wheelchairs, chairs, balls

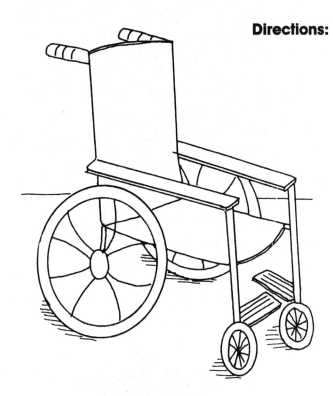

Directions: If you cannot find wheelchairs for this activity, rent a video about Special Olympics. If you are fortunate enough to be able to borrow a few wheelchairs, let the children take turns learning how to use the chairs. Once they have gained a little confidence, try having some races or playing ball. For added effect, place four regular chairs in a row in front of four other chairs. Have eight children take a seat. Give four children balls. Ask them to play catch with the opposite person. The key is not to get off the seat for any reason. Do not give any dropped balls back to the children. When all four pairs have dropped their balls and are unable to retrieve them, discuss the frustrations they may have experienced. Discuss how their regular chair is different than a wheelchair is for a handicapped person. Discuss how each person could make life easier for a handicapped person.

Mouth Painting

Objective: To discover the difficulty of quadriplegia

Materials: paintbrushes, paper plates, paint, paper, tape

Directions: Discuss what the children think it would be like to not be able to move any part of their body except their neck and head. Tape a bunch of paper plates to the tops of the children's work space and set paint out on them. Tell the children that they are going to pretend that they are quadriplegics but can still paint a picture. See if the children can discover how they would accomplish such a task. Eventually, give the children a piece of paper taped to their work station and a paintbrush to use in their mouth. Prior to this exercise, be sure all the brushes have been washed well. To help remind the children not to use their hands, have them fold their hands behind their backs. Later, discuss what it was like to paint with one's mouth.

Park Walk

Objective: To develop total body fitness

Directions: Take the children on a walk to a local park. The purpose of this walk is to use whatever you encounter as an opportunity for total body fitness. For instance, if you come across a large puddle, have the children see how far past the puddle they can jump. A little further on, perhaps you encounter a bridge. Have the children hop on one foot across the bridge. Along the sidewalks, have the children tightrope walk the cracks. If you run into steps, have the children hop with two feet up the steps and have them walk backwards down the steps. Be creative and try to involve as many parts of the body as possible.

Fitness Circles

Objective: To develop total body fitness

Materials: chalk, a large playing area

Directions: Draw four sets of circles (five-feet in diameter) in a line. Draw a starting line and a finish line. Divide the class into two teams. At a whistle start, have the first contestants from each team run to the Circle Number 1. In this circle, the children must do ten jumping jacks. When each player has completed the activities in Circle Number 1, he/she must run to Circle Number 2. In this Circle Number 2, each contestant must do ten sit-ups. In Circle Number 3, they must hop on one foot ten times. Finally, in Circle Number 4, they must do ten donkey kicks. (See diagram.) From Circle Number 4, the contestants must run to cross the finish line. Have ribbons for everyone who finishes.

59

Crazy Olympics

Objective: To increase stamina, coordination, strength and flexibility

Materials: tape measure, ribbons, notebook, pen, timer, chalk

Directions: Set up the following stations around the school property.

1. The Long Jump Station: Children jump as far as they can from a given point.
2. The Short Jump Station: Children take the smallest jump from a given point.
3. Backward Speed Walking Station: Children walk backwards as fast as they can from a given point.
4. The "Circle the School" Run: Children run around the school as fast as they can.
5. Crab Crawling Station: Children crab walk as fast as they can from a given point.
6. The "20-yard Bunny Hop Station:" In a sack, children hop as fast as they can from a given point.

Time events and measure distances for the children's records. Place the results in a notebook entitled *Crazy Olympic Class Records*. Encourage the children to beat their personal records instead of each other's records. Give ribbons for participation.

Sports Movements

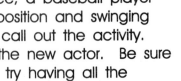

Objective: To use imagination while stretching most major muscle groups in the body

Directions: This activity works very well on a rainy day. Have all the children sit in a large circle. Choose one child to be a mime athlete. Whisper a sport or a sporting position into the mime athlete's ear. He/she must act out the secret activity. For instance, a baseball player might be mimed as an individual assuming the batting position and swinging with an imaginary bat. The children in the circle should call out the activity. The first person to guess the correct sport can become the new actor. Be sure to let all the children have a turn. Call out a sport and try having all the children act out that sport at the same time.

Healthy Eating Bulletin Board Bulletin Board

Objectives: To display the names of those children who are aiming to be health conscious as well as providing a decorative environment

Materials: 2 large sheets of construction paper, marker, scissors, posterboard, stapler, ruler

Directions: Cover a bulletin board with a decorative paper. Cut three-inch wide strips of posterboard and write a child's name on each. Staple two large sheets of construction paper together to form an envelope. After writing the title, "Health Conscious Students," on the front of the envelope, pin it to the center of the bulletin board. Cut an arrow out of construction paper and staple it to the bulletin board pointing straight down to the envelope. (See illustration below). Title the bulletin board, "Healthy Eating Starts Here!" Let the children show you their low-sugar health conscious lunches for a week. Stick the names of the children who ate healthy lunches into the envelope.

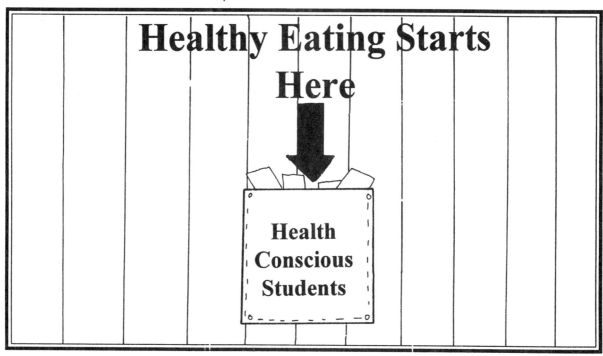

Health News Bulletin Board Bulletin Board

Objective: To reinforce healthy eating habits through visual reminders

Materials: empty cartons from health foods, markers, stapler, construction paper, scissors

Directions:
1. Divide a bulletin board into six equal sections. Use different colored construction paper to differentiate between the sections.

2. Give each section one of the following labels:
   1. Milk, Yogurt, Cheese Group
   2. Meat, Poultry, Fish, Dry Beans, Eggs & Nuts Group
   3. Vegetable Group
   4. Fruit Group
   5. Fats & Sweets
   6. Bread, Cereal, Rice & Pasta Group

3. Collect packaging containers for each of the six sections. Attach these empty packages to the appropriate section on the bulletin board. Discuss with students which foods are healthy and which are unhealthy.

Art

Emphasis in this chapter has been placed on seasonal art activities. The goal is to give the children an opportunity to develop their creativity and express themselves artistically.

The children are presented with a huge variety of different mediums to explore. Wax, paints, markers, chalk, crayons, wood, ink, manmade materials and natural materials are just a few of the items explored. The children are given the opportunity to try a variety of marking tools as well. Outside of the usual paintbrush, crayon and marker, the children discover many new ways to express themselves. Hopefully through their explorations they will learn to examine the world in which they live more carefully and respectfully.

As art should be shared, it is hoped that by making the art activities seasonal, the final products can be displayed on the walls, ceilings and halls of the school. You can help the children build confidence in their work by respecting and displaying their art. Encourage the children to explain their art to you and their peers to also promote their artistic expression.

Outstanding Work

Objective: To display children's work creatively

Materials: butcher paper, sponges, paint, paint trays, scissors, basket, yarn, push pins or glue, stapler

Directions:

1. Cover a bulletin board with a solid color.

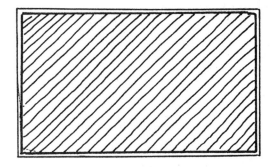

2. Out of butcher paper, cut a large hot air balloon.

3. Have the children sponge paint a hot air balloon.

4. Pin or glue the hot air balloon to the the center of the bulletin board.

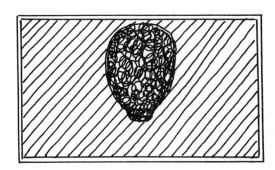

5. Attach four strands of yarn to a basket. The other ends should be stapled to the hot air balloon on the bulletin board.

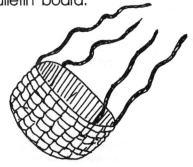

6. Put the children's outstanding papers into the basket for display.

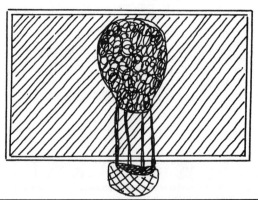

Soda Straw Designs

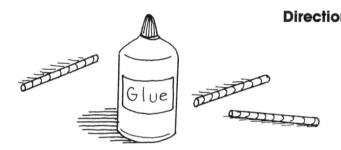

Objective: To create a relief picture using soda straws

Materials: drinking straws, glue, scissors, cardboard

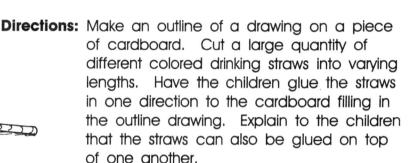

Directions: Make an outline of a drawing on a piece of cardboard. Cut a large quantity of different colored drinking straws into varying lengths. Have the children glue the straws in one direction to the cardboard filling in the outline drawing. Explain to the children that the straws can also be glued on top of one another.

Wood Scrap Sculpture

Objective: To manufacture a sculpture using wood scraps

Materials: wood scraps, wood glue, acrylic paint (a seasonal choice of colors), paintbrushes, toothpicks

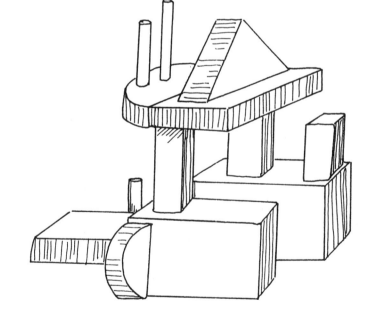

Directions: Contact a local lumberyard to see if they might be willing to donate some scrap wood. Before beginning this project discuss how sculpture has three dimensions and a paper has only two dimensions. Have the children choose pieces of scrap wood that fit together well. When the arrangement is satisfying, have the children glue all the pieces together. Remind the children to hold the pieces being glued together for enough time before adding another block. A lot of glue is not necessary. Finally, have the children paint the sculpture.

The Hall of Fame

Objective: To display children's art work in an honorable and creative fashion

Materials: thin Plexiglas, black posterboard, frame clips, hammer, tiny picture nails, scissors

Directions: Title a bulletin board, "Hall of Fame." Cover the bulletin board with a solid color of paper. Follow the steps below to make frames to display the children's artwork.

1. Cut black posterboard in large rectangles.

2. Cut thin Plexiglas in the same size rectangles as the posterboard.

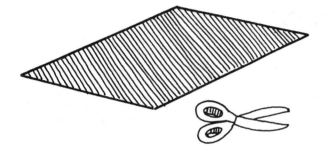

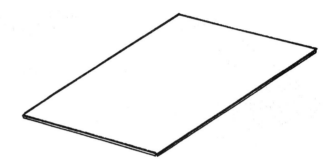

3. Place art work between Plexiglas and posterboard.

4. Clip the sides of the frames and hang them from nails on the bulletin board.

Doodle Designs

Objective: To form a picture from a musically inspired design

Materials: music of different tempos, pencils, music player, drawing paper, crayons

Directions: Ask children to listen to the music with their eyes closed. With a pencil, have them draw a continuous line on their paper. The line should reflect the music. Remind them not to look or lift their pencil from their paper until instructed to stop. Stop the music and have the children look at what they have created at that point. Instruct them to look for things in their design. Have them color the things they find.

Magic Lines

Purpose: To create a design using a wax resist.

Materials: white wax crayons, white paper, watercolor paint, paintbrushes, water containers, music and a music player

Directions: Play music and ask the children to follow the music movement with their white crayons on their white paper. Explain that they will not see any design. After playing several selections of music, have the children put away the white crayons. Using watercolor paint, have the children brush the entire surface of their white paper. Watch as the children discover their magical designs.

Texture Designs

Objective: To create a design using textured wallpaper

Materials: wallpaper scrapbook, scissors, glue, 8 1/2" x 11" paper

Directions: Give each child a sheet of paper. The children should make a design by cutting various scraps of wallpaper and placing them in a pleasing formation on their paper. Encourage the children to overlap their scraps. Then, each child should glue their design in place. Discuss the various textures in each design with the children.

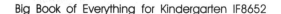

Leaf Art

Objective: To incorporate natural leaves into a picture

Materials: leaves, twigs and branches, string, pipe cleaners, glue, scissors, construction paper, any other scraps for decorating

Directions: Have the children collect leaves, twigs and branches from outside. (Colorful leaves work best.) Have children make creatures on construction paper by pasting leaves onto the paper and adding other materials to create the decorative features. Display these works of art to get everyone excited about fall.

Leaf Printed Flower Pots

Objective: To decorate terra cotta pots with colorful leaf prints

Materials: small leaves, small terra cotta pots, paintbrushes, acrylic paint

Directions:

1. Have each child place his/her pot on its side.

2. Instruct the children to brush a thin layer of paint onto the back of a leaf.

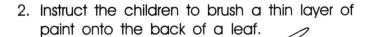

3. The children can then press the leaf onto the pot and observe the print when it is removed. Tell the children to do one side of the pot at a time. When the side they first worked on is dry, they can then repeat the design or create a new one on the other side of the pot.

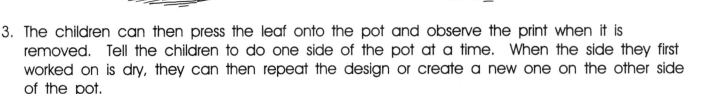

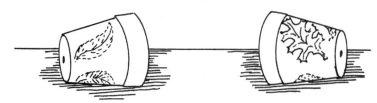

Magnetic Leaves

Objective: To design magnetic leaves for decorative purposes

Materials: flour, salt, water, wax paper, rolling pin, acrylic paint of autumn colors, Popsicle sticks or toothpicks, paintbrushes, magnetic strips, glue, marking tools, measuring cup, mixing bowl

Directions:

1. Mix two cups flour, one half cup salt, three-fourths cup water. Knead until smooth.

2. On wax paper, roll dough with a rolling pin to one quarter inch thickness.

3. Using a Popsicle stick or toothpick, have the children cut leaf shapes out of the dough.

4. After several days of drying, the children can paint the leaves autumn colors.

5. Show the children how to attach a magnetic strip to the back of their leaf. Tell the children to be sure to let the glue dry before hanging their leaf on their refrigerator.

The Pumpkin Patch

Objective: To create a bulletin board for Halloween

Materials: orange construction paper, sponges, photos of the children in the classroom, different shades of green paint, scissors, butcher paper, glue

Directions: Cover a bulletin board with butcher paper. Using orange construction paper, cut out different pumpkin shapes and sizes. Be sure to have a pumpkin shape for each child. Show students how to cut a window in each pumpkin shape to use to display their photo. The children can tape their photo to the back of the pumpkin shape. Have each child glue his/her pumpkin onto the butcher paper. Then, using the pattern below, cut vine shapes out of the sponges. Have the children sponge paint vines connecting all the pumpkins. Use varying shades of green paint for an interesting effect.

Trick-or-Treat Bags

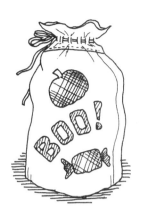

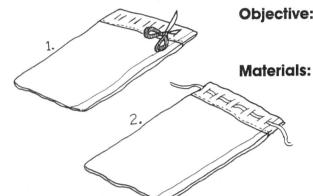

Objective: To produce a bag for trick-or-treating

Materials: Indelible, thick felt-tip markers (orange, black, brown); small white pillowcases; scraps of Halloween fabric; orange and black ribbon; felt scraps; scissors; fabric glue; plastic creatures, yarn, etc.

Directions: Have children bring small white pillowcases from home. Set out the materials mentioned above on a table. Tell the children they are going to decorate their pillowcases to become trick-or-treat bags. Talk about safety during Halloween outings while the children are working on their bags. Help the children cut slits in their pillowcase border so that they can insert a drawstring. Then, show the children how to weave the string through the slits. (See diagram for further explanation.)

Pumpkin Painting

Objective: To paint a pumpkin for the Halloween season

Materials: pumpkins, acrylic paint, paintbrushes, black permanent markers, pipe cleaners, construction paper, yarn, glue, aprons, a wash bucket

Directions: If you can arrange to take a field trip to a pumpkin patch, this project is even more delightful. Provide each child with a small pumpkin. Because carving pumpkins is so difficult at this age, talk about decorating pumpkins with paint and other materials. Discuss making animals or characters that do not have the typical jack-o'-lantern grins. Give students the supplies and let them create some perfectly precious pumpkins.

Paper Bag Mask

Objective: To assemble a mask from a paper bag

Materials: paper bags large enough to fit over a child's head, glue, scissors, paint, paintbrushes, yarn, colored paper, buttons, bottle caps, fabric, pipe cleaners, ribbons

Directions: Each child should slip a paper bag over his/her head. (Sometimes the sides of the bags will need to be cut so that they fit comfortably). Make a mark to show where the eyes will go. Have the children remove the bags and cut out large openings for viewing using the marks you made. Remind the children before they decorate their mask that the opening of the bag will be the bottom of their mask. Finally, let the children decorate their mask with the materials provided.

• •

Tissue Paper Candy

Objective: To make "candy" out of tissue paper

Materials: many colors of tissue paper, scissors

Directions: This activity is perfect to implement during nutrition or Halloween safety lessons.

1. Cut tissue paper into 3" squares.

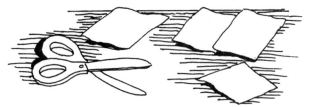

2. Show the children how to roll a square of paper into a ball.

3. Have the children use another square of the same color of paper and wrap it around the ball of tissue paper.

4. Instruct the children to twist the ends in opposite directions. Let them fill a bowl with the candy or decorate a trick-or-treat bag.

Headdress

Objective: To create a headdress for Thanksgiving

Materials: construction paper, scissors, clear tape, cranberries, blueberries, fresh green leaves or blades of grass, mixing bowls, paintbrushes, stapler, headband and feather pattern on page 74

Directions:

1. Using construction paper and the feather and headband pattern, have each child trace and cut out 4 or 5 feathers and one headband for his/her headdress.

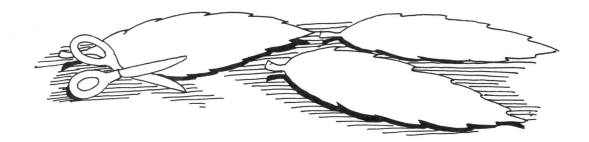

2. Crush the berries in separate bowls. Explain to children that when the settlers first arrived in America, painting was done using things from nature. Discuss the vibrant colors the Native Americans used in decorating. By rubbing leaves or grass and painting with crushed berries, have the children decorate the feathers and headband.

3. Size a headband to each child's head. Staple the ends together. Have the children tape their feathers to the headband. Staple the feathers for reinforcement.

Feather and Headband Patterns

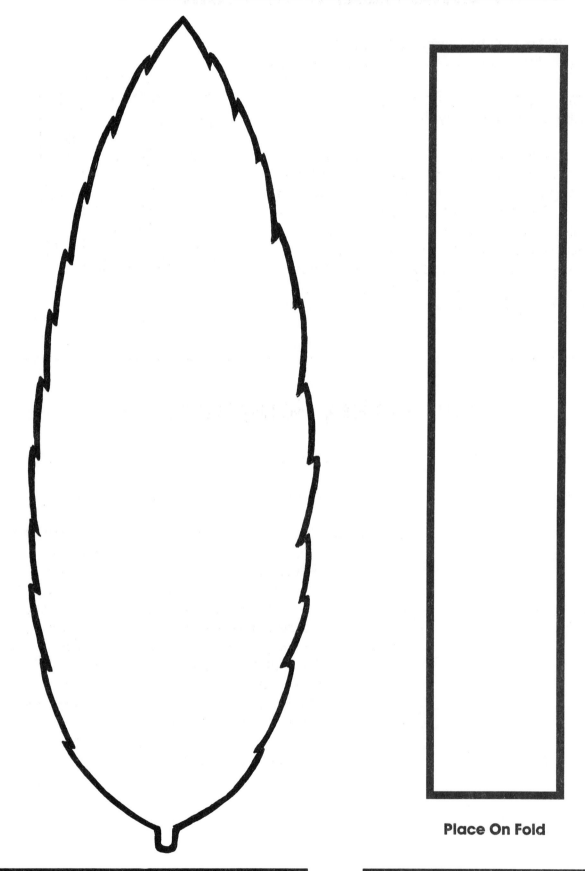

Place On Fold

Native American Vests

Objective: To create a paper bag vest that resembles a Native American vest for Thanksgiving clothing

Materials: large paper grocery bag, large, felt-tip markers, scissors, crayons

Directions: For each child, cut a large paper grocery bag up the center and make a hole large enough for a child's head to fit through the top. Cut a hole in both side panels of the bag for armholes. Have the children decorate all sides of the bag using crayons, large felt-tip markers or any other creative marking tools. Show the children how to cut fringe along the base of the bag to give it some authenticity.

Stuffed Turkey Sculptures

Objective: To design a Thanksgiving Turkey centerpiece

Materials: newspaper, glue, paint, paintbrushes, water container with water

Directions: Give each child a turkey shape design that they can use as a pattern to cut four sheets of newspaper. Glue two of the shapes together. Then, have them glue the other two shapes together. Help the children glue the two sets together along the edge leaving a space for stuffing. Let the shapes dry well. When they are dry have the children stuff their turkeys with crumpled newspaper. Let them paint their turkeys. Finally, instruct the children to use their turkeys as a centerpiece for their thanksgiving dinner.

75

Dinner Napkin Rings

Objective: To make a set of napkin rings for Thanksgiving dinner

Materials: paper towel and/or toilet paper rolls, scissors, ribbon, glue, beads, beans, dry macaroni, dry spaghetti, tiny pebbles, sand, tiny shells, fall colors of paint, paintbrushes, shellac spray

Directions:

1. Cut paper towel or toilet paper rolls into 2"-long cylinders.

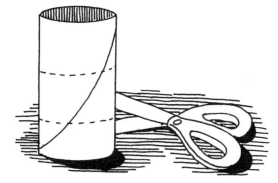

2. Tell the children to decorate the cylinders by gluing any materials listed above to cover the entire roll.

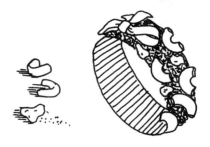

3. The children can let the cylinders dry and then paint them using paintbrushes and fall colors of paint.

4. When the paint is dry, help the children spray the cylinders with a shellac spray. They can then tie a ribbon around the roll and use a dot of glue to hold the ribbon in place.

5. Tell the children to use the rolls as napkin rings for Thanksgiving dinner.

Snowflakes

: To make enough snowflakes to decorate the classroom

s: any type of decorative paper, scissors

Directions:

1. Demonstrate to the children how to fold a sheet of paper to create a snowflake. Follow the steps below.

a.    b. 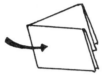   c.

2. Show the children how to cut along folded sides. Let them open up their paper and delight in the discovery of their very own snowflake design.

Splatter Paint

Objective: To make a snow scene using a splatter technique of painting

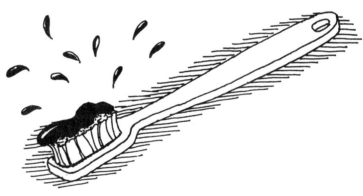

Materials: dark paper, white tempera paint, water, toothbrushes, old screen, construction paper, scissors, glue

Directions: Have the children use construction paper to cut out designs of trees, houses or any other creative ideas. Have them glue the designs to a dark sheet of construction paper. Next, they dip a toothbrush into diluted white tempera paint. Show them how to hold a screen above the design and rub the toothbrush vigorously over the screen. The paint will spatter through the screen and create a snowy effect.

Ivory® Soap Snowmen

Objective: To mold snowmen out of moistened Ivory® soap flakes

Materials: Ivory® soap flakes, water, Popsicle sticks, construction paper, toothpicks, yarn and other decorating scraps

Directions: Add water to Ivory® soap flakes to create molding clay. Instruct each child to mold the soap into three balls. The children then push a Popsicle stick through the center of their two balls to hold them together. Tell the children to decorate their snowman using yarn and other odds and ends. Let the sculptures dry overnight.

Snow Scene Jars

Objective: To make a snow scene in a jar

Materials: baby food jars, silver glitter, super glue, plastic animals or figures, water

Directions: Help the children glue a plastic figure to the inside of a baby food lid. Be certain to let the super glue harden completely. Next, the children should fill the jar with water. Show them how to sprinkle a significant amount of glitter into the water. Tell them next to tighten the lid and turn the jar upside-down. Now they can shake their jar and watch the pretty snow fall on the figure.

Bouquet Garni

Objective: To make a gift that could be given over the Hanukkah week

Materials: parsley flakes, dried thyme leaves, bay leaves, mixing bowl, string, vegetable soup recipe, copy of the recipe card below, muslin or cheesecloth, felt-tip markers, hole punch

Directions: This gift is a traditional way of seasoning home-cooked dishes. It is particularly tasty in soups or casseroles.

1. For each sachet, help the children mix one teaspoon parsley flakes, 1/4 teaspoon dried thyme leaves and one bay leaf.

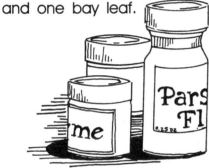

2. Cut each child a 6" diameter circle of muslin or cheesecloth.

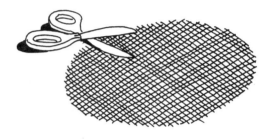

3. Help each child place the herbs in the center of the muslin and secure it tightly with a long piece of string to form a sachet.

4. Using felt-tip markers, have the children decorate the recipe card below containing a hearty vegetable soup recipe. Punch a hole in a corner of the card and attach it to the string from the sachet.

3 to 4 stalks celery	1 can corn
3 carrots	1/4 head cabbage, shredded
3 potatoes	1 can tomatoes
2 to 3 onions	1 Tbsp. savorex
1 can peas	2 Tbsp. salt

Clean and dice all vegetables. Cover with water. Cook until tender, several hours on low heat. Allow bouquet garni to seep for one half hour.

Wrapping It Up

Objective: To design wrapping paper for the Hanukkah season

Materials: feathers; string; thin light gray paper; blue, white and silver paint; paintbrushes; large paint trays; rattan string; tape

Directions:

1. Tape a piece of gray paper down for each child on his/her work place.

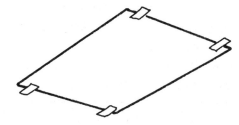

2. Have the children paint the paper blue, white or silver using a feather or a string.

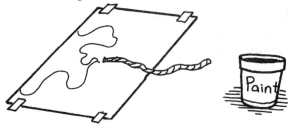

3. After the paper dries, have the children roll the paper into a cylinder and tie a rattan string around the roll. Direct the children to use the paper at home to wrap gifts.

Making Candles

Objective: To make candles that can be used to celebrate the Festival of Lights

Materials: paraffin wax, crayons, muffin trays, candlewicks, sand, butter, toothpicks

Directions: Melt paraffin wax according to package instructions. Place a half of a crayon (color of choice) into the melting wax. Butter the muffin trays thoroughly. Line muffin trays with sand. Pour melted paraffin into the trays and place a toothpick with a candlewick dangling down into each muffin cup. Let the wax harden and then pop them out of the tray.

The 3-D Christmas Tree

Objective: To make a bulletin board celebrating the Christmas holidays

Materials: green posterboard, scissors, Cheerios® or popcorn, string, dull needles, shiny paper, a string of Christmas lights, stapler, electrical source, butcher paper, tape, glue

Directions:

1. Trace a Christmas tree pattern on green posterboard twice and cut out both shapes.

2. Staple one tree to the bulletin board. Fold the other tree in half. Tape and glue the folded tree to the bulletin board as displayed below. Little posterboard wedges work well to support the folded tree.

3. Decorate the tree with lights by stapling the lights to various points on the tree. Be sure there is enough cord left to reach an electrical source.

4. Cut spiral decorations, as shown below, out of shiny paper and string popcorn or colored Cheerios® for added decorations.

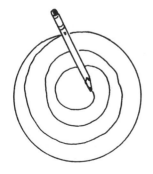

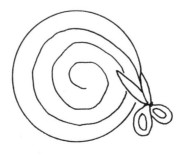

Apple Santa

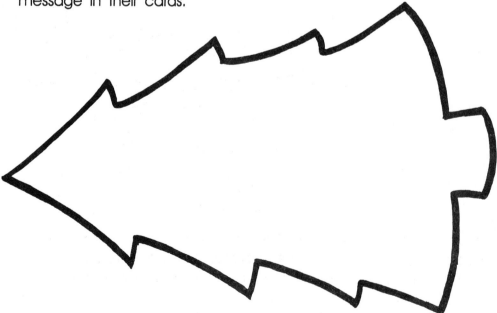

Objective: To make a Santa table decoration or party favor

Materials: toothpicks, marshmallows, cotton, red and black gumdrops, large red apples

Directions: Using toothpicks, show the children how to stick the five marshmallows into a large red apple to form the head, arms and legs of Santa. Next, they place a large red gumdrop on Santa's head to form his hat. Have the children place two red gumdrops for Santa's gloves and two black gumdrops for his boots. Tell the children to use a small piece of cotton for his beard and tiny pieces of gumdrops for his other features.

Colorful Christmas Cards

Objective: To make decorative Christmas cards

Materials: hole punch, tissue paper, green construction paper, glue, markers, tree cutout pattern

Directions: Cut a tree pattern from green construction paper for each child. Using hole punches, have the children perforate their tree cutout. On the back of the cutout, the children then should glue colored tissue paper squares over the holes to create the effect of colored ornaments. Show the children how to fold an 8 1/2" x 11" sheet of posterboard in half. Instruct the children to glue their tree pattern to the posterboard. Finally, the children should write their Christmas message in their cards.

Candy Cane Reindeer

Objective: To decorate a candy cane reindeer Christmas ornament

Materials: pipe cleaners, candy canes, scissors, construction paper, glue, small red cotton balls, string or ribbon

Directions: Have the children cut two eyes out of construction paper for the reindeer. They can then glue them on the curve of the candy cane. Next, show the children how to wrap a pipe cleaner around the top of the candy cane curve. they should glue it in place and bend the pipe cleaner into an antler shape. Finally, at the bottom of the curve of the candy cane, the children should glue a small red cotton ball to form the reindeer's nose. A string or ribbon should be tied to the top of the candy cane so that it can be used for decoration.

Junk Print Wrapping Paper

Objective: To create Christmas wrapping paper using miscellaneous printing objects

Materials: red and green paint, old sponges, string, feathers, bottle caps, toothbrushes, corrugated paper, springs, plain newsprint, ribbon, trays or paper plates

Directions: Using the sponges, strings, feathers, etc. listed above, show the children how to decorate newsprint to create wrapping paper. Use trays or paper plates for the paint. You will want to tell the children to let one color of paint dry before applying the second color. A string can then be tied around the roll of wrapping paper when it is dry. See how much fun the children will have wrapping gifts.

Christmas Tree Decorating

Objective: To make and decorate a paper Christmas tree

Materials: green construction paper, spools, dowels, glitter, glue, cotton, foil, scissors, yarn, colored construction paper

Directions: For added fun, before beginning this project, sing "O' Christmas Tree," or read a story about tree decorating.

1. From green construction paper, help the children cut out half circles.

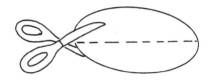

2. Show them how to glue the sides together to form cones.

3. Next, have the children stick a dowel in a spool. A drop of glue can now be placed in the top of the cone. Tell the children to rest the cone on top of the dowel.

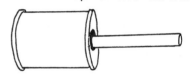

4. Tell the children to decorate their "tree" using the items mentioned above.

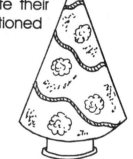

Sweet Ornaments

Objective: To make Christmas ornaments from a simple orange and decorative materials

Materials: oranges, ribbon, cloves, wire hangers (for ornaments)

Directions: Give each child an orange. Have the children stick cloves into the peel of the orange. Next, the children can tie two ribbons around the orange. Help them hook a wire hanger to use to hang the ornaments.

Party Hats

Objective: To make a paper hat for the New Year

Materials: scissors, glue, tape, ribbon, colored construction paper, stapler

Directions:

1. Help the children form a cone out of colored construction paper.

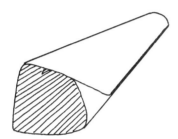

2. Tell the children to tape the cone closed on the inside of the cone and run a bead of glue on the edge of the top of the cone.

3. The children then trim the bottom of cone to form an even circle base.

4. A tassel can now be made for the top of the hat by cutting slits in a sheet of construction paper.

5. The children next tape the cut paper in place on the top of the hat.

6. Staple a piece of ribbon to the opposite sides of each child's hat. Let the children have fun wearing the hats!

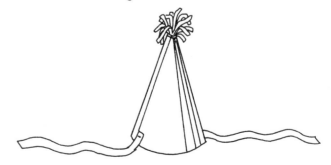

Extension: Practice a countdown and a celebration that would follow a New Year's Eve celebration.

The Dream of Equality

Objective: To design a bulletin board that reinforces the ideas Martin Luther King Jr. impressed upon the people of the United States

Materials: black felt, white posterboard, Velcro®, colorful felt-tip markers, scissors

Dream of Equality

Directions: Cover the bulletin board with black felt. Title it, "The Dream of Equality." Discuss Martin Luther King Jr. with the children and his beliefs. Be sure to include discussions of equality and peaceful problem solving. Discuss how each child in the classroom is different, but all people have the same rights. Have each child trace an outline of his/her hands on posterboard. The children should use markers to decorate the hands and cut them out of the posterboard. The children should then attach a small piece of Velcro to the back of each posterboard hand. Have the children stick the Velcro hands they made onto the bulletin board. Make sure the hands are touching. Encourage the children to think like Martin Luther King Jr. Help the children see how different each hand looks from the others on the bulletin board.

Casting Shadows

Objective: To outline the shadow a child casts

Materials: large sheets of butcher paper, black markers, scissors, direct sunlight

Directions: Choose a well-lit area of the classroom or do this activity outside on a sunny day. Divide students into pairs. Have the pairs take turns tracing their partner's shadow. Then, discuss the significance of the groundhog seeing its own shadow. Have the children cut out the tracings of their shadows and place them around the room. Be sure to have the children write their names on their own shadow.

Opaque Shadows

Objective: To make a profile shadow tracing of each child

Materials: opaque projector, chalk, black construction paper, scissors, glue, white paper

Directions: Have a child sit on a chair so that you have his/her profile view. Shine an opaque projector against the side of the child's head. With chalk, trace the outline of the profile being projected onto a piece of black construction paper. Have the child cut out the profile and mount it onto a sheet of white paper larger than the head shape.

The Key to My Heart

Objective: To design a decorative Valentine's Day bulletin board that promotes positive thinking and caring

Materials: white paper, stapler, scissors, yellow or gold and red construction paper, red yarn or red ribbon, lace ribbon, crayons, drawing paper, glue (optional)

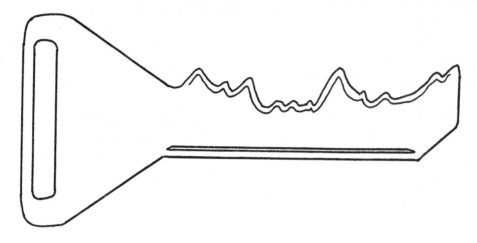

Directions: Cover a bulletin board with white paper. Cut a very large heart shape out of red construction paper. Staple or glue the lace ribbon to the edge of the heart shape. Staple the sides and bottom of the heart to the center of the bulletin board so that it creates a pocket. Cut a large key shape out of yellow or gold construction paper (See pattern above). Attach a red ribbon or piece of yarn to the end of the key. Attach the other end of that ribbon or yarn to the bottom of the heart. Title the bulletin board, "The Key to My Heart." Have the children draw pictures of things or people they love. Place the drawings into the heart pocket. Pull out drawings on occasion and discuss the children's individual loves.

Valentine Awareness

Objective: To assemble a valentine collage

Materials: construction paper hearts of all different sizes and colors, paper plates, paper, glue

Directions: Make hearts of all different colors, sizes and dimensions. Give each child a paper plate with various hearts. Ask the children to hold up a heart that is large/small, tall/short, red/blue/yellow, half/whole, etc. At the end of the activity, ask the children to arrange all their hearts into a collage. Discuss overlapping and make sure the children cover the entire sheet of paper. Mat pictures and decorate the classroom or hallway.

Valentine's Wash

Objective: To design a valentine's wash

Materials: crayons, water, red paint, paintbrushes, 8 1/2" x 11" sheets of white paper

Directions: With the children, discuss ideas about Valentine's Day. Include hearts, red, pink, cupid, caring, etc. Show the children how to fold a sheet of paper into eight equal parts. In each part, have the children color their own valentine idea using crayons. Finally, have the children paint over their paper with a red, watercolor wash. For added effect help the children mount their artwork against black construction paper after it dries.

Sponge-Painted Hearts

Objective: To design wrapping paper or a wall poster for Valentine's Day

Materials: manila or butcher paper, masking tape, pre-cut heart-shaped sponges, red and white paint provided on paper plates, aprons, wash bucket

Directions: Tape a large sheet of paper to a desk or table for each child. Allow the children to sponge paint using red and white paint. Talk about overlapping hearts and color-mixing with the children. Be sure the children's papers dry before using them for wrapping paper or a wall poster.

Classroom Mailbox

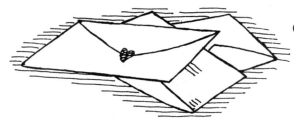

Objective: To decorate a mailbox to use for Valentine's Day

Materials: an old mailbox; red, pink, and white tissue paper; glue; ribbons; lace; scraps of fabric; buttons; glitter; hearts; doilies

Directions: Set all sorts of decorating materials on a large table. Place an old mailbox in the center. Have the children work in groups decorating the mailbox. As children bring their valentines to school, have them place them in the mailbox. Choose various children to distribute the mail on Valentine's Day. Save the mailbox after Valentine's Day. It may serve as a great resource for other writing projects (i.e. letters to Santa, a suggestion box for ideas for the classroom, etc.).

Pine Cone Bird Feeder

Objective: To build a bird feeder to attract birds

Materials: pine cones, string, peanut butter, plastic knives, bowl with wild birdseed, small plastic plates, drinking straws, scissors

Directions:

1. Give each child a pine cone. Help the children tie a string around the base of their pine cone.

2. The children next smear peanut butter on their pine cone.

3. Tell the children to roll their pine cone in the bowl of wild birdseed.

4. Help the children punch a small hole in center of a plastic plate.

5. Cut drinking straws in half and give one to each child.

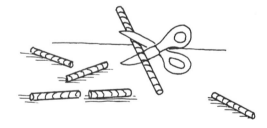

6. Help the children thread the string attached to the pine cone through the straw and the plastic plate.

7. Finally, help the children make a knot above their plate.

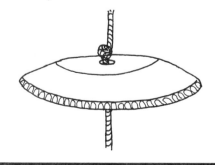

8. The children are now ready to hang their feeder outside to invite birds to their home or school.

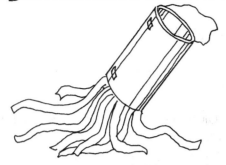

Windsocks

Objective: To design a paper windsock for indoors

Materials: construction paper, stapler, yarn, tape, felt-tip markers

Directions: Using felt-tip markers, have the children decorate a large sheet of construction paper. Next, they roll the construction paper into a cylinder shape and tape it together. The children now cut strips of ribbon or construction paper and tape them along the bottom of the cylinder shape. Have the children tape a strand of yarn to the top of the cylinder. Put a staple through the taped yarn for added strength. Hang for decoration!

Pebble People

Objective: To use nature for a craft

Materials: smooth stones, enamel paint, paintbrushes, glue, yarn, felt, strings, beads and seeds

Directions: Have the children look for smooth stones. Suggest that they might find these stones along a riverbed or seashore. Have them wash and dry their stones. Suggest that they paint people faces on the pebbles using enamel paint. Once the paint has dried, have the children add other features using the items mentioned above. These pebble people could be displayed in an aquarium or on a window shelf. They could also be used as a paperweight.

Shell Service

Objective: To make a craft from nature

Materials: 3 large scallop shells per child, 1 wire clothes hanger per child, plaster of Paris, mixing bowl, spoon, 1 plastic container lid per child

Directions: Have each child choose three scallop shells from a shell assortment. Give each child a wire clothes hanger and a plastic container lid. Mix the plaster of Paris with water to the consistency of cream. Let the children scoop the plastic into their plastic container lids. Bend a clothes hanger for each child to place in the center of the plaster. While the plaster is still soft have the children place their shells into the mixture. Once the plaster has hardened, demonstrate how the serving tray works. This craft makes an ideal gift too!

St. Patrick's Day Collage

Objective: To make a cheerful St. Patrick's Day collage

Materials: posterboard, glue, green glitter, green yarn, shamrocks, green felt-tip markers, green crayons, macaroni, Popsicle sticks painted green, any other scraps that could be made green

Directions: Give each child a piece of posterboard that has been cut into a shamrock shape. Allow the children all the freedom they choose in decorating their shamrock with whatever green scraps are available.

Extension: During the activity, serve a clear beverage to which green food coloring could be added.

  # Leprechaun Hats

Objective: To make a leprechaun hat for St. Patrick's Day

Materials: light colored construction paper, green foil paper, glue, decorating scraps, stapler, hat pattern on page 94, scissors

Directions:

1. For basic hat shape, follow the pattern on page 94.
2. Let the children be creative in the decorating of their basic hat shape that they cut out of light colored construction paper.
3. Show the children how to cut out shamrock shapes using the green foil paper.
4. Help the children staple the basic hat shape to the headband as illustrated below.
5. Size each child's headband to his/her head and staple the ends of the headband together.

Leprechaun Hat Patterns

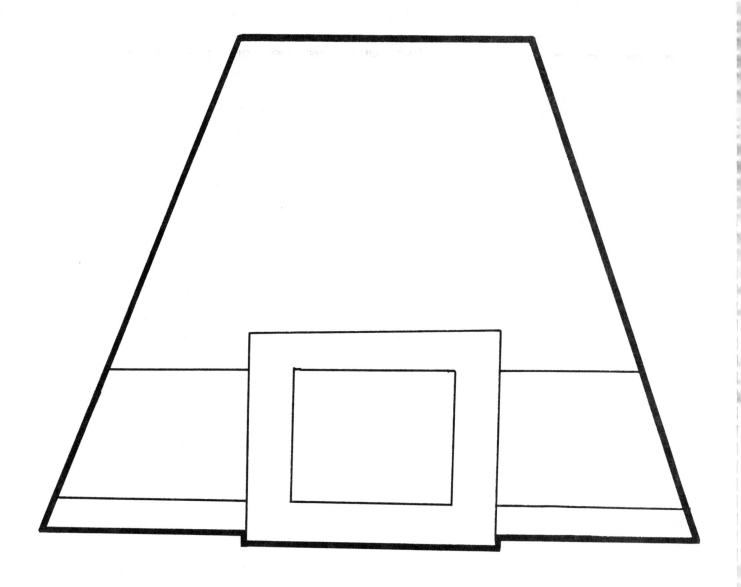

Place On Fold

94

Enormous Easter Eggs

Objective: To make a large Easter egg

Materials: newspaper, scissors, wheat paste thinned to the consistency of cream, large container for mixing paste, balloons, pastel-colored tempera paint, paintbrushes, clear plastic spray, small Easter or spring items (i.e. eggs, chicks, candy, etc.)

Directions:

1. Let the children help you cut newspaper into strips about one-half inch wide.

2. Prepare a large container with wheat paste the consistency of cream.

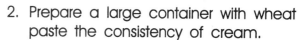

3. Blow up a small balloon for each child to the desired egg size.

4. Let the children begin covering the balloon by dipping a strip of newspaper into the paste, squeezing off the excess and laying it on the balloon.

5. Show the children how to overlap all the newspaper strips on the balloon until the entire balloon is covered.

6. Allow the papier-mache to dry thoroughly and then spray them with a clear plastic spray.

7. Let the children use tempera paint to make their Easter egg designs.

8. When the tempera paint has dried, show the children how to cut the egg shape in a jagged fashion through the center.

9. The children can then fill their egg with a small chick, Easter grass, flowers or any other spring items.

May Day Baskets

Objective: To make May Day baskets for special friends

Materials: paper drinking cups, Easter grass, construction paper, glue, stapler, glitter in spring colors, various treats to put into the baskets, scissors

Directions:

1. Let the children each decorate a paper drinking cup with glitter designs.

2. Have the children staple a strip of construction paper to opposite sides of the cups.

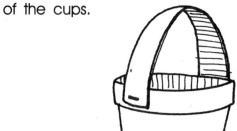

3. Let the children fill their cups with grass.

4. They can now fill their cups with various wrapped Easter treats.

5. Instruct the children to take their May Baskets home and hang them on a friend's door, ring the doorbell and hide. Tell them to watch as their friend enjoys the surprise!

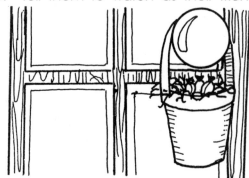

May Day Flowers

Objective: To make and piece together a
flower puzzle

Materials: pictures of flowers from
magazines, glue, cardboard,
construction paper, scissors

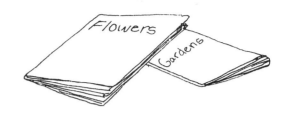

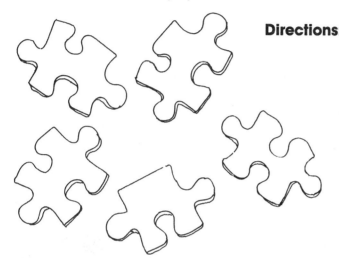

Directions: Cut out pictures of flowers from a flower or
garden magazine and paste them on
pieces of cardboard. Cut across each
picture in an irregular fashion. Pass the
pieces around the group. Have the
children try to find the match that will
complete the flower. Let them put the
pieces together until the whole flower is
formed. Eventually, the completed puzzles
can be pasted onto a sheet of
construction paper and displayed for the
springtime.

Tissue Paper Vases

Objective: To produce a decorative
vase for Mother's Day
Materials: multiple colors of tissue
paper, white glue, water,
bowl, paintbrushes, clear or
white plastic bottles

Directions: Give each child a clear
plastic bottle, a pile of different colored tissue paper and a paintbrush. Dilute a
bowl of white glue using water. Tell the children to paint over a small portion of
the bottle with the dilluted glue. Next, they should lay tissue paper strips in the
painted areas. Show the children how to overlap the tissue paper and discover
new colors. Encourage the children to cover the entire bottle with the tissue
paper. Finally, have the children paint over all the tissue paper with an even
layer of glue. This ensures that all the paper edges adhere to the bottle. Let it
dry.

Extension: Take the children on a nature walk and let them collect flowers to put in their
new vases.

Necklaces Extraordinaire!

Objective: To create a necklace out of homemade beads

Materials: salt, flour, water, food coloring, toothpicks, ribbon or string, mixing bowl

Directions: Mix three parts salt and one part flour. Add enough water to form a doughlike consistency. If the children want to add color, add food coloring. Knead the color through the dough. Divide the dough so that each child has a ball. Have the children break off small pieces and form them into beads. Instruct them to pierce each bead with a toothpick making sure they go all the way through the bead. Allow the beads to dry. When dry, the children can string the beads on a ribbon or colorful string and give them to their mothers for Mother's Day.

Jewelry Boxes

Objective: To make a decorative jewelry box to give as a Mother's Day gift

Materials: small empty boxes, glitter, glue, colored sand, buttons, shiny stones, crayons, fabric pieces, shiny paper

Directions: Have the children decorate the boxes for their mothers using the materials listed above. Discuss with them the function of a jewelry box. Perhaps the jewelry box could serve as a home for the necklace mentioned in the activity above.

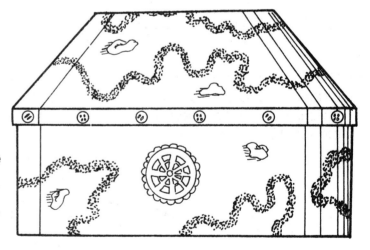

Pressed Nature Cards

Objective: To design Mother's Day cards using natural products

Materials: flowers, grass, ferns, leaves, scissors, posterboard, newsprint, clear contact paper, glue, straight pins

Directions:

1. Go on a nature walk with the children and collect the nature products listed above. Dry and press them between newsprint for approximately one week.

2. Cut the posterboard to the desired card size. Give one to each child.

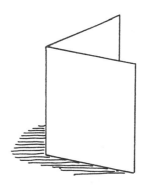

3. Have the children arrange the natural products on the card using a very small amount of glue.

4. Cut each child a square of clear contact paper large enough to extend beyond his/her card's edges.

5. Show the children how to peel the backing from the contact paper and press it firmly in place. Use a pin to prick bubbles of air that might form on the child's card. The children can then press them out using their finger tips. Trim the excess contact paper around the edges.

Sand Painting

Objective: To create a summer beach scene using the technique of sand painting, measuring spoon

Materials: large sheet of construction paper, large paintbrushes, felt-tip markers, sand, yellow tempera paint, measuring spoon

Directions: Talk about what a beach might look like on a summer day. Mix two tablespoons of sand with each cup of paint. With large paintbrushes, have the children paint a sandy beach scene. When the paint is dry, have the children draw things they might see on a summer day at the beach. The drawing should be done with felt-tip markers.

Tie-Dye T-Shirts

Objective: To design a wild T-shirt for the summer months

Materials: a white T-shirt, boxed dyes, rubber bands, mixing buckets

Directions:

1. Gather sections of a T-shirt and wrap them tightly with a rubber band. (See possible wrapping techniques).

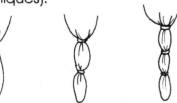

2. Mix a bucket of your lightest colored dye. Dip the whole shirt into the dye. Ring it out.

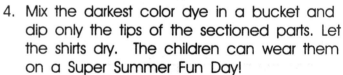

3. Mix a medium color dye and dip only the sectioned parts.

4. Mix the darkest color dye in a bucket and dip only the tips of the sectioned parts. Let the shirts dry. The children can wear them on a Super Summer Fun Day!

Bare Feet

Objectives: To feel the summer sand with bare feet and to make an impression of the feet to keep as a reminder when the weather turns cool

Materials: shoe boxes, sand, plaster of Paris, aluminum foil, water, mixing bowl, spoon

Directions:

1. Help each child line a shoe box with aluminum foil.

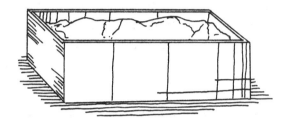

2. The children then fill the shoe box half full with sand. Wet the sand with enough water to make it hold together.

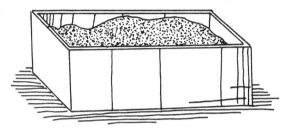

3. The children can leave an imprint in the sand by stepping in the box with one bare foot.

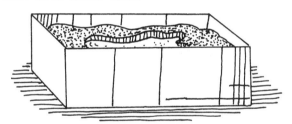

4. Add water to plaster of Paris making it the consistency of thin cream.

5. Help the children pour the plaster of Paris filling the imprint to the edge.

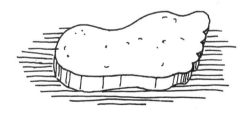

6. After a week of drying, show the children how to take out the footprint and brush off extra sand.

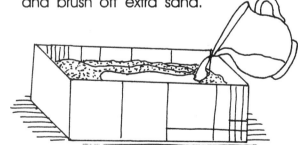

7. The children can leave the footprint as is, or they can decorate it with scraps or paint. This works great as a paperweight!

Puzzle Picture Frames

Objective: To make a picture frame from puzzle pieces to give as a Father's Day gift

Materials: corrugated cardboard, glue, acrylic paint, paintbrushes, scissors, old jigsaw puzzles, shellac, ruler

Directions:

1. Cut two 7" x 9" rectangles out of corrugated cardboard. Cut a 5" x 7" rectangle opening out of the center of one of the rectangles. Give one of each of the rectangles to each child.

2. Give each child an old jigsaw puzzle that can be painted with acrylic paint. Let the children paint the puzzle pieces and spray them with a shellac.

3. Using the painted puzzle pieces, have the children cover the cardboard rectangle with the opening in it. Instruct the children to overlap and mix the different colored pieces around the frame's edge. When the child is pleased with his/her arrangement, have him/her glue the pieces into place.

4. Help the children glue the other rectangle of corrugated cardboard to the back of the puzzle-covered frame. Instruct the children to glue the cardboard pieces together by putting a bead of glue along the sides and bottom of the frame.

5. Have the children draw a self portrait on a 5" x 7" sheet of drawing paper. Slide the picture into the frame from the opening in the top.

T-Shirts for Dad

Objective: To design a T-shirt for a Father's Day gift

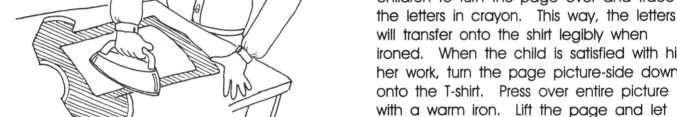

Materials: fabric crayons, drawing paper, T-shirts for dads, iron

Directions: Have the children bring a T-shirt that would fit their dad. Using fabric crayons on white drawing paper, have the children draw a picture of their Dad and themselves. In pencil, on the back and below the child's drawing, help the children print the sentence, "Me and my Dad." Instruct the children to turn the page over and trace the letters in crayon. This way, the letters will transfer onto the shirt legibly when ironed. When the child is satisfied with his/her work, turn the page picture-side down onto the T-shirt. Press over entire picture with a warm iron. Lift the page and let the T-shirt cool.

Note: Be very careful with a warm iron in the classroom.

Handprints for Dad

Objective: To design a poster for Father's Day

Materials: posterboard, tempera paint, smocks, trays for paint

Directions: Have each child decorate a large piece of posterboard by dipping his/her hands into paint and making handprints over the whole page. Let the handprints dry and have each child finger print, "I Love You Dad," in the center of the page. It may help to write this phrase somewhere large enough so that every child can read it.

Fireworks

Objective: To create a fireworks display using a crayon etching

Materials: crayons, black India ink or thick black tempera paint, paintbrushes, scraping tools (i.e. toothpicks, hairpins, nail files, Popsicle sticks, etc.), manila or white drawing paper

Directions: Have the children cover the entire surface of a sheet of paper using a heavy coat of bright colors of crayon. Stress to the children the importance of coloring the paper entirely and very heavily. The children should not be concerned about creating a picture. The children then paint over the colored surface of crayon with black India ink or black tempera paint mixed at a thick consistency. Rubbing the crayon surface with a cloth first will help get the covering to adhere to the waxy crayon surface. When the covering is dry, have the children use scraping tools like a toothpick, hairpin, nail file or Popsicle stick to scrape a fireworks design into the surface. Watch the children's delight as the colors show through the dark covering.

Festive for the Fourth

Objective: To design picnic items for the fourth of July

Materials: white felt, red and blue fabric paints, wooden craft rings, paintbrushes, water and a water container, glue, glitter

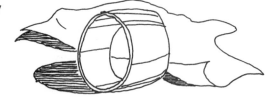

Directions: Discuss the significance of the fourth of July. Talk about activities that people do on the fourth. Give each child an 8" x 12" rectangle of white felt. Tell the children that they are going to be making a place mat for themselves for the holiday. To decorate their place mats, have the children use blue and red fabric paints. Encourage the children to make any design they would like. Give each child a wooden craft ring to cover in glue and roll through a mixture of red, blue and silver glitter. When the glue dries, place a napkin inside the ring. Instruct the children to use the craft rings as napkin holders.

Flags, Flags, Flags

Objective: To design a 4th of July flag

Materials: white drawing paper; red, white and blue construction paper; glue; scissors; markers; string; tape

Directions: Before creating the flags, discuss with the children what the significance of flags is and what different flags look like. Be sure to display the United States flag when discussing the 4th of July.

1. Instruct the children to cut out the body of the flag on white drawing paper but have them be sure to leave one end straight.

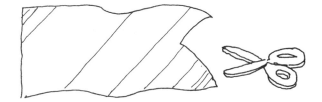

2. Next, the children use red and blue construction paper to cut out decorative shapes such as stars, stripes, circles, hearts, organic shapes, etc. and use markers to add detail.

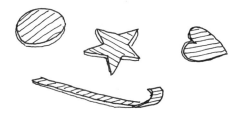

3. Have the children glue the decorations onto the white drawing paper and tape them in place.

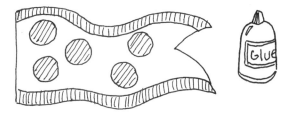

4. The children then fold the straight edge of the paper over about one inch.

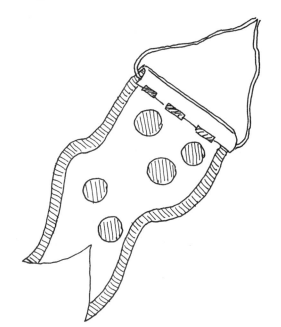

5. Have the children thread a string through the taped casing they just made. They can make a large loop by tying the string ends together.

Abstract Expressionism in the Classroom

Objective: To provide children with some art history

Materials: thinned tempera paints, large paintbrushes, drop cloth, old white tablecloth, bowls for paint, examples of Jackson Pollock's art (i.e. *One-Number 31, 1950)* tape, smocks, table

Directions: Show the children pictures of Jackson Pollock's art. Ask the children to give their impression of his art. Cover the following points about this abstract expressionist.

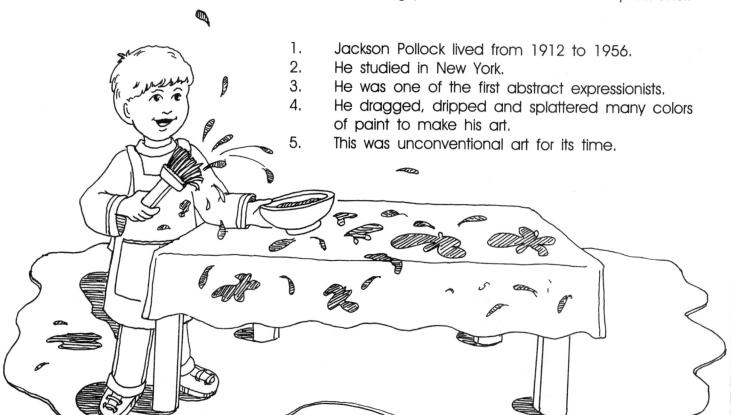

1. Jackson Pollock lived from 1912 to 1956.
2. He studied in New York.
3. He was one of the first abstract expressionists.
4. He dragged, dripped and splattered many colors of paint to make his art.
5. This was unconventional art for its time.

Tell the children that they are going to serve as Jackson Pollock's apprentices. Tell them that they are going to use his technique of painting to make a tablecloth. Cover a large outdoor space with a drop cloth and tape it into place. In the center of the drop cloth, place a table. Cover the table with a white tablecloth. Require each child to wear a smock. Fill several bowls with paint. Give a bowl with a single color of paint to a couple of children to share. Distribute several bowls of paint at a time. Remind the children to drag, splatter or drip the paint as Jackson Pollock did. Establish the rule that there is no spraying each other with paint. Let the masterpiece dry in the sun before removing it from the table.

Holiday Bulletin Board Calendar

Objective: To create a seasonal bulletin board that provides information regarding activities for the month

Materials: holiday wrapping paper, scissors, 31 envelopes, rubber stamps, red and green ink pads, markers, 31 index cards, push pins

Directions: Cover a bulletin board with holiday wrapping paper. Title the bulletin board, "December Activities." Have the children help you create this bulletin board. Using rubber stamps with green and red ink, have the children decorate white note card envelopes. Write a number from one to thirty-one on each envelope. Pin the envelopes to the bulletin board arranging them in a calendar format. Stick an index card in each envelope. On the index cards, write activities/events that will occur during the month of December. Remember to include things like holiday parties, gift exchange days, school break days, etc. Place the index cards back into their appropriate dates. Each day of the month, pull out the index card designated for that particular date and read the activities/events on it to the children.

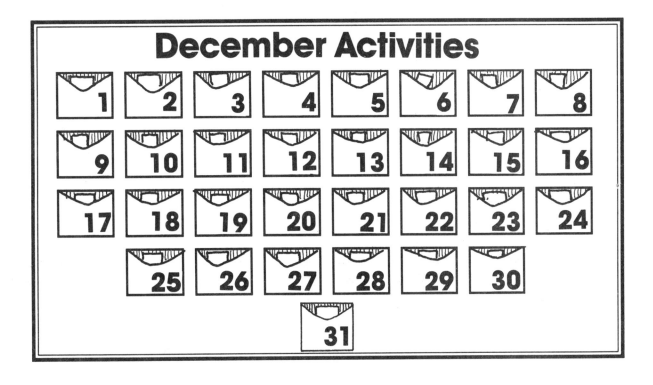

Bulletin Board

Mix a Color Bulletin Board

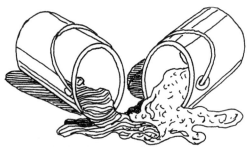

Objectives: To teach color mixing and to create a colorful classroom environment

Materials: red, blue, yellow, white, green, orange, black and purple construction paper; push pins; scissors

Directions: Out of colored construction paper, cut one blue, one red and one yellow 18" diameter circle. Cover the bulletin board with black construction paper. Pin the three circles in a triangle formation, overlapping each other, onto the center of the bulletin board. In the areas that overlap, trace a pattern shape out of thin, white paper. Use this tracing to cut a purple, green and orange overlapping section. Pin these on the bulletin board over the appropriate overlapping area. (See bulletin board illustration below, for greater detail.) Explain to the children that when the certain colors are mixed, they create new colors. Go on to explain and show them how blue and red mixed together create purple, etc. Title the bulletin board, "Let's Mix!"

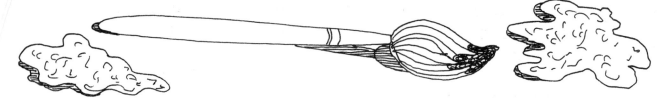

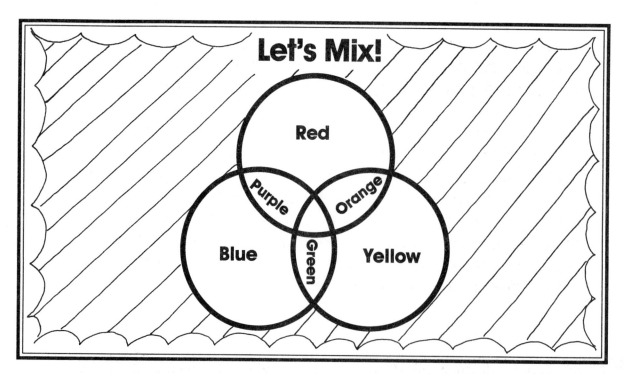

Cooking

Having children feel competent about their cooking skills is one goal of this chapter. To build this competency, the cooking chapter includes fifteen basic skills for cooking. Activities complement each skill.

The second part of this chapter includes recipes from the six food groups on the Food Guide Pyramid. These recipes give the children another opportunity to practice their cooking skills. Because food is often prepared the same way every time it is made, these recipes include silly and playful presentations.

As eating should be a nutritious and enjoyable experience, another goal of this chapter is to have the children take their cooking experiences home. In our environments and lifestyles today, preparing a healthy meal can sometimes be a challenge. Having the children learn to prepare nutritious, simple recipes with basic cooking skills might help in food preparation at home. Encourage the children's parents to utilize their children's skills at home.

Yogurt Pie

Objective: To make a nutritious yogurt pie

Ingredients/:
Materials graham cracker pie shell, one quart of strawberry flavored yogurt, spoon, mixing bowl, strawberries, plastic knives

Directions: Tell the children that they are going to make a nutritious snack from the milk, yogurt and cheese group. Have a child empty a one-quart container of strawberry yogurt into a large mixing bowl. Have other children scoop yogurt from the mixing bowl onto the graham cracker pie shell. Encourage the children to spread the yogurt evenly over the crust. Have the children slice strawberries as shown below. Be sure to supervise this part closely. Then, they can decorate the pie with the fruit. Put the pie in the freezer till it becomes firm. Enjoy!

Strawberry-Banana Cooler

Objective: To make a healthy, dairy drink

Ingredients/:
Materials blender, straws, oranges, plastic knives, clear plastic cups, frozen unsweetened whole strawberries, 2 ripe bananas, buttermilk, strawberry jam

Directions: Have the children put two to two and one half cups of frozen strawberries into a blender. Then, place two bananas and enough buttermilk in the blender to make the blender spin easily. Have a child add a little strawberry jam to the mixture. Taste to see if the mixture is sweet enough. Add more jam if necessary. Have the children cut the orange slices in half and garnish their plastic cups. Tell them to place a straw in the mixture and savor the flavor!

Cheesy Kabobs

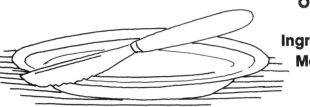

Objective: To make a healthy cheese kabob snack

Ingredients/: a decorative toothpick for each child,
Materials cheddar cheese, Swiss cheese,
mozzarella, Monterey Jack cheese, celery,
pickles, plastic knives, paper plates

Directions: Talk about the nutritional value of cheese with the children. Discuss where cheese comes from and how it is made. Have the children wash their hands thoroughly. Give each child a paper plate. Give each child a small block of each of the cheeses mentioned above. With their plastic forks, have the children cut one-half inch cubes out of the cheese. Give each child a portion of a celery stalk and some pickles. Have the children cut the celery into one-half inch slices. Then, give each child a decorative toothpick. Ask the children to arrange the items on their paper plates into a cheese kabob. Have the children alternate the celery, pickles and cheese on their toothpicks. Refrigerate till ready to eat.

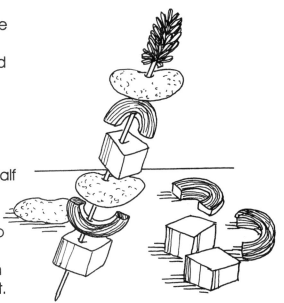

Cookie Cutter Cheese

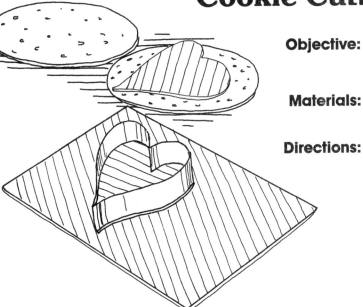

Objective: To mix play time with snack time to encourage eating wholesome cheese

Materials: cookie cutters, slices of healthy cheese, crackers, paper plates

Directions: Give each child a paper plate to prepare his/her food on. Then, give each child four crackers and two slices of healthy cheese. Provide cookie cutters for the children to use to press into their cheese slices. Let the children eat the shapes plain or let them put the shapes on their crackers. Encourage the children to eat their cheese scraps.

Crispy Cheesy Celery

Objective: To make a nutritious snack

Ingredients/:
Materials Rice Krispies® cereal, cheese spread, celery, brownie pan, plastic knives, paper towels

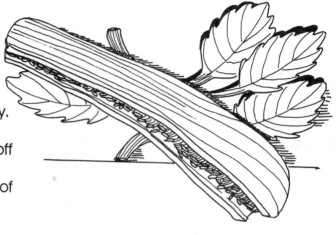

Directions: Give each child a stalk of celery. Have the children wash their celery stalk, cut the leafy ends off and pat it dry. Using a plastic knife, have them fill the groove of the celery stalk with a cheese spread. Fill a brownie pan with Rice Krispies® cereal. Have the children roll their cheese celery in the cereal. If the cereal does not stick well to the cheese, encourage the children to press the cheese portion down into the cereal.

Unique Yogurt Cones

Objective: To prepare and present food in an enjoyable way to encourage eating what normally may not have been a popular snack

Ingredients/:
Materials sugar cones, paper towels, plastic spoons, fruit-flavored yogurt, granola cereal

Directions: Give each child a sugar cone, paper towel and plastic spoon. Have the children fill their cones with fruit-flavored yogurt. Place a paper towel around the bottom of the cone to prevent leaks. Then, have them sprinkle granola cereal on the top of the yogurt. The children can eat their treat with a plastic spoon immediately or you can place the cones in the freezer and enjoy later.

Extension: Using fresh fruit, have the children flavor a plain yogurt. Supplement the mixture for the commercially prepared fruit-flavored yogurt suggested in the unique yogurt recipe above.

Cinnamon Toast

Objective: To make a cinnamon toast mixture

Ingredients/:
Materials bread, toaster, sugar, cinnamon, funnel, shaker, adhesive labels, paper plates, paper cups, spoon, markers, plastic knives, butter, measuring cups and spoons

Directions: Have each child bring a shaker to school for this activity. Allow the children to enjoy basic mixing by helping them measure one-half cup of sugar and two tablespoons of cinnamon per child. Place the mixture in a paper cup for each child. Let the children stir the mixture till it is an even color of brown. Using a funnel, let each child pour the mixture into his/her shaker. Have them put the top back on their shaker. Provide each child with an adhesive label. Have the children decorate their label and stick it to their shaker. Make a slice of toast for each child. Let the children butter their own toast using a plastic knife. Let the children shake the cinnamon toast mixture onto their bread and enjoy!

Raspberry Corn Muffins

Objective: To make delicious raspberry corn muffins

Ingredients/:
Materials flour, sugar, cornmeal, baking powder, salt, eggs, milk, cooking oil, fresh or frozen raspberries, mixing bowls, wooden spoon, muffin tray, measuring cups and spoons

Directions: In a medium mixing bowl, stir together the following:

3/4 cup of flour
3/4 cup of yellow cornmeal
3/4 cup of sugar
2 teaspoons of baking powder
1/4 teaspoon salt

Set the above ingredients aside and in another bowl mix:

1 egg beaten
3/4 cup milk
1/4 cup cooking oil

Combine the ingredients from both bowls and fold in 3/4 cup of raspberries. Fill greased muffin cups three-fourths full. Bake in 400° F preheated oven for 20-25 minutes. This recipe serves twelve people. Cool slightly and serve.

Fancy French Toast

Objective: To make unique French toast

Ingredients/: 3 eggs, half and half milk, sugar, vanilla, cinnamon, 1/2 a bagel per child,
Materials knife, butter, frying pan, confectioners sugar, mixing bowl, measuring cups and spoons

Directions: In a large mixing bowl have the children mix:

3 eggs
1 cup half and half milk
1/4 cup sugar
1/4 teaspoon vanilla
dash of cinnamon

Slice the bagels and give each child a half. Have them soak their bagel in the mixture. Melt butter in a frying pan and place the bagel in the pan. Serve on paper plates with confectioners sugar and some fresh fruit.

· ·

Bizarre Biscuits

Objective: To prepare a snack that involves food from several of the six food groups

Ingredients/: deviled ham, cheddar cheese,
Materials refrigerated biscuit dough, milk, muffin tray, pastry brush, mixing bowl, plastic spoons

Directions: In a mixing bowl, have the children combine the following: two 2 1/4-ounce cans of deviled ham and one cup of shredded cheddar cheese. Give each child a refrigerated dough biscuit. Have the children flatten and spread the biscuit in a four-inch circle. Next, with plastic spoons, have the children spread a tablespoon of the ham and cheese mixture onto the biscuit. Have them roll up their biscuits and place them two, side-by-side, in a greased muffin cup. Let them brush their biscuits with milk. Bake in a 350° F preheated oven for approximately 20 minutes. Serve the biscuits warm.

Inside Out Pizza

Objective: To make a nutritious snack for sharing

Ingredients/: Materials four 6" tortillas, grated cheddar cheese, mozzarella cheese, peppers, tomatoes, olives, pizza sauce, wax paper, microwave-safe plate, microwave, paper plates, knife

Directions: Cover a work table with wax paper. Tell the children that they are going to be making a pizza type snack. Have them place a tortilla on the wax paper and sprinkle half of the tortilla with cheddar cheese and the other half with mozzarella cheese. Add the other toppings mentioned above and let them cover them with another tortilla. Next, the children should place their tortilla on a microwave-safe plate and cover it with a piece of wax paper. Microwave on high for ninety seconds. Cool and cut into wedges for sharing.

Build-It-Yourself Subs

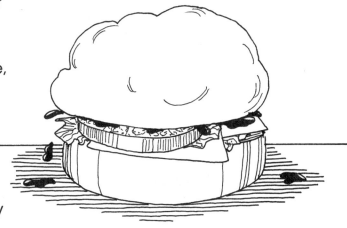

Objective: To have the children build their own sub sandwich

Ingredients/: Materials rolls, a variety of deli meats, tomato slices, shredded lettuce, vegetable oil, mayonnaise, a variety of deli cheese slices, plastic knives, paper plates

Directions: Have the children wash their hands before beginning this activity. Give each child a paper plate and a knife. They should cut the roll in half and begin placing their toppings on the roll. Encourage the children to apply the oil and mayonnaise first, if they choose to put it on their sub. Build up an appetite and eat well!

Rice Experimentation

Objective: To examine the process of cooking rice

Ingredients/: Materials dry white instant rice, water, salt, saucepan, spoon, measuring cups and spoons

Directions: Cooking rice can be a great science experiment. The children will be amazed to watch the water in the saucepan disappear as the rice is cooked. To cook rice, have the children help you follow the directions on the package. Remove from the heat. While the rice is cooking, discuss what is happening to the water. Ask the children what causes the water to disappear. Let the children taste the rice. Ask them to think of ways they could enhance the flavor.

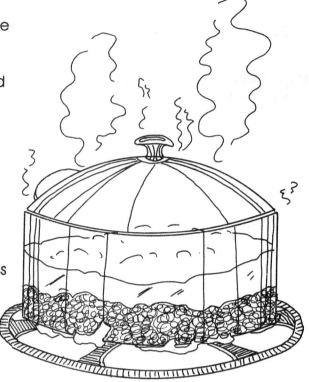

Super Spaghetti

Objective: To make a spaghetti lunch

Ingredients/: Materials spaghetti noodles, spaghetti sauce, saucepans, strainer, salt, measuring spoons and cups, water, paper plates, plastic forks

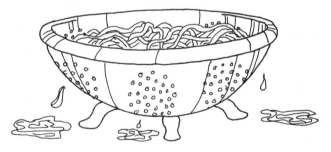

Directions: Bring two quarts of water to a boil in a large saucepan. Have the children add two teaspoons of salt. When the water comes to a boil, add the spaghetti. Let the water return to its boiling state. Cook the spaghetti uncovered, letting the children stir frequently. When it is done, help the children drain the spaghetti in a strainer and rinse in hot water. Heat your favorite spaghetti sauce to pour over the spaghetti and enjoy!

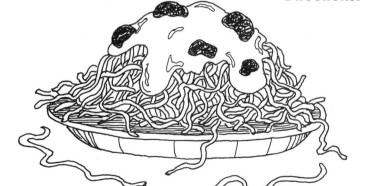

Sipping Strawberries

Objective: To make a blended fruit drink

Ingredients/: Materials blender, plastic cups, orange for garnishing, plastic knives, straws, strawberries, orange juice, vanilla ice cream, ice cream scoop, measuring cups

Directions: Have the children measure and combine the following ingredients in a blender:

6 cups fresh or frozen unsweetened strawberries
1 1/2 cups orange juice
2 scoops vanilla ice cream

Cover and blend till creamy and smooth. This recipe will yield about eight servings. Have the children pour the mixture into plastic cups. Have them cut up orange slices to use to garnish their cups. They can add a straw and sip a strawberry!

Frozen Fruity Surprise

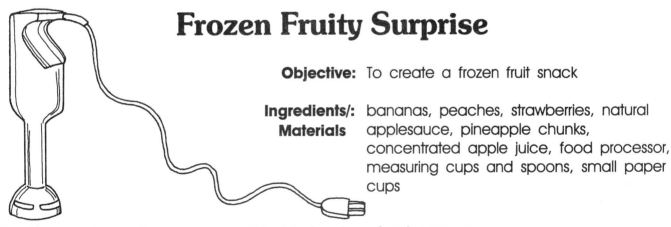

Objective: To create a frozen fruit snack

Ingredients/: Materials bananas, peaches, strawberries, natural applesauce, pineapple chunks, concentrated apple juice, food processor, measuring cups and spoons, small paper cups

Directions: Place the ingredients listed below in a food processor.

4 bananas
4 hulled strawberries
4 cups peeled and chopped peaches

2 cups natural applesauce
2 cups pineapple chunks
4 tablespoons of concentrated apple juice

Process the food for a short time, keeping the fruit in small chunks. Have the children fill paper cups with the mixture. Place the cups in the freezer and serve frozen.

Fruit Pizza

Objective: To make a nutritious fruit pizza

Ingredients/: Materials seasonal fruit, flour, sugar, butter, vegetable oil, water, vanilla, cream cheese, fork, mixing bowl, pizza sheet, rolling pin, non-stick cooking spray, plastic knives, pizza cutter, measuring cups and spoons

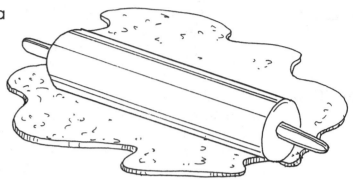

Directions: To make the pizza crust, preheat oven to 375° F. In a large mixing bowl, combine 11/2 cups flour and 1/4 cup sugar. Cut in 1/4 cup butter and mix till resembles a coarse meal. Using a fork, stir in cup of oil. Add 3 tablespoons of water (one at a time). Spray pizza sheet with non-stick spray. Place dough formed into a ball shape on the pizza sheet. Using a lightly floured rolling pin, roll the pastry over the entire pizza sheet. Bake till light brown (approximately 12 minutes). Let cool. Prepare the pizza crust before class if time does not allow for entire preparation.

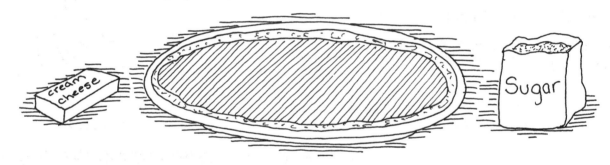

For the pizza "sauce," have the children combine one 8 oz package of cream cheese, 1/4 cup of sugar and a 1/2 of a teaspoon of vanilla. Have the children use plastic knives to spread the cream cheese mixture over the pizza crust to represent the pizza sauce.

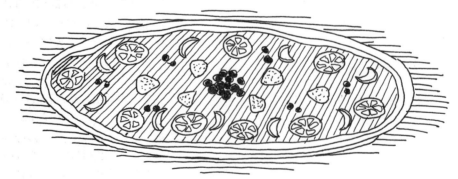

For the pizza toppings, have the children use their plastic knives to cut the fruit in slices. Next, have them layer the pizza with a decorative design of fruit toppings. Use a pizza cutter to divide the pizza. Enjoy!

Fruit Juicer Juice

Objective: To make fruit juice

Ingredients/: hand held juicer, lemons, oranges,
Materials mandarins, grapefruits, paper cups, knives

Directions: Talk to the children about making juice. Have the children recall some of the juices they have tasted. Show the children how to squeeze juice from oranges, lemons, grapefruits and mandarins. First, have the children press and roll the fruit on a table to soften the fruit. Then help them cut the fruit in halves. Using a hand held juicer, have the children next press and rotate the fruit to make juice. Have the children clean out the strainer before beginning to make a new juice. Let the children taste the fruit juices just after they are made. Have them talk about how the fresh squeezed juices taste relative to store-bought juices.

• •

Caramelized Bananas

Objective: To caramelize bananas

Ingredients/: unsalted butter, dark brown sugar,
Materials bananas, shallow casserole dish,
microwave oven, plain yogurt, granola
cereal, paper bowls, plastic spoons, metal
spoon, plastic knives, lemon

Directions: In a shallow casserole dish, have the children place four tablespoons of cubed, unsalted butter and four tablespoons of dark brown sugar. Let the children set the microwave on high for one minute. Using plastic knives, let them cut four bananas in 1/4 inch slices. Ask one child to squeeze a lemon over the bananas. Next, combine the bananas with the melted butter and sugar mixture. Cook the combination for one minute and forty-five seconds on high. Stir the mixture again. Have the children scoop plain yogurt into paper bowls. Have them spoon the caramelized bananas on the yogurt and sprinkle a little granola cereal on the top of the bananas. Go bananas and enjoy!

Kiddie Hors d' Oeuvres

Objective: To prepare a nutritious snack from the fruit group

Ingredients/:
Materials bananas, plastic knives, peanut butter, honey, apple butter, paper bowls, plastic spoons

Directions: Remind the children to wash their hands before beginning this activity. Give each child a banana and a plastic knife. Have the children slice the banana into their own paper bowl. Ask them to carefully pour a little honey, scoop a little peanut butter and spread a little apple butter on the top of their banana slices. Give the children a plastic spoon and let them "dig in!"

Apple Cider

Objective: To make a delicious cup of warm apple cider

Ingredients/:
Materials cinnamon sticks, nutmeg, apple cider, large cooking pot, ladle, Styrofoam cups, apples, measuring spoon

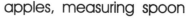

Directions: Have the children pour a gallon of apple cider into a large cooking pot. Let them measure a teaspoon of nutmeg and place it into the apple cider. Next, let a child place cinnamon sticks into the apple cider. Simmer the drink on the stove for fifteen to twenty minutes. While the cider is simmering, have the children cut apple wedges to use to garnish their cups. Also, have them place a cinnamon stick in each cup. Serve the cider by letting the children use a ladle to fill their cup. Remind the children to sip the cider slowly in case it is too hot.

Crunchy Cooked Broccoli

Objective: To get children interested in trying cooked broccoli

Ingredients/: Materials microwave-safe casserole dish, microwave, paper towels, sesame seeds, broccoli

Directions: Talk to the children about their interest in eating cooked green vegetables. The response will likely involve a lot of turned-up noses. Explain to the children that you are going to give them the opportunity to learn how to cook a green vegetable that tastes great. Children typically do not like soft, overcooked vegetables. Vegetables cooked this way lose a lot of their nutritional value as well. Broccoli stays bright green and crunchy when cooked in a microwave. Have the children microwave sesame seeds on a paper towel for three and a half minutes on high. Next, have them wash a head of broccoli. They should put the broccoli, floret side down, in the casserole dish. They add two tablespoons of water to the broccoli and cover tightly. Let someone set the microwave on high for four minutes. Cook, remove and let the broccoli stand for a few moments. Choose someone to sprinkle the sesame seeds on the broccoli. Let the children taste test the broccoli by cutting a small floret off the head for each child. Tell the children that they might want to prepare this part of their family's dinner some night.

Baked Potato Filler

Objective: To add extra flavor to everyday potatoes

Ingredients/: Materials microwave, microwave-safe plate, paper towels, potatoes, forks, broccoli, cheddar cheese, paper plates

Directions: Have the children wash and then pierce four potatoes with a fork. Have them wrap each potato in a paper towel and organize them on a microwave-safe plate. Next, have a child set the microwave on high for five minutes. Cook and rotate the potatoes after five minutes on high. Then, have a child set the microwave on high for another five minutes. (Check periodically as microwave strength varies.) When soft inside, let the potatoes cool. With a plastic knife, cut a cross on the top of each potato. To turn the potatoes into something special, add a scoop of melted cheddar cheese and a few steamed florets of broccoli. Sprinkle bacon bits over the entire potato. Cut the potatoes in slices to let the students sample their work.

Creamed Peas, Onions and Mushrooms

Objective: To prepare vegetables so that the children will try them

Ingredients/:
Materials frozen peas, frozen creamed onions, sliced, drained mushrooms; grated Parmesan cheese; microwave-safe, 2-qt. dish; microwave, plastic forks, paper bowls

Directions: In a microwave-safe, two-quart dish, have the children put the following ingredients:

1 package (10 oz) frozen peas
1 package (10 oz) frozen creamed onions
1 jar (4 oz) of sliced, drained mushrooms

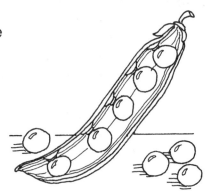

Have the children cover the dish tightly and microwave on high for seven and a half minutes. Remind the children to stir the mixture several times throughout the cooking time. Sprinkle with Parmesan cheese and serve in paper bowls with forks.

Grilled Cheese Broccoli Sandwiches

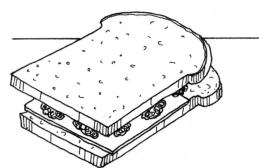

Objective: To make grilled cheese sandwiches with broccoli

Ingredients/:
Materials bread, cheese slices, crunchy-cooked broccoli (see page 121 for recipe.), softened butter, frying pan, plastic knives, paper plates, spatula

Directions: With their plastic knives, have the children butter several slices of bread. Next, they should place a cheese slice on the unbuttered side of one slice of bread. The children should top the cheese with crisp-cooked broccoli florets. The other slice of bread should be placed (butter side up) on top of the cheese and broccoli. Place a pat of butter in a frying pan and melt on medium heat. Have the children place a few sandwiches in the pan. Cook until the bread is light brown. Use a spatula to turn the sandwiches over. Cook about two minutes per side. Remove the sandwiches from the pan and have the children cut the bread into quarters. Serve on paper plates.

Frogs on a Log

Objective: To enjoy a playful, healthy snack

Ingredients/: celery, raisins, peanut butter,
Materials plastic knives, paper towels

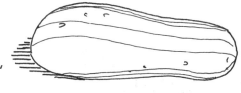

Directions: Have the children wash celery
and remove the leafy greens on the ends.   Next, have them pat the celery
dry with paper towels   Give each child a stalk of celery and allow him/her to
make frogs on a log.   Using plastic knives have the children spread peanut
butter in the celery groove.   Explain that the celery stalk, filled with peanut
butter, is the brown log.   Let raisins represent the frogs.   Each child should
determine how many frogs he/she would like to place on his/her log.   You
might want to sing *Five Green and Speckled Frogs* while making this snack.
The lyrics are below.

Five green and speckled frogs,
Sat on a speckled log,
Eating some most delicious bugs (yum, yum).
One jumped into the pool,
Where it was nice and cool,
Now, there are four, green, speckled frogs (glum, glum).

The song is designed to continue, subtracting a frog each verse till there are no frogs left.

· ·

Pumpernickel Cucumber Sandwiches

Objective: To encourage children to eat cucumbers

Ingredients/: dill, one (2" square) loaf of pumpernickel
Materials bread, softened cream cheese, cucumbers,
plastic knives, paper plates

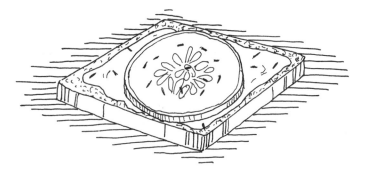

Directions: Have the children slice cucumbers as thin
as they possibly can. Set aside the
cucumbers. Next, have the children
spread cream cheese on one side of
two-inch squares of pumpernickel bread.
Have them lay a slice of cucumber on
the cream cheese and sprinkle a small
amount of dill on top. These bite-size
sandwiches are really refreshing!

Deli Sliced Kabobs

Objective: To provide an easily prepared, high protein meat snack

Ingredients/:
Materials thin, deli sliced meats, wooden skewers, mandarin slices, grape halves, kiwi wedges or whatever fruits are in season

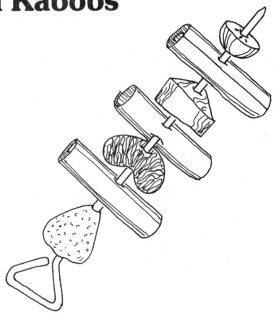

Directions: Have the children make their own kabobs. Give each child a skewer and explain safety rules surrounding it. Provide a tray of thin, deli sliced meats and fruit pieces from fruits that are in season. Have the children arrange the fruit and meat on their skewers in a pleasing fashion. Encourage the children to alternate between placing a fruit piece and meat slice on the skewer. Cover and refrigerate covered until snack time.

Tuna Boats

Objective: To get children to eat a playful snack containing tuna

Ingredients/:
Materials tortilla chips, canned tuna, mayonnaise, soft bagels, mixing bowl, spoons, measuring cups, pepper

Directions: Have the children create tuna boats by mixing six and one half ounces of canned, drained and flaked tuna to one half cup of mayonnaise. Let them add a little pepper and mix well. Give each child one half of a soft bagel. Let him/her spread the tuna mixture on the bagel. Last, the children should place a tortilla chip (pointed part up) on top of the tuna mixture for the sail of the boat. Enjoy!

The Sack Snack

Objective: To make a nutritious trail mix snack

Ingredients/: medium-sized paper sacks, Chex® cereal, raisins, shelled peanuts, yogurt chips,
Materials small resealable bags

Directions: In a medium paper sack, have the children combine the following ingredients:

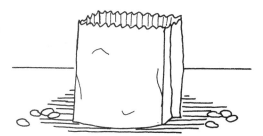

4 cups of Chex® cereal
2 cups of raisins
2 cups of shelled peanuts
1 1/2 cups of yogurt chips

Let the children mix the ingredients by holding the paper sack tight and shaking it. Pour the mixture into small resealable bags. Explain to the children, the significance of a trail mix to a hiker who cannot carry perishable meats. Talk about the protein and high energy parts of this mixture.

Taco Flavored Drummies

Objective: To spice up a common meal of chicken drumsticks

Ingredients/: corn chips, butter,
Materials taco seasoning mix: chicken drumsticks, bowls, fork, medium-sized shallow casserole dish, measuring cup and spoons.

Directions: Preheat oven to 425° F. Have the children prepare the seasoning and coating by crushing the corn chips. Then, they place three cups of the crushed corn chips in a bowl. Have a child mix three tablespoons of melted butter and one envelope of taco seasoning. Let the children dip a chicken drumstick into the seasoning mixture and then in the crushed corn chips. Then, the drumsticks should be arranged in a shallow, greased casserole dish and baked for 35 minutes until golden brown.

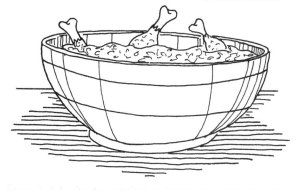

Deviled Eggs

Objective: To make deviled eggs as a protein alternative to meat

Ingredients/:
Materials eggs, relish, mayonnaise, paprika, small mixing bowl, spoon, large saucepan, water, plastic knives, fork, parsley, measuring spoons

Directions: Help the children boil water. Place six eggs in the boiling water for approximately four minutes. Next, replace the boiling water with cold water and let the eggs cool. When the eggs are cool, let the children crack and peel the shells. Using their plastic knives the children should cut the eggs in half and drop the yolks into a small bowl. One child should mash the yolks with one and one half tablespoons of relish and three tablespoons mayonnaise. Help the children fill the egg halves with the yolk mixture and sprinkle them with a trace of paprika. If you can obtain some sprigs of fresh parsley, place a tiny piece on each egg.

Layered Bean Dip

Objective: To provide a protein vegetarian snack

Ingredients/: refried beans, salsa, avocados, sour
Materials cream, sharp cheddar cheese, tortilla chips, glass pie plate

Directions: Preheat oven to 350° F. Have the children spread layers of ingredients in a 9" inch glass pie plate. Below is the amount and order of the ingredients as they should be layered.

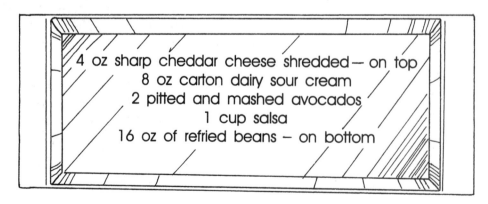

4 oz sharp cheddar cheese shredded — on top
8 oz carton dairy sour cream
2 pitted and mashed avocados
1 cup salsa
16 oz of refried beans — on bottom

Cover with foil and bake for fifteen to twenty minutes. Serve with tortilla chips.

No-Fuss Frozen Fruit Pops

Objective: To make a healthy, frozen fruit snack

Ingredients/: Materials craft sticks, fresh fruit (e.g. whole strawberries, complete pineapple rings, whole bananas, watermelon, fresh wedges of cantaloupe, etc.), sandwich bags

Directions: On a hot day, prepare and share this snack with the children. Let the children choose a fresh fruit. To assemble the fruit pops, have the children slide a craft stick into the piece of fruit. Cover the fruit part of the pop with a sandwich bag and freeze for four hours. Enjoy!

Valentine Pops

Objective: To practice decorating by making valentine cookies on a stick

Ingredients/: Materials dough from a favorite sugar cookie recipe, heart-shaped cookie cutter, craft sticks, icing in a tube, plastic knives, waxed paper, flour, rolling pins, cookie sheets, non-stick cooking spray

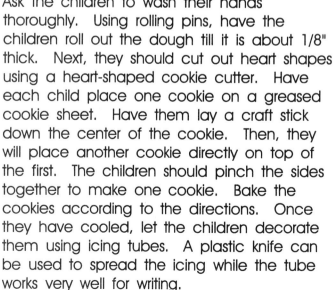

Directions: Make your favorite sugar cookie recipe prior to class. Have the dough well-chilled. Preheat the oven to 350° F. Have a work table covered with wax paper. Lightly flour the surface. Ask the children to wash their hands thoroughly. Using rolling pins, have the children roll out the dough till it is about 1/8" thick. Next, they should cut out heart shapes using a heart-shaped cookie cutter. Have each child place one cookie on a greased cookie sheet. Have them lay a craft stick down the center of the cookie. Then, they will place another cookie directly on top of the first. The children should pinch the sides together to make one cookie. Bake the cookies according to the directions. Once they have cooled, let the children decorate them using icing tubes. A plastic knife can be used to spread the icing while the tube works very well for writing.

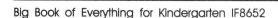

Chunky Chocolate Chippers

Objective: To make delicious, chocolate chip cookies

Ingredients/: Materials cookie tray, spatula, mixer, spoon, ingredients listed below, mixing bowls, measuring cups and spoons, cooling rack

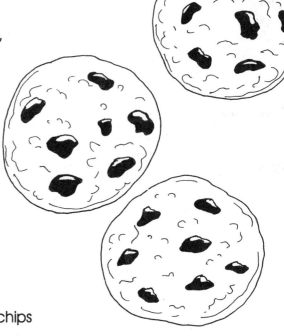

Directions: Preheat the oven to 350° F.

      2 cups all-purpose flour
      1 teaspoon baking soda
      1/2 teaspoon salt
      1/2 cup shortening
      1/2 cup chunky peanut butter
      2 eggs
      1 cup granulated sugar
      1/2 cup brown sugar
      1 teaspoon vanilla
      1 tablespoon of water
      1 (12 oz) package chocolate chips

In a bowl, have the children stir together flour, baking soda and salt and set aside. Let them beat the shortening, peanut butter, eggs, sugars, vanilla and water until the mixture appears creamy. Add the dry ingredients and let the children blend it well. The children can pour in a package of chocolate chips and stir well. Have them drop the dough by spoonfuls onto a cookie sheet. Bake for ten minutes. Using a spatula, help the children remove cookies from the cookie sheet and place them on a cooling rack.

Chocolate-Dipped Pineapple

Objective: To satisfy a sweet tooth with chocolate-dipped pineapple

Ingredients/: Materials plastic knives, microwave, microwave-safe bowl, wax paper, baking sheet, pineapple rings, slivered almonds, bittersweet chocolate

Directions: Have the children cut pineapple rings into quarters. Let them break bittersweet chocolate into pieces and place them in a microwave-safe bowl. Microwave the chocolate on medium for two minutes. Stir. Place a sheet of wax paper over a baking sheet. Let the children dip one side of the chocolate ring into the chocolate mixture and place it on wax paper, chocolate side up. Next, have them press a slivered almond into the chocolate. Refrigerate at least fifteen minutes. Eat up!

Cherry Cobbler

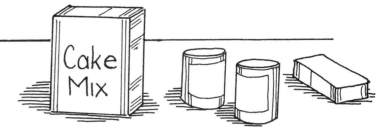

Objective: To make a tasty treat

Ingredients/: Materials cherry pie filling, 9" x 13" baking dish, yellow cake mix, butter, knife, non-stick cooking spray

Directions: Preheat oven to 350° F. Have the children pour two cans of cherry pie filling in a 9 x 13 inch baking dish, lightly sprayed with non-stick cooking spray. Then, have them sprinkle the entire box of yellow cake mix over the filling. Next, the children cut one and one half sticks of butter into slices. Have them place the slices on the cake mix. Bake for one hour. Let cool and enjoy!

Eggs in a Nest

Objective: To make an edible bird's nest and eggs

Ingredients/: Materials shredded-wheat biscuits, butter, brown sugar, honey, cinnamon, mini jellybeans, measuring cups and spoons, large mixing bowl, muffin tray, muffin baking cups

Directions: Preheat the oven to 350° F. In a large mixing bowl, have the children mix together:

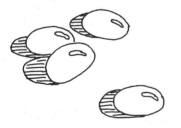

6 crumbled, large shredded-wheat biscuits
1/4 cup of butter
1/4 cup of brown sugar
2 tablespoons of honey
1/2 teaspoon cinnamon

Have the children grease a muffin tray. Then, each child should fill a muffin cup with the mixture. Encourage them to press down gently on the center of their mixtures to create a small indentation. Bake for ten minutes. Remove from the oven and let the mixture cool in the trays. Remove carefully from trays and let the children fill them with mini jellybeans.

Candy Popcorn

Objective: To make a sweet popcorn snack

Ingredients/: Materials mixing bowl, 9" x 13" baking pan, spoon, saucepan, ingredients listed below, measuring cups and spoons

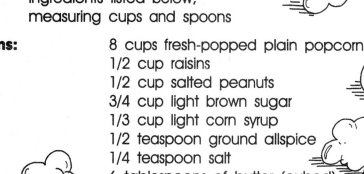

Directions:
8 cups fresh-popped plain popcorn
1/2 cup raisins
1/2 cup salted peanuts
3/4 cup light brown sugar
1/3 cup light corn syrup
1/2 teaspoon ground allspice
1/4 teaspoon salt
6 tablespoons of butter (cubed)
1 teaspoon vanilla extract

Preheat the oven to 250° F. In a large mixing bowl, have the children measure and mix the popcorn, peanuts and raisins. Then, have them place the mixture in a 9" x 13" baking pan. Set aside. In a saucepan, combine brown sugar, corn syrup, allspice and salt until blended. Have the children cut the butter in cubes and add to the saucepan. Bring mixture to a boil using low heat and stirring constantly. Increase heat and let cook for five minutes without stirring. Remove from heat and add vanilla. Immediately pour liquid over popcorn mixture. Let the children stir the mixture with a spoon to cover the popcorn completely. Bake for fifty minutes remembering to stir several times while cooking. Remove from oven and let the mixture cool. Have the children break the treat into bite-sized pieces once it has cooled.

Almond Chocolate Balls

Objective: To make tasty chocolates

Ingredients/: Materials milk chocolate, raisins, chopped almonds, wax paper, microwave-safe bowl, microwave, airtight container, measuring cup

Directions: Have the children microwave 250 grams of milk chocolate broken into pieces. Set the microwave on high for two minutes. The children can combine 150 grams of chopped almonds, one cup of raisins and the melted chocolate. Then, they should drop the mixture by spoonfuls on wax paper. Allow the mixture to sit in a cool place. Seal it in an airtight container.

Sifting Skills

Objective: To learn and practice sifting skills

Ingredients/: Materials flour, sifter with a crank, 2 large mixing bowls, measuring cup

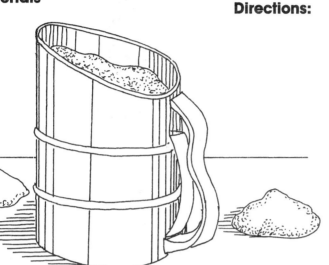

Directions: Fill a large mixing bowl with flour. Place a crank sifter in another large mixing bowl. Tell the children that they are going to have an opportunity to practice their sifting skills. Give the children a measuring cup to scoop flour from the large mixing bowl and put into the sifter. Keep the sifter inside the large mixing bowl to prevent the flour from flying all over the place. Let the children sift the lumps out of the flour. (Sugar could be substituted for flour.) Ask the children to compare the texture of the sifted and unsifted flour.

Rolling Skills

Objective: To practice the rolling skills involved in baking

Ingredients/: Materials rolling pin, flour, wooden cutting board, mixing bowls, wax paper, measuring cups and spoons

Directions: Have the children make the simple cookie dough recipe below.

2 cups butter softened
2 cups sugar
1 egg
1 teaspoon vanilla.

1/4 teaspoon salt
1 teaspoon baking soda
4 1/4 cups flour

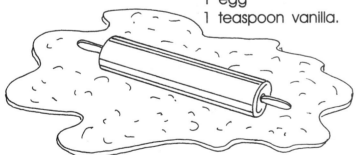

Let the children combine the wet ingredients in one bowl. Then, they should combine all the dry ingredients in another bowl. Last, have them mix both together and refrigerate.

Cover a table with wax paper. On this table have the children practice rolling out the dough using a lightly floured rolling pin and lightly floured wax paper. Remind the children to roll from various angles of the dough and not in one direction only.

131

Crazy Cut-outs

Objective: To practice cutting with cookie cutters

Ingredients/: Materials cookie cutters, Jell-O ® jigglers mix, wax paper, pan for Jell-O ®

Directions: Cover a table with wax paper to promote easy clean-up. Prepare a flat pan of Jell-O ® jigglers mix by following the simple directions on the package. Once stiff, give each child a square of Jell-O ® to use to practice making cutouts using cookie cutters. Let the children enjoy eating the jiggler cutouts and encourage them to try the scraps too.

Extension: Let the children try making cutouts from play dough. The dough can be pressed by hand or rolled with a rolling pin.

Preparing Fresh Produce

Objective: To demonstrate the necessity and technique of washing fresh produce

Ingredients/: Materials wash basin, water, head of lettuce, salad spinner, clean dish towel

Directions: Fill a water basin half full of cool water. Place a head of lettuce in the basin and show the children how the lettuce holds tiny particles of dirt. Have the children break the leaves apart and rinse them individually. Then, they should place the leaves in a salad spinner. Help them spin the lettuce dry. Empty the spinner onto a clean dish towel and have the children pat the leaves dry. Refrigerate the lettuce in the crisper of the refrigerator.

Chopping, Dicing, Mincing

Objective: To practice chopping, dicing and mincing skills

Ingredients/: Materials large head of lettuce, plastic knives, cutting boards

Directions: Discuss the difference between chopping, dicing and mincing. Give the children plastic knives and cutting boards to work on. Demonstrate how to chop the head of lettuce in half, how to dice and mince the lettuce by cutting it in cubes and very tiny tidbits. Let the children practice cutting the lettuce themselves. When finished experimenting, feed the lettuce scraps to a classroom pet if there is one.

Whip It Good!

Objective: To practice using an electric blender

Ingredients/: electric blender, large mixing bowl, carton
Materials of whipping cream, spatula

Directions: Have the children pour a carton of whipping cream into a large mixing bowl. Show them how to assemble the electric blender and discuss the safety needed in using one. Help the children hold the blender in place. Let the children explore with the different speeds. Occasionally, scrape the sides of the bowl with a spatula to mix all the ingredients thoroughly. Then, discuss what happened to the whipping cream over a period of whipping it using an electric blender. Supervise this activity very closely.

Separating Eggs

Objective: To practice separating egg yolks from their whites

Ingredients/: eggs, mixing bowls
Materials

Directions: This skill is a favorite of young children. Demonstrate how to crack and pull apart the egg with your thumbs. Over a mixing bowl, cup the bottom part of the shell in one hand and pull the top away. The children will see that some of the egg white will pour over on top of your hand and into the mixing bowl below. Show them how the bottom portion of the egg can be poured into your cupped hand. The whites will siphon through your slightly separated fingers into the mixing bowl below. Place the egg yolk into another mixing bowl. Let the children practice. Save the cracked eggs and let the children use them to practice beating with a whisk.

Beat the Eggs

Objective: To practice using a whisk

Ingredients/: eggs, whisks, mixing bowls
Materials

Directions: Demonstrate how a whisk works and have the children practice beating eggs. Suggest that the children help at home with beating eggs for quiches, scrambled eggs and in baking recipes.

I Can Help Too!

Objectives: To inform the children's parents about the cooking skills their child is learning at school and to have parents reinforce them at home

Materials: activity sheet (below), crayons

Directions: Have each child circle and color the kitchen tools below that he/she has learned to use. Copy some recipes that the children have made at school and encouage the parents to try making the same recipes at home.

· ·

Color the kitchen tools you have learned to use at school.

Can Opener Crazy

Objective: To practice opening cans with a hand-held can opener

Materials: hand-held can opener, empty tin cans

Directions: Collect as many old tin cans as possible. Lay the cans on a table and give the children hand-held can openers. Demonstrate how to use the can opener in front of the children. Be sure to discuss safety in using the openers and holding open metal cans. Let the children practice opening the cans. Remind them to put the opened cans and lids in a designated trash can.

Kitchen Time

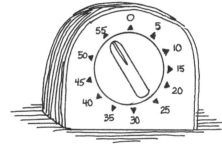

Objective: To learn how to set a kitchen timer

Materials: a kitchen timer

Directions: Demonstrate how a kitchen timer works. Let the children set the timer throughout the day. Plan to do an activity, estimate how long it will take and set the timer. When the buzzer sounds, see how close your time estimate was.

Grating Away

Objective: To practice grating

Materials: graters, potatoes, mixing bowls

Directions: Demonstrate how a grater works. Discuss what foods might need to be grated for a recipe. Talk about the safety factors involved in using a grater. Let the children take turns trying to grate a potato using a grater. Discuss how difficult it is to do and what foods might be easier to grate.

Measuring and Mixing

Objective: To practice measuring and mixing skills

Materials: measuring cups, measuring spoons, funnel, small mixing bowl, glass jar with tight-fitting lid, adhesive labels, markers, ingredients listed below

Directions: To practice measuring and mixing dry and wet ingredients, have the children measure and mix the following ingredients to make a spinach salad dressing.

1 teaspoon salt
2 tablespoons sugar
2 tablespoons vinegar
1/4 cup of vegetable oil
-dash of Tabasco® sauce
-dash of pepper

Ask the children to use a funnel to pour the dressing from the small mixing bowl to a glass jar with a tight-fitting lid. Tell the children to use markers to create an adhesive label for their glass jar. Help the children label their jars. Encourage them to share their dressing with their family or friends.

Safety First

Objective: To remind children of the safety requirements with cooking

Materials: chart paper, marker

Directions: Discuss the safety risks involved in cooking. Tell the children that you would like them to give you some cooking rules. Write the children's rules on the chart paper and read them frequently for safety reminders. Be sure to include the rules listed below.

1. Never use stoves or knives without supervision of an adult.
2. Always wash your hands before preparing foods.
3. No taste-testing with fingers or mouths while preparing food.

Food Guide Pyramid

Color the Food Guide Pyramid below. Draw a line from the foods outside the pyramid to the group they belong to (See example).

• •

Name _____

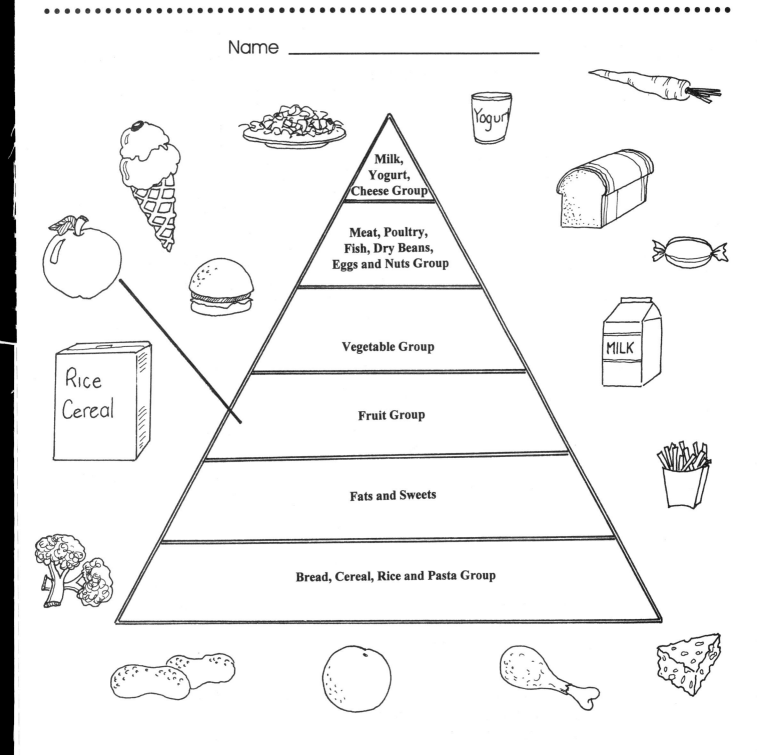

Bulletin Board of Top Secret Recipes

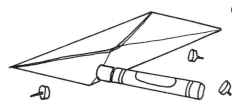

Objectives: To foster parent involvement and brighten the classroom environment

Materials: Six 6 1/2" x 9 1/2" white envelopes, markers, butcher paper, stapler, push pins

Directions: Ask the children to help design this bulletin board. Have the children use markers to decorate enough butcher paper to cover the bulletin board. Tell the children to draw all different kinds of food on the butcher paper. Cover the bulletin board with the butcher paper. Write a single food group title from the Food Guide Pyramid on each white envelope. Pin the envelopes to the bulletin board. Title the bulletin board "Top Secret Recipes." Then, encourage the children to bring their favorite recipes from home. Ask the children to get help from their parents with this activity. When the child brings a recipe to school, help him/her place it in the appropriate food group envelope. Eventually, remove all the recipes from the envelopes and correlate them into a recipe book. Let the children decorate a cover for the book and send it home as a gift idea.

Favorite Class Recipes

Top Secret Recipes

Fats and Sweets Group

Fruit Group

Bread, Cereal, Rice and Pasta Group

Meat, Poultry, Fish, Dry Beans, Eggs and Nuts Group

Milk, Yogurt and Cheese Group

Vegetable Group

Language Arts

The language arts activities presented in this book have been designed to build upon one another. The goal is to help children develop and reinforce the whole language skills of **Reading, Speaking, Listening and Writing.** Although the chapter is organized more according to development, the children will be involved in many activities dealing with more than one of these skills at the same time.

To help children develop **Reading** skills, the introductory activities included in this chapter involve basic letter recognition and sound, small word building and recognition, and short sentence structure. Opposites and rhyming word activities are also included.

Throughout the chapter, the children are challenged to develop their **Speaking** skills. Puppet play is promoted in the activities as it helps reduce the fear of public speaking for many children.

The many **Listening** skills activities presented in this chapter include following directions, sequencing, poetry, memory and riddle activities. All serve to enhance this very necessary and important skill.

To help the children acquire **Writing** skills, this chapter includes many writing activities. These activities are integrated with all the whole language activities and can be found throughout the chapter.

By doing the activities included in this Language Arts chapter, the children will have an enjoyable first experience building whole language skills. The hope is to help children appreciate literature and the language arts of our world.

The Alphabet Jar

Objective: To introduce and reinforce alphabet letters and their sounds

Materials: large clear plastic jar, objects beginning with the letter of the week, chart paper, markers, masking tape

Directions: Each week, choose a letter to be the featured "letter of the week." Place a piece of masking tape on the jar marking it with the featured letter. Each day of that week, add an object to the jar that begins with that letter. (Encourage the children to bring a small object from home that would belong in the jar.) On Friday, use chart paper to record all of the objects that went into the jar over the course of the week. The children may be able to help write the words.

Extension: At the end of the week, allow the children the opportunity to guess how many objects are in the letter jar without opening the lid to the jar.

Alphabet Jewelry

Objective: To reinforce alphabet letters and their sounds

Materials: craft barrettes, dry macaroni, string, posterboard, markers, glue

Directions: Make letter cutouts out of posterboard. Give each child a letter and have him/her decorate it using markers. Explain that they are going to be making alphabet jewelry. Provide dry macaroni for beads, string for bracelets and necklaces and any other materials students might need. See example below for an idea.

Letter Bags

Objective: To reinforce the beginning sounds and recognition of the letters p, b and d

Materials: 5 objects beginning with p, 5 objects beginning with d and 5 objects beginning with b, three paper grocery bags

Directions:

1. Lay all the objects randomly on the floor.

2. Put three large grocery bags at the front of the room. Label separate bags with p, b and d, respectively.

3. Ask for volunteers to choose an object and place it in the proper bag, matching beginning sounds.

Toss and Tell

Objective: To reinforce the difficult letters: p, b, d and q

Materials: chalk, concrete playground space, a beanbag

Directions:

1. Using chalk, draw a grid on the concrete. (See diagram to right.)

2. Fill in the grid squares with the letters p, b, d and q.

3. When all the squares have been filled, let the children take turns tossing a beanbag into a square.

4. The child who tosses must hop to the beanbag via the available squares. As the child hops on the square, the group should help call out the letter the child is standing on before the child proceeds.

Puppet of the Week

Objective: To introduce a new letter and its sound in a non-threatening fashion

Materials: paper lunch bags, markers, glue, crayons, yarn, buttons, paper scraps, etc.

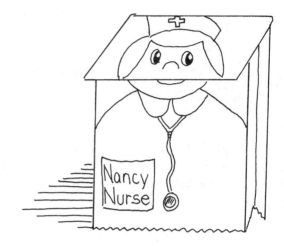

Directions: Make a paper bag puppet to represent the letter of the week. Look through old coloring books for help if you are not the type to draw freehand. For example, make a nurse for the letter **N**. Decorate the puppet and laminate it if possible. Then, let the children use the puppet during free time. Be sure to write both the upper and lower-case versions of the letter on the puppet.

. . . .

It's a Party!

Objective: To reinforce the "letter of the week"

Materials: construction paper, markers, stapler

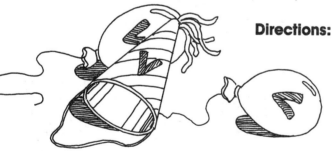

Directions: Ask the children to imagine that they are going to host a party for the letter of the week. Design invitations telling what is going to take place at the party. Explain that everything at the party must be associated with the letter of the week (i.e. the food, games, decorations, party favors).

. . . .

Skywriting

Objective: To reinforce letter recognition

Directions: Ask the children if they have ever been to an air show. Discuss how the airplanes can leave messages in the sky. This is called skywriting! Then, tell the children that they can skywrite the alphabet by drawing letters in the sky with their fingers. Sing the alphabet song together and skywrite each letter as you sing.

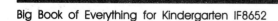

The Mail Carrier Match

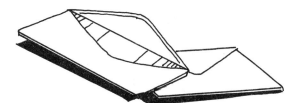

Objective: To practice matching upper- and lower-case letters

Materials: 10 large milk cartons, markers, scissors, 10 envelopes

Directions:

1. Collect ten large milk cartons and label each one with an upper-case letter. Choose letters with which the children have difficulty matching upper- and lower-cases. Decorate the cartons to look like houses.

2. Cut a slit in the top of each carton. Make the slits large enough for the envelopes to fit.

3. Label 10 envelopes with lower-case letters matching those you wrote on the milk cartons.

4. Choose a volunteer to deliver the mail. He/she should match the envelopes to the cartons.

Just for Fun: Try to find a mail carrier uniform to use for this game.

Alphabet Inventions

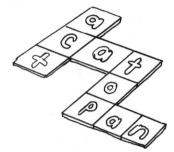

Objective: To practice using lower- and upper-case letters in original games

Materials: crayons or colored felt-tip markers, colored construction paper, scissors

Directions: 1. Cut 26 squares out of the construction paper.

2. Draw an upper-case **A** on one side and a lower-case **a** on the other side of a single square. Do this same process on the rest of the squares using the remaining letters of the alphabet.

3. Now let students make words using the letters. Let them build on words by using a common letter as in a crossword puzzle. They can also spell classmates' names. See who can make the longest word. Be creative!

Molding the Alphabet

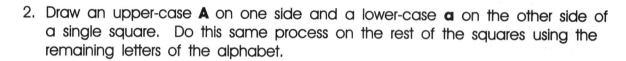

Objective: To reinforce upper- and lower-case letters

Materials: play dough, tongue depressors

Directions: 1. Make a large bowl of play dough. Have the children help. Use your favorite recipe or try the one below.

2 cups salt
2 cups flour
2 tablespoons powdered alum
Mix with water to consistency of putty.

2. Give each child a handful of play dough.

3. Have students roll the play dough into strings. Then, they can cut it using a tongue depressor.

4. Next, ask the children to make upper- and lower-case letters out of the play dough.

5. On the chalkboard, write the letter you are requesting the children to form. Ask them to look at the board to check their work.

ABC and You and Me

Objective: To make a book using drawings and beginning sounds for each letter of the alphabet

Materials: Each child will need the following: one 18" x 24" sheet of colored construction paper, seven sheets of white or manila lightweight paper, markers or crayons

Directions:

1. Instruct the students to fold each sheet of paper in half. Have the students insert the manila pages inside the colored cover page.

2. Help students staple the pages together along the folded edges.

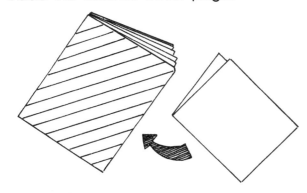

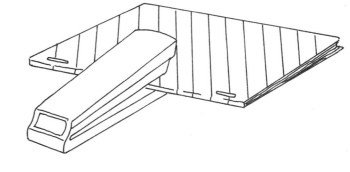

3. Using the front and back sides of each page, have the students write each letter of the alphabet starting with the letter A on the first page. Have the children include both the lower- and upper-cases of each letter.

4. Tell the children that they will be making a book for a special friend. Have the children write and/or draw something on each page that starts with the letter written on it. When they are finished with the inside of the book, have them decorate the cover. Give the children several days to complete the project to avoid rushing. Remind the children to make the book for a special friend.

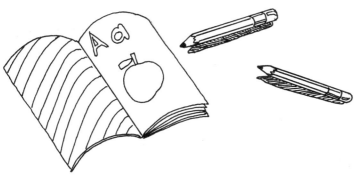

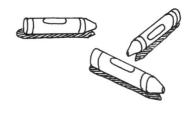

145

Sighting the Days

Objective: To recognize the days of the week

Materials: a copy of the activity sheet below for each child

Directions: Give each child a copy of the activity sheet below. Read the days of the week while the children follow along the left column. In the right column, have the children draw things they might like to do on each of the corresponding days.

Draw things that you do beside each day below.

Sunday	
Monday	
Tuesday	
Wednesday	
Thursday	
Friday	
Saturday	

Letter Practice Opportunity

Objective: To practice and reinforce recognition of the letters of the alphabet

Materials: oaktag, salt, glue, scissors, emery boards, fine sandpaper, paint, shaving cream, play blocks

Salt and Glue Letters:
Let children squeeze glue on a piece of oaktag to form a letter. Then, they pour salt on the glue. When it is dry, allow children to trace the letter with their fingers.

Sandpaper Letters:
The children will enjoy cutting letters out of sandpaper and gluing them to oaktag. Have the children trace the letters when the glue is dry.

Yarn and Bean Letters:
Have students place glue on paper to form a letter. Then, they place yarn or beans on the glue. Try to give students colorful items to use.

Shaving Cream and Sand Letters:
Students follow the same directions for finger-painting letters but substitute shaving cream or sand for the paint.

Emery Board Letters:
Students can cut and glue pieces of emery boards onto a piece of oaktag to form a letter. Have children trace the letter when the glue is dry.

Finger Paint Letters:
Place a small scoop of paint on a table top. Let each child practice making letters in the paint using their finger tips.

Big Block Letters:
Let students use the large blocks from the play area to create large letters on the floor. Students can trace the letters by balance walking on the blocks.

Other Letter-Making Items:
Try having students make letters out of cold cooked spagetti, ribbons, marbles, noodles or crushed eggshells.

147

Letter Mobiles

Objective: To reinforce a letter and its sound

Materials: wire coat hangers, yarn, scissors, colored construction paper, glue, white drawing paper, crayons, string

Directions:

1. Choose a letter to be the featured letter. Or, let students choose their own letter.

2. Have students wrap yarn around a wire hanger.

3. Next, they cut seven shapes out of white paper. Students should write the featured letter on one of the shapes.

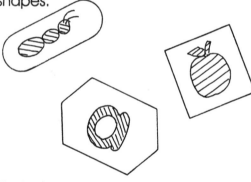

4. Instruct the students to illustrate six things that begin with the featured letter on the remaining white shapes.

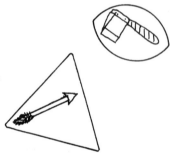

5. Students next glue all of the shapes on a sheet of construction paper. Have them cut around the shapes leaving a 1/4" border.

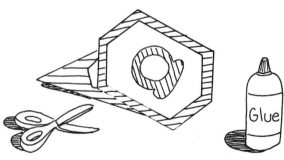

6. Students then cut seven strings of varying lengths to use to attach the shapes to the wire hanger. Tell the students to attach the shape with the letter written on it to the top of the hanger and the picture shapes to the bottom of the hanger.

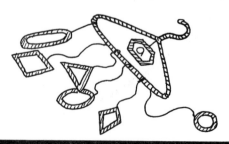

148

Clothespin Matching

Objective: To match appropriate letters to beginning sounds of objects

Materials: 26 clothespins, copy of the gameboard pattern below, marker, resealable bag

Directions: Using a marker, write a letter on each clothespin. Cut out, color and laminate the gameboard below. Have the children attach the appropriate clothespin to the picture on the gameboard whose beginning sound matches the letter on it. Store the pieces to this activity in a resealable bag.

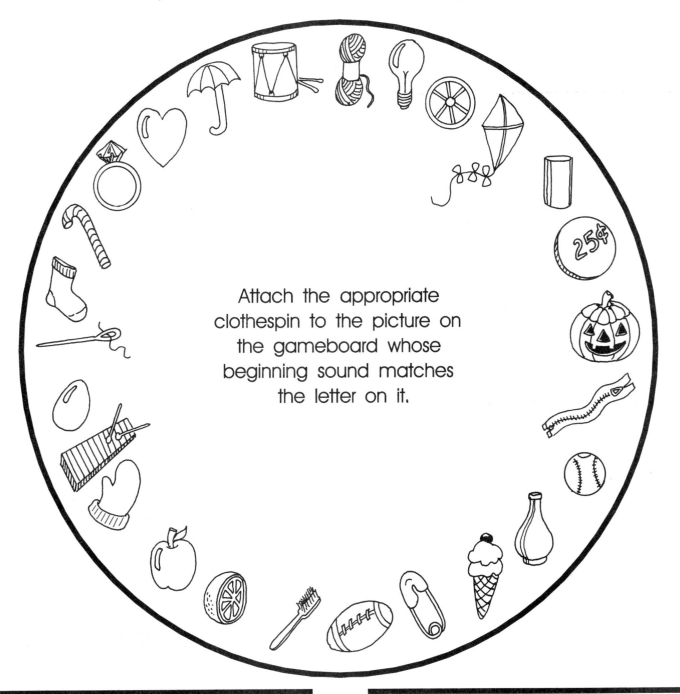

Attach the appropriate clothespin to the picture on the gameboard whose beginning sound matches the letter on it.

149

The Towering Alphabet

Objective: To introduce and reinforce alphabet letters and sounds

Materials: 26 empty coffee or infant formula cans, construction paper, thick felt-tip markers, glue, scissors

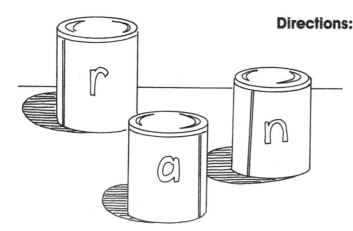

Directions: Cover each can with brightly colored construction paper. Using a thick-tip marker, draw a lower-case letter of the alphabet on each can. All 26 letters must be used. Allow children to arrange cans in a tower formation and in alphabetical order. Use the cans to introduce words containing just a few letters. Perhaps begin with the "a" and "n" cans. Then, ask children to retrieve a can that could make a three-letter word like "ran".

Extension: Leave the cans in a designated play area of the room. Allow children to build with the cans in their free time.

- -

Stacked Carton Words

Objectives: To reinforce alphabet sounds and to begin development of small word building

Materials: 3 sturdy cardboard cartons per child, poster paint, tape, paintbrushes

Directions: Give each child three sturdy cardboard cartons similar in size and have the children tape the cartons shut. Direct the children to paint each box using poster paint. Then, have them paint the letters b, c, d and f on the sides of one carton, a, u, o and i on the sides of another carton and t, p, g and n on the sides of the third carton. Talk about the sounds these letters make while leading them along in their painting. After the paint has dried, let the children stack their cartons and phonetically make three-letter words.

Hanging Out the Alphabet

Objective: To create a classroom display of various letters

Materials: construction paper, markers, string and clothespins, clothesline cutout patterns below and on pages 152 and 153

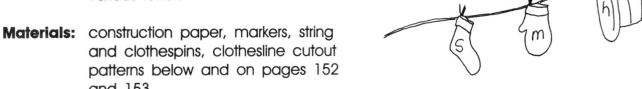

Directions:

1. Using construction paper, cut out the shapes of the items listed below.

   A = Apron
   B = Boots
   C = Coat
   M = Mittens

   Q = Quilt
   R = Rug
   S = Sock
   U = Underwear

   V = Vest
   H = Hat
   T = Tie

2. Have the students decorate the cutouts using markers or any other scraps.

3. Write the lower-case letter each item begins with on the object itself.

4. Hang a clothesline in the classroom. Using clothespins, attach the items to the line for letter viewing anytime.

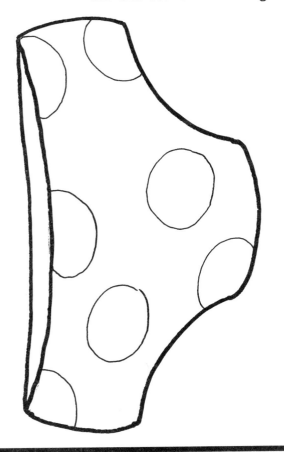

Clothesline Cutouts

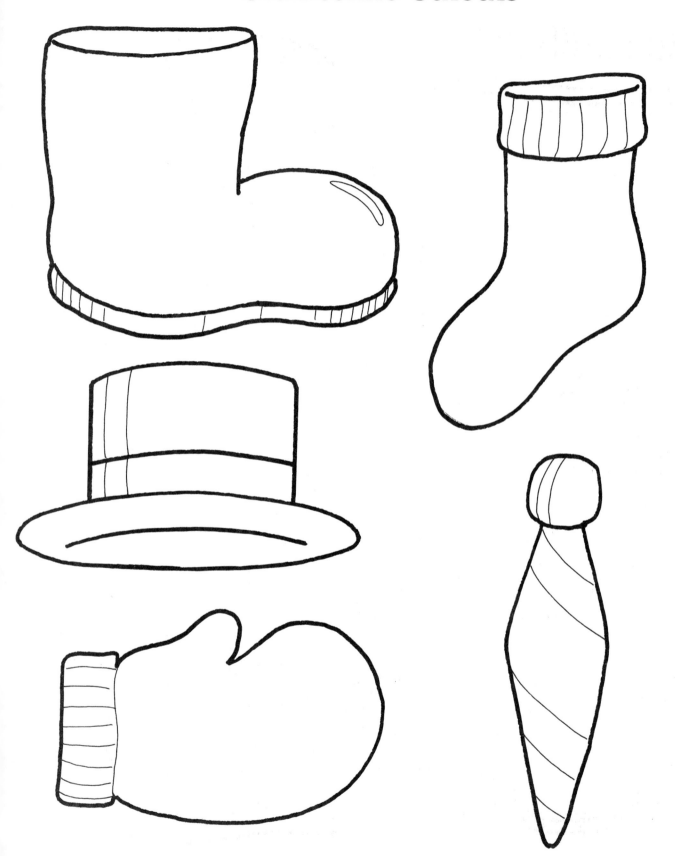

Clothesline Cutouts

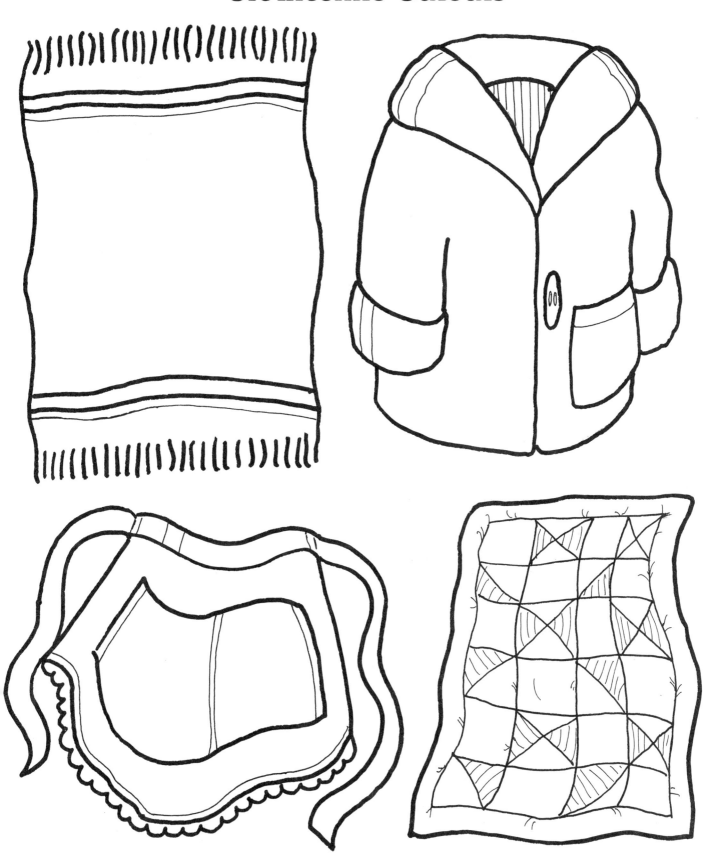

Decorating Words

Objective: To introduce new words

Materials: posterboard, markers

Directions: Write words on posterboard as shown above. Have the children decorate the words to show their meaning. Some word choices may include cold, wet, hot, winter, summer, fall, spring.

Extension: Make a collage of a word by cutting out pictures of the word from magazines and newspapers or by using miscellaneous scraps from the art center to create them. Remind the children to focus on the meaning of the word.

Shopping Lists

Objective: To develop confidence in phonetics

Materials: a copy of the activity page below for each child, pencils, crayons

Directions: Give each child a copy of the activity page below. Encourage the children to try to spell words by sounding the letters out. Tell them that they are going to create their own grocery shopping list. Tell them to use the drawings as a guide for the food groups. Then, have them illustrate the remainder of the words on their lists.

Write a grocery list. Draw and color a picture of each item you list.

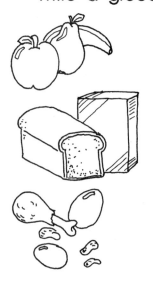

Spinning Word Wheels

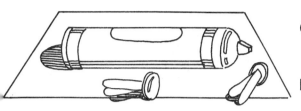

Objective: To introduce children to words in a non-threatening fashion

Materials: cardboard, construction paper, brads, markers, scissors

Directions: Make the spinning wheel following the directions below. Cut a circle with an 11-inch diameter out of cardboard. Cut a circle with a 14-inch diameter out of construction paper. On the smaller circle of cardboard, cut out a 2 1/2-inch square as illustrated. To the right of the square opening, write a two- or three-letter word ending of your choice.

Center the small circle on top of the large circle. Push a brad through the center of both circles allowing them to rotate freely. In the square opening of the small circle, write a letter that forms a word with the ending you have chosen. Rotate the circles and add another letter until there are no longer any empty spaces. Let the students enjoy making new words!

155

Puzzling New Words

Cat

Objective: To create new words in a playful manner

Materials: 4" x 5" cards, marker, scissors, drawing paper

Directions: Cut 4" x 5" cards in half using unusual cutting lines. Using a marker, write a word ending (e.g. the ending "at") on the right half of each cut card. On the left side, write a letter or group of letters that form a three or four-letter word when the two pieces are joined. Have the children put the puzzle pieces together. Have them write the word they formed and draw a picture to illustrate it.

Rubber Stamp Sounds

Objective: To introduce phonetic spelling

Materials: rubber stamps of the letters of the alphabet, drawing paper, markers

Directions: Divide the class into several groups. Provide the groups with ink pads, drawing paper and rubber stamps of the letters of the alphabet. Have each group work together to make phonetic words by stamping the letters in the appropriate order. Have the groups share their words. Leave the stamps and ink pads on a tray for future independent work time.

Body Language

Objective: To initiate small word building

Materials: large floor space

Directions: Write a three-letter word on the board. Have the children find an open space on the floor. While standing, have the children read the word on the board. Tell the children they will be spelling words using their entire body. Spell the word out loud for the children. Have them maneuver their bodies into each letter of the word as it is called out.

Word Search

Objective: To have children focus on the specific spelling of words

Materials: one copy of the puzzle per child, pen or pencil

Directions: Give each child a copy of the puzzle below. Have him/her find each word listed.

 nut
bird
tree
 dog
hat
water
 snake
sky
cat
 leaf
flower
rat

v	h	y	u	l	r	b	s
c	a	t	t	e	d	o	n
d	t	u	w	a	o	s	a
o	n	o	i	f	l	k	k
g	l	t	r	e	e	y	e
f	a	a	w	a	t	e	r
r	t	b	i	r	d	x	z

Theme Boxes

Objective: To begin small word recognition through phonetics and sight words

Materials: 4 old cigar boxes, small objects as categorized below, strips of paper, marker, rubber bands

Farm Objects	Tool Objects	Beauty Objects	School Objects
cow	saw	brush	pen
pig	nail	comb	ruler
hay	hammer	mirror	pencil
tractor	wrench	lipstick	paper
barn	chain	toothbrush	eraser

Directions:
1. Put each category of objects in a box.
2. Using a marker, write the name of each object on a strip of paper.
3. Put a rubber band around the strips of paper belonging together and place them in their appropriate box.
4. Children should choose one box to work on at a time.
5. Children should lay objects on a table and match appropriate words with objects before beginning a new box.

Find the Food

Objective: To develop word recognition through sight words

Materials: empty refrigerator box, empty food containers, plastic fruits and vegetables, markers, construction paper, scissors, drawing paper

Directions: Find an empty refrigerator box and cut out shelves to fit inside the box. (See illustration.) Collect empty food containers and plastic fruit and vegetables. Cover the empty food containers (i.e. the boxes) with construction paper so that the visual aid of the product is covered. Using a marker, label all the food items. Place the food items in the mock refrigerator. Read each label to the children. Then, choose one child from the class to find the item in the refrigerator by reading the label on the product. Through repetition, the children will recognize the word.

Extension: Eventually, write the labels of the products on the board and have the children illustrate the same products on a piece of paper.

Magic Muffins

Objective: To think creatively while using some introductory phonetics

Materials: recipe cards, recipe box, pencils

Directions: Read a story involving magic to the students (i.e. *Jack and the Bean Stalk, Cinderella, Snow White,* etc.). Tell the students they are going to make magic muffins. Have the children brainstorm about what they might put into the batter of magic muffins. Give each child a recipe card containing the information that is seen on the one below. Let the children create their own magic muffin mix and the ingredients spelling the words phonetically. Focus on creative thinking. When each child is done, place his/her card in a recipe box. Each day, read at least one recipe!

Magic Muffins
1/2 Cup _____
1 Tsp. _____
1/4 Tbsp. _____
4 Cups _____
dash of _____

Extension: Have children draw a picture of their magic muffin on the back of their recipe card.

Planting Letters

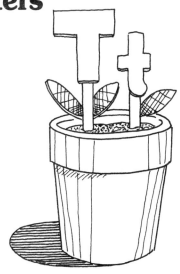

Objective: To reinforce upper- and lower-case letters

Materials: construction paper, tongue depressors, Styrofoam cups, scissors, sand, glue

Directions: Give each child a Styrofoam cup filled with sand and two tongue depressors. Give a construction paper cutout of the upper- and lower-case featured "letter of the week." Have the children glue each cutout to a tongue depressor. Have them cut and glue leaf shapes onto their tongue depressors. Once the glue has dried have, the children plant their upper- and lower-case flowers in their Styrofoam cups.

Creature Movements

Objectives: To introduce new sight words and to exercise some large muscle groups by playing a game

Materials: strips of posterboard, pictures of animals, markers

Preparation: On each strip of posterboard, write the name of a different animal. Begin using short name animals like cat, dog, fish, cow, bird, worm, ant, rat, lion, bear, seal. Then, use unique spelling words like elephant, kangaroo, hippo, spider, snake, monkey. Glue a picture of the animal to the back of the strip for initial introductions to the words.

Game: To play, hold up a strip containing an animal's name and say the following to students letting them fill in the blank with the animal's name: "If I were a _____, I would..." Let the students act out that particular animal. Encourage animal sounds and movements. Remember that repetition causes recognition. Have FUN!

Environmental Signs

Objective: To teach environmental sign recognition for the childrens' safety

Materials: copies of the environmental signs below

Directions: Make enlarged copies of the signs below, color them and glue them to heavy posterboard. Laminate the cards. Display the cards and help the children read them. Repeat reading the cards several times. Have the children take turns identifying the environmental signs and pantomiming the appropriate actions.

Stop

Yield

Pedestrian Crossing

Signal Ahead

Railroad Crossing

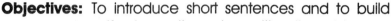

Mini Messages!

Objectives: To introduce short sentences and to build self-esteem through positive thoughts

Materials: art easel, large sheet of posterboard, marker, hole punch, two plastic adhesive hooks, 18" x 5" strips of posterboard

Directions: Set an art easel in a highly visible location of the room. Set a sheet of posterboard on the easel. Stick two adhesive hooks 12" apart and centered on the posterboard. Write short sentences on the posterboard strips using a marker. You can write one on either side. Punch two holes in the top of the strip (twelve inches apart.) Hang these sentences, phrases or messages from the adhesive hooks. Create one message a week. Introduce the sentence on Monday and invite the children to read it during the remainder of the week.

Short messages and ideas:

You did it! I love you! I am thinking of you!
I am glad you are you! Enjoy today! Please smile!
Be happy! You are beautiful! You make me glad!
Hug someone! Be a friend! Play fair!

The "I Can" Graph

Objective: To build self-esteem and confidence

Materials: chart paper, marker, drawing paper, colored pencils

I Can...							
sing	jump	paint	draw	skip	hop	run	bike
✔	✔	✔	✔	✔	✔	✔	✔
✔	✔	✔	✔	✔	✔	✔	
✔	✔	✔	✔		✔	✔	
✔	✔				✔		
✔					✔	✔	
✔					✔	✔	

Directions: Discuss things that children like to do (i.e. sing, dance, hop, run, camp, hike, draw and bike). Ask the children if they are able to do these things. Give each child a sheet of drawing paper titled "I Can..." Using colored pencils, have the children draw something they can do. Collect all the children's artwork and graph the activities illustrated by the children. Discuss how wonderful all the children's abilities are.

Once Upon A Time

Objective: To practice using full sentence structure

Materials: pictures of people, places, things and actions (biking, jumping, smiling, frowning), glue, 5" x 7" rectangles of heavy paper, blue and red markers

Directions:
1. Have students glue pictures of nouns to one side of a 5" x 7" rectangle of heavy paper.

2. Then, they glue the verb pictures to the opposite side of the paper.

3. Have students mark the noun side of card with a red marker dot and the verb side of the card with a blue dot.

4. Have each child describe in a sentence what the card is telling him/her. Ask the children to begin their sentence using the side with the red dot on it and end their sentence using the side with the blue dot on it.

Extension: Give each child two or more cards. Allow the children to use their sentences to build a story.

Silly Sentence Stories

Objective: To practice using full sentence structure

Materials: story starter ideas below

Directions: Discuss what whole sentences are and how to use them in a story. Tell the children that they are going to have the opportunity to be the authors of silly stories. Choose one child to begin. Give the child a story starter from the list below. Ask the child to tell what would happen next in the story. Help the child to use full sentence structure. Have Fun!

1. The whale had something very wrong with his tail.
2. There was a mouse who lived in a very funny house.
3. Inside the chocolate sandwich cookie, there was something very unusual.
4. There was something very slippery in the boy's pocket.
5. Farmer Fritz found that there were strange things going on in the barn.

Story Telling Strips

Objective: To teach the concept of sequencing through drawings

Materials: 5" x 16" strips of drawing paper, markers or crayons

Directions: Give each child a strip of drawing paper. Show the children how to fold the strips in half lengthwise and then to fold them in half lengthwise again. There should be four equal rectangles when the strip is unfolded. Tell the children to label each rectangle with the numbers 1 through 4. Have the children draw pictures in each rectangle to tell a story in sequential order from left to right. Ask for volunteers to show and tell their stories.

What Comes Next?

Objective: To discover the sequence of events

Materials: activity sheet below, markers

Directions: make a copy of the activity strips below for each child. Have the children complete the strips by drawing in the blank square.

Fill the blank box with a picture that completes the sequence. Color the strip.

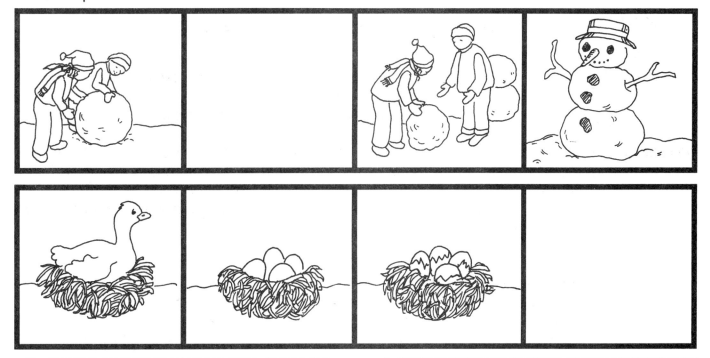

Run To Read?

Objective: To teach children to read from left to right

Materials: chalk, sidewalk or playground, book

Preparation: Using chalk, draw what looks like a large sheet of paper on the concrete. Write, "I love to run" on the first line. The next line should read, "I love to jump and I love to walk to school." Remember to leave a space between the lines, keep in mind that the children will be moving between the spaces of the lines.

Game: Read a book to the students and discuss how a book is read from left to right. Have a volunteer trace the direction of reading (a few lines) in front of the group. Then, use the playground project to reinforce the idea. Have a volunteer stand on the word "I." Have that person walk to the end of the line. The child then returns between the lines to the word "run." The child should run to the end of the line. After dropping down to the word "jump," the child should jump to the end of the line. The child should repeat the action and walk to the end of the word "school."

Word Search Collage

Objective: To develop word recognition skills

Materials: scissors, magazines or newspapers, paper, marker, glue

Directions: Give each child a paper titled, "Words I Know." Have the children look through magazines and newspapers for words they recognize. Tell the children that they are going to be making a collage by cutting out the words they recognize and gluing them on a paper. Have the children read their collages to each other.

Finger Play Recitation

Objective: To develop word recognition through repetition

Materials: a favorite finger play, chart paper, marker

Directions: Write the words of a favorite finger play on chart paper. Have the children follow along as it is recited. Eventually, have a child lead the recitation, pointing at each word as it is read by the class.

Calendar Craze

Objective: To introduce the days of the week and months of the year in written and oral form

Materials: 2 large pieces of posterboard, marker, yardstick, scissors, masking tape

Directions:

1. On a large piece of posterboard draw a 14" x 14" square.

2. Using a yardstick, draw six horizontal lines every 2" from the left side of the square.

3. Next, draw six vertical lines every 2" from the bottom up to the second to the last horizontal line.

4. Cut thirty-one 2" squares out of another piece of posterboard. Each square must be marked with a number of one of the days of the month (i.e. 1-31).

| 1 | 2 | 3 | 4 | 5 | | | | | |

5. Cut twelve 2" x 12" strips of posterboard. Write the name of a month on each strip.

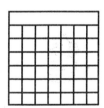

January

February

March

6. Write the days of the week in the seven squares of the second horizontal row from the top.

7. Begin each day by letting the children put up the correct month and date. Use masking tape to stick these pieces to posterboard. Each day, the children can recite through the days, months and numbers.

The News

Objectives: To reinforce the calendar information and to introduce children to sight words for weather, days of the week, months of the year

Materials: posterboard, markers, masking tape, scissors

Directions:

1. On a large sheet of posterboard, write a small paragraph like the one below.

The News

Today is _____,
the ___ of _____.
It is _____ and
_____ outside.

2. With a marker, write weather words, months of the year, days of the week and dates on pieces of posterboard. Cut them out.

3. Each day, let the children tell the news for the day. Have them tape up the correct words for the blank spaces.

4. Read the news aloud together.

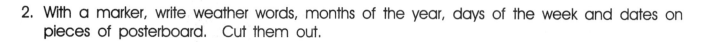

Opposites Table

Objective: To introduce opposites to children

Materials: large table, objects that are opposite (i.e. brick/pillow, big block/small block, cotton ball/rock, sandpaper/wrapping paper, basket full of apples/empty basket, an old teddy bear/a new teddy bear, etc.)

Directions: On a table, put opposite objects side by side. After discussing them, mix objects up and allow children to organize them by matching opposites.

Object Match-Up

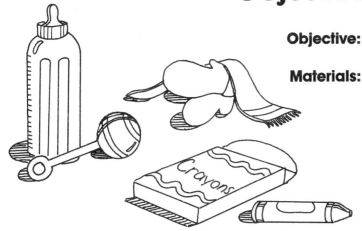

Objective: To build vocabulary and reasoning skills

Materials: labels, objects that belong together like those below:
shoe and shoelace
scarf and mittens
pen and cap
fork and spoon
bottle and rattle
empty crayon box and crayons

Directions: On a table, randomly set out the objects. Ask for volunteers to match the objects that belong together. Be sure each child describes why he/she has made the match he/she did.

Similar or Different?

Objective: To find similarities and differences between the children

Directions: Divide the class into pairs. Have the children discuss what makes their physical appearance similar and different. Consider hair style and hair color, eye color, height, weight, gender, skin color and attire.

167

Opposites Pantomime

Objective: To practice opposites

Materials: opposite words that students can act out

Directions: Have the students sit together in a big circle. Have a volunteer act out a word. The students should guess the word and act out the opposite of that word. Some ideas for pantomime words are, sit/stand, happy/sad, smile/frown, laugh/cry, whisper/shout, sleep/awake, like/hate. Let the children create their own opposites.

Twisting the Text

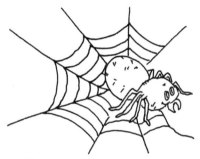

Objective: To practice opposites

Materials: nursery rhymes, chart paper, marker

Directions: Choose a nursery rhyme like the one below. Write the nursery rhyme on chart paper and underline the words that have opposites. Read the nursery rhyme with the children. Rewrite the rhyme, replacing each *italicized* word with its opposite.

Little Miss Muffet,	*Big* Miss Muffet,
Sat on her tuffet,	*Stood* on her tuffet,
Eating her curds and whey,	*Drinking* her curds and whey,
When along *came* a spider,	When along *went* a spider,
And *sat down* beside her,	And *stood up* beside her,
And frightened *little* Miss Muffet away.	And frightened *big* Miss Muffet away.

The Mysterious Bag

Objective: To develop creative thinking and memory skills

Materials: large paper bag, many different objects

Directions:
1. Fill a bag full of objects.
2. Have a volunteer reach into the bag and describe the object he/she is touching.
3. The other children should try to guess the object. If they cannot, have them ask probing questions to the volunteer to help them.

Sentence Solutions

Objective: To develop creative thinking skills

Materials: sentence starters below, marker, chart paper

Directions: Write the sentence starters below on chart paper. Ask the children to use their creativity to compose endings for the sentences. Use the children's answers to complete the sentences on the chart paper.

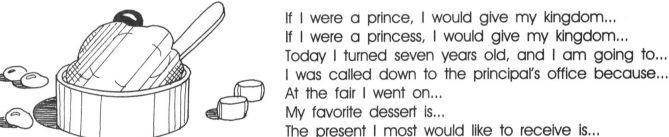

If I were a prince, I would give my kingdom...
If I were a princess, I would give my kingdom...
Today I turned seven years old, and I am going to...
I was called down to the principal's office because...
At the fair I went on...
My favorite dessert is...
The present I most would like to receive is...

Language Lunch

Objective: To use creative thinking skills

Materials: paper lunch bags, posterboard, chart paper, markers

Directions: On chart paper write the following sentence, "In my lunch I would like..." Discuss the foods children like to have in their lunch. Write the children's responses on the chart paper. Give each child a paper lunch bag. Tell them to write their name on their bag. Then, give each child a 5" x 7" strip of posterboard titled, "In my lunch I would like..." Instruct them to write words from the chart paper which represent foods they would like for lunch. Have the children take their list with them in their lunch bag.

Memory Matching

Objective: To match picture cards that have the same beginning sounds

Materials: posterboard, magazines, scissors, glue

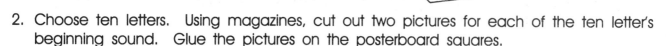

Directions:

1. Cut twenty 2" squares out of posterboard.

2. Choose ten letters. Using magazines, cut out two pictures for each of the ten letter's beginning sound. Glue the pictures on the posterboard squares.

3. Place all 20 cards face down on the floor. The first player must draw two cards. If the pictures on the cards have the same beginning sound, there is a match and the player keeps the two cards. This player takes another turn and continues until a match is not made.

4. The next player then draws two cards and play continues. The students should try to remember where the pictures are laying.

5. When all the cards have been matched, the player with the most cards is the winner.

• •

Letter Memory Tray

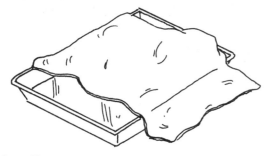

Objective: To develop memory skills while reviewing beginning sounds

Materials: dinner tray, 10 objects beginning with the same letter and sound, a large handkerchief

Directions:

1. Place 10 objects with the same beginning sound and letter on a serving tray.

2. Hold up and identify each object to the class.

3. Let children memorize what is on the tray for 30 seconds. Cover the tray with large handkerchief.

4. Ask a volunteer to recall the items on the tray from memory.

Extension: Take one object away and see if the children can tell you which one it is.

Challenging Changes

Objective: To teach children to look for details

Materials: miscellaneous objects (e.g. hats, ties, ribbons, buttons, shoes, shirts, etc.), a partition

Directions: Set up a partition with miscellaneous objects hidden behind it. One at a time, let students go behind the partition and change their appearance slightly. Let the children return to the group. The group must identify what is different about each child's appearance. Remind the children that they must look carefully at their classmate and remember what he/she looks like.

Detail Detective

Objective: To learn to look for details

Materials: activity sheet below

Directions: Have the children look for the unusual items hidden in the picture below. Remind the children to pay attention to detail.

Find the unusual items in the picture below.

Mr. and Miss Muffet

Objective: To provide additional practice with rhyming words

Directions: Explain to the children that in the nursery rhyme of "Little Miss Muffet," the words "muffet" and "tuffet" rhyme. Let the children play a silly rhyming game with their names. Omit the words "muffet" and "tuffet" and have children fill in their names and a silly, rhyming thing they might sit on. Use the examples below to demonstrate the activity.

Little Miss Sue
Sat on her shoe
Eating her curds and whey,
When along came a spider
And sat down beside her
And frightened Miss Sue away.

Little Mr. Joe
Sat on his toe
Eating his curds and whey,
When along came a spider
And sat down beside him
And frightened Mr. Joe away.

- -

What's Missing?

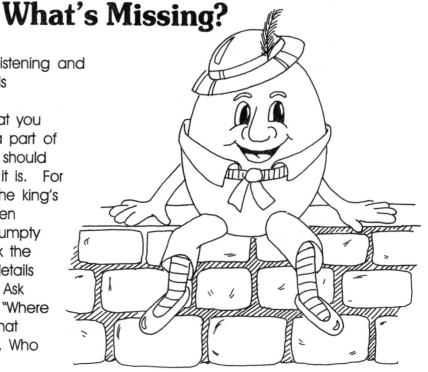

Objective: To develop good listening and comprehension skills

Directions: Tell the children that you are going to say a part of a rhyme and they should guess what rhyme it is. For example, say "All the king's horses." The children should respond, "Humpty Dumpty." Then ask the children to recall details about the rhyme. Ask questions such as, "Where did Humpty sit?, What happened to him?, Who tried to help?"

Extension: Have children draw a line of the rhyme and help write the line below the drawing.

The Nonsense Dance

Objective: To perform actions to rhyming words

Directions: Have the children listen to the following nonsense rhymes and perform the actions suggested.

Humpty, dumpty, dand.
Please get up and <u>stand</u>.

Humpty, dumpty, do.
Touch the tip of your <u>shoe</u>.

Humpty, dumpty, dee.
Touch the top of your <u>knee</u>.

Humpty, dumpty, dingers.
Clap all of your <u>fingers</u>.

Humpty, dumpty, dap.
How loud can you <u>clap</u>?

Humpty, dumpty, dace.
Rub around your <u>face</u>.

Humpty, dumpty, doe nails.
Reach down for your <u>toenails</u>.

Humpty, dumpty, deat
Find a comfortable <u>seat</u>.

Extension: Repeat the rhymes and omit the underlined words. Let the children call out the missing rhyming word and do the action described.

Rhyme Time

Objective: To teach children to identify rhyming words

Materials: nursery rhyme books, graph paper, markers

Directions: Establish a Nursery Rhyme Book Day. Have the children bring a nursery rhyme book from home. Ask each child to pick his/her favorite nursery rhyme. Over a couple of days, read each child's favorite rhyme to the class. Pick out all the rhyming words with the children's help. Write the rhyming words on a big sheet of graph paper. Periodically, review the words on the graph paper. Have the children give the rhyming word to the teacher to read.

Yes/No Cards

Objective: To practice rhyming words

Materials: paper plates, markers, tongue depressors, glue

Directions: Have the students glue a tongue depressor to a paper plate. On one side of the plate, students write the word "no." On the other side, they write the word "yes." Call out rhyming words or similar sounding words. If the words rhyme, the children should hold up the side that says "yes!" If they do not rhyme, they should hold up the side that says "no!"

Acting Out

Objective: To review rhyming words

Materials: nursery rhymes

Directions: Recall and discuss nursery rhymes with the children. Have the children pick out the rhyming words in the nursery rhymes. Ask for volunteers to act out the characters while the class sings or recites the words. Suggested nursery rhymes include *Hickory Dickory Dock, Humpty Dumpty, Hey Diddle Diddle* and *Little Bo Peep.*

Extension: For added encouragement, visit your local library and obtain nursery rhyme music tapes. Let the tapes complement the activity.

Direction Following Fun

Objective: To develop strong listening skills

Materials: flash cards, markers

Directions:

1. Make flash cards which give students 2-, 3- and 4-step directions. (See example below.)

2. Have children take turns choosing one card. The child must then follow the directions given on the card. Have the group verbally repeat the sequence of directions without reading the flash card.

Walk to the classroom door. Shake a friend's hand. Return to your seat.

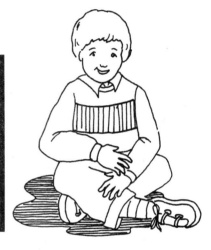

Direct the Artist

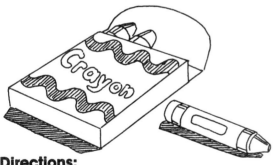

Objective: To reinforce strong listening skills while developing fine motor skills

Materials: coloring book, crayons, overhead projector, a large sheet of butcher paper, masking tape

Directions:

1. Tear out a page from a coloring book.

2. Using an overhead projector, project the image to the front of the room onto a large sheet of butcher paper. This paper should be taped to the wall or chalkboard.

3. Give directions to the children on coloring parts, adding things and making alterations. Have fun!

Sequencing

Objective: To develop listening and comprehension skills

Materials: posterboard, tongue depressors, glue, markers

Directions:

1. Read a popular story to the students such as "The Three Bears" or "Little Red Riding Hood."

2. Make signs containing the main characters' names. (See diagram.) Use tongue depressors for handles. Have volunteers hold the signs up for the group to read.

3. Have another volunteer move the individuals holding the signs into the order they were introduced in the story.

4. Verbally discuss the sequence of events.

First and Last

Objective: To develop sequencing ideas through the concepts of first and last

Materials: short story

Directions: Read a short story to the children and have them pick out the first and last words on each page. Then, line up five children and have the remaining children identify the first and last persons in line. Repeat this procedure after reorganizing the same children in a different order.

Verbal Cues!

Objective: To follow verbal directions

Materials: activity page below, crayons, verbal directions below

Directions: Give each child a copy of the activity page below. Have the children follow verbal directions to complete the activity page.

1. Color the Birthday Boy's hat blue.

2. Put six candles on the Birthday cake.

3. Draw some Birthday gifts on the table.

4. You can come to the party, too! Draw yourself at the party.

5. Color the balloons red and yellow.

6. Count the number of guests, including yourself, that are at the party.

7. On the back of this paper draw or write what you would like to give to the Birthday boy.

Riddle Resolution

Objective: To develop listening, comprehension
and creative thinking skills

Materials: riddles below

Directions: Read the riddles below, one sentence at a time. Have the children try to solve
each riddle before all the clues are given.

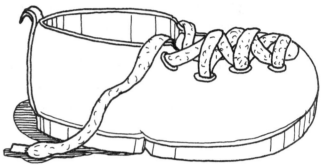

1. I am usually dirty.
    I come in different sizes.
    People wear me when they go outside.
    To close me, pull my laces.
    What am I?_____. (shoe)

2. I am shiny and long.
    I am at every meal.
    I must be used to eat soup.
    What am I?_____. (spoon)

3. I am an instrument.
    I have strings.
    People use their chin and shoulder to
    play me.
    What am I?_____. (violin)

4. I live on a farm.
    I am large and heavy.
    I eat grass.
    I make milk.
    What am I?_____. (cow)

Extension: Have the children draw a picture book of their favorite riddle. Each page
should be a clue. The final page should give the answer. Some children may
be able to create their own riddles.

Puppet Play

Objective: To build listening and public speaking skills

Materials: yarn, buttons, paper, scraps of cloth, stapler, cotton balls, glue, markers, construction paper, scissors

Directions: Choose a popular children's story to read to the students. Have them recall the characters and events of the story. Give each child a copy of the puppet pattern below. Out of construction paper, have them cut two copies of the puppet pattern. Then, glue and staple the edges together. Instruct the students to decorate the puppet using miscellaneous items. The students should try to make the puppet resemble a character from the story that was read. While reading the story, have volunteers act out the story using their puppets.

Character/Setting/Plot

Objective: To introduce the components of a story

Materials: large sheet of butcher paper, crayons

Directions: Read a story to the students and ask them to describe the people or animals in the story. Explain the concept of characters. Talk about when and where the story is taking place and tell students that this is the setting. Lastly, discuss what is happening in the story and how this forms the concept of plot. Fold a piece of paper in three parts. Label each part with one of three concept headings you discussed with students. Have the children draw a picture of the concepts relating to the story which was read. Use the words when, where, why and what to help the children.

Authoring/Illustrating

Objective: To teach the functions of an author and illustrator

Materials: chart paper, drawing paper, construction paper, crayons, stapler

Directions: Read a short story to the children. Introduce them to the author and illustrator names on the cover of the book. Ask the children what these individuals do. Tell the children that they are going to be authors and illustrators, too. Have the class write a story by dictating their ideas. Write each child's thoughts on chart paper. When the story is complete, divide the class into small groups and give the groups a sheet of drawing paper with a sentence from their story on the bottom of the page. Have the children illustrate their sentence. After everyone is finished, put all the pages together and staple a construction paper cover to form a book.

Extension: Take the children on a field trip to a printing center so that they can see how books are put together.

The Memory Picnic

Objective: To build memory skills

Materials: picnic basket

Directions: Have the students sit in a circle. Place a picnic basket in the middle of the circle. Begin the game by saying, "If I were going on a picnic, I would take _____" and fill in the blank. The next person should repeat what you would take and add one thing of his/her own. See how far around the circle you can go before the students forget things.

 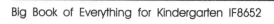

Classroom Library

Objective: To make books accessible to children and their families while promoting daily reading experiences

Materials: as many books as possible, oaktag, sign in/out sheet, hole punch

Directions: Collect as many books as possible. Parents often like to give gifts to the school or teachers during the holidays. Send a note recommending donations of used books or cash donations for new books. Keep all books in an accessible place. Give each child a "library card" for the month. Make this card out of oaktag with the numbers 1-20 written around the border. The child's name should also be written on the card. Establish a set of policies about borrowing the books. Punch out a number on the child's card each time he/she checks out a book. Also, record it on the sign in/out sheet. Include the title and date of the book being borrowed and the person borrowing the book.

Field Trip: Visit a local library. Arrange for a story telling tour or puppet show.

Extension: Choose a child each week to be the librarian. The librarian's responsibilities may include organizing the books.

Book Care

Objective: To reinforce respect for books

Materials: an old worn or abused book

Directions: Show the children an abused book and discuss why and how it might have been abused. Discuss proper book handling using the following reminders: Use clean hands while you look at a book. Use a bookmark instead of folding page corners back. Keep food and drinks away from books. Place books in a safe place after reading them. Write your name in your own books so that they can be returned to you if they are lost. Make copies of the following bookmark to give to the children who use proper book handling.

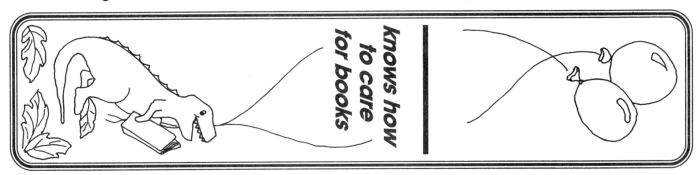

knows how
to care
for books

Poetry With Maracas

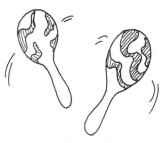

Objective: To teach poetry rhythm

Materials: poetry; empty, non-breakable bottles with lids; beans, small stones, sand or nuts

Directions:

1. Have each child make a maraca. To do this, students fill a non-breakable container with one of the materials mentioned above.

2. Read some poetry to the children and discuss rhythm.

3. Clap some rhythm patterns.

4. Shake a maraca to a poem's rhythm. Have the students join in by shaking their own maraca creations.

Expressive Poetry Movement

Objective: To interpret poetry

Materials: action poems, chart paper, marker

Directions: Write an action poem on chart paper and read it to the children while tracking the words with your finger. Have the children suggest how to act out the action words. Then, have them pantomime the poem as it is read again.

An alligator can walk.
An alligator can run.
But what an alligator really likes
Is to nap in the bright sun.

Name Calling

Objective: To teach children recognition of their classmates' names

Materials: felt strips, felt board, fabric paints

Directions: Give each child a felt strip with his/her name written on it in fabric paint. To the tune of "Frère Jacques," sing:

> "Where is _____?"
> "Where is _____?"

Fill in the blank with a child's name. This child should continue the song singing:

> "Here I am!"
> "Here I am!"

You then continue with:

> "How are you today_____?"

The child should then walk to the front of the room and stick his/her felt name tag to the felt board for all the children to see.

The child sings:

> "Very well, I thank you."

You finish singing:

> "Run away. Run away."

Extension: Try singing the words of the song to your own tune. Or, make up a whole new song!

Decorate Your Name

Objective: To recognize classmates' names

Materials: adhesive name tags, markers, glitter, glue, rice, sequins, colored sand

Directions: Using a marker, write each child's name on an adhesive name tag. Instruct each child to trace his/her name using glue. Then, let each child decorate his/her name by gluing any of the items mentioned above. Encourage the children to wear their name tags.

Telephone Language

Objectives: To teach verbal courtesy and to practice phone numbers and addresses

Materials: 2 phones to use for fun, one copy of the phone pattern below for each child

Directions:

1. Remember to unplug the phones before using them with the students.

2. Discuss emergency numbers with students and the seriousness of their use.

3. Talk about telephone courtesy.

4. Role-play the discussion ideas using both phones.

5. Give each child a copy of the phone pattern below and have the children practice writing their phone numbers and addresses on it.

- -

Fill in your phone number and address on the telephone below.

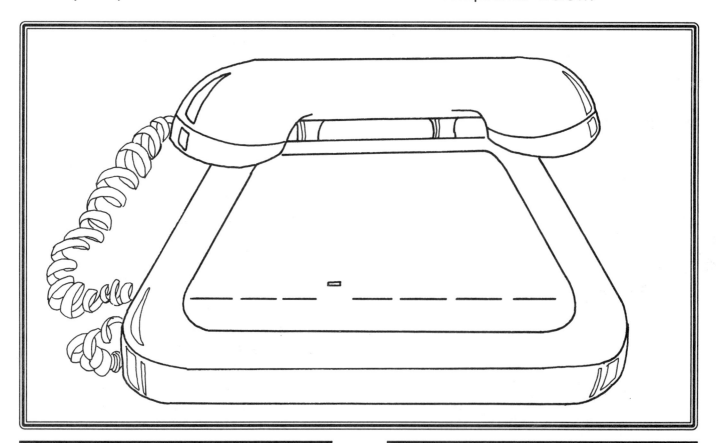

Real and Make-Believe

Objective: To discriminate between real and make-believe

Directions: Discuss with the students the differences between things that are real and things that are make-believe. Read each sentence below and ask the children to tell whether this is something that could really happen or something that is just make-believe. Then let students give examples of things that are both real and make-believe.

1. Our dog drove the car to the park to take his owners for a walk.
2. He tied his shoelaces so he would not trip.
3. The girl ate the house she lived in because she was still hungry.
4. The fish walked over to the cat sitting on our porch.
5. The boy studied hard and did all his homework.
6. The mother elephant just waltzed in through the front door.
7. The mouse flew over our house, but he could not find his cheese.
8. The birthday cake had 10 candles on it.
9. The hot dog ran down the street chasing a cat.
10. Susie loves to play with snakes, spiders and rabbits.

Make-Believe Creatures

Objective: To create make-believe characters

Materials: 8 1/2" x 11" sheets of paper, lengthwise, markers

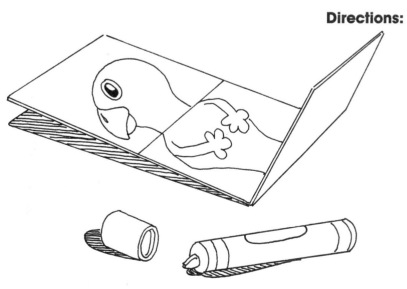

Directions: Cut each 8 1/2" x 11" sheet of paper in half lengthwise. Take a strip of paper and fold it three ways. Have a volunteer draw a head on the top section, leaving neck lines visible for the next volunteer who, unaware of the first drawing, should add a body on the next section leaving leg lines for the next drawer. The last volunteer, unaware of any drawings, should complete the creature in the last section. Open up the strip of paper and see what kind of make-believe creature was created. Let the children make all kinds of creatures.

Birthday Bulletin Board

Objectives: To teach children to give without spending money and to reinforce name recognition

Materials: large construction paper circles, push pins, construction paper, scissors, crayons/markers

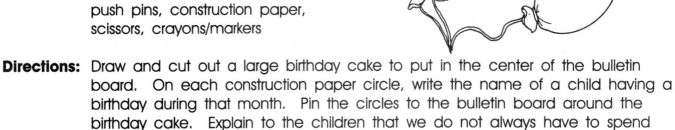

Directions: Draw and cut out a large birthday cake to put in the center of the bulletin board. On each construction paper circle, write the name of a child having a birthday during that month. Pin the circles to the bulletin board around the birthday cake. Explain to the children that we do not always have to spend money to give someone a gift. Have the children discuss what other things they could give to their friends. Ask them to draw pictures or cut out pictures of the things they mentioned. Pin their drawings and pictures to the names of the children on the bulletin board.

Patchwork Quilt

Objective: To create an alphabet bulletin board

Materials: scraps of fabric, posterboard, scissors, glue, felt, ruler

Directions: Cut posterboard into 26 squares that are 6" x 6." Give each child a square to decorate with scraps of fabric. Discuss quilt-making and its history. Arrange the children's squares on a bulletin board making all the edges meet. Designate a letter of the alphabet for each square. Cut the letters out of felt and glue them each on a square. Make extra squares, if necessary, to fill up all the space on the bulletin board.

Weekly Words Bulletin Board

Weekly Words

☆ Stop   ☆ Sun
☆ Pet   ☆ Cat
☆ Kit

Objective: To reinforce new words learned during the week

Materials: construction paper, scissors, stapler, posterboard, marker, bright colored paper

Directions: Cover a bulletin board with a bright colored paper. Use the pattern below to make star shapes out of construction paper. Write the new words of the week on strips of posterboard. Staple the stars in a vertical row down the bulletin board. Beside each star have the children staple a new word. Review the words on the bulletin board frequently.

Bookworm Corner

Objectives: To inform parents of books being read in the classroom and to decorate the wall of the classroom

Materials: 8 1/2" x 11" sheets of colored construction paper, thick-tip black marker, stapler, seasonal wrapping paper, bookworm pattern on page 189

Directions: Cover a bulletin board with seasonal wrapping paper. Title the board "Books We Have Read in _____." (Write the appropriate month in the blank.) Enlarge and cut out a bookworm using the pattern. Every time you read a book in class, write its title and the author's name on an 8 1/2" x 11" sheet of construction paper. Eventually, the bulletin board should be covered with books.

Books We Have Read in February

The Rainbow Fish By Marcus Pfister

Corduroy By Don Freeman

The Giving Tree By Shel Silverstein

Love You Forever By Robert Munsch

One Zillion Valentines By Frank Modell

The Berenstain Bears and Too Much Junk Food by Jan and Stan Berenstain

Come a Tide By George Ella Lyon

Bulletin Board Bookworm Pattern

Names Bulletin Board

Objectives: To reinforce name recognition and to create an eye-appealing and inviting environment

Materials: individual classroom photographs, push pins, posterboard, thick-tip black marker, scissors

Directions: This bulletin board idea is particularly beneficial as an instruction tool if used in the beginning of the school year. Cover the bulletin board with a seasonal color. (For example, if you are displaying in October, use orange paper.) Title the bulletin board, "A Great Bunch!" Collect a class photograph of each child. Using push pins, display each child's picture on the bulletin board. Cut three-inch strips of posterboard. Using a black marker, write a child's name on each strip. Pin each strip under the appropriate picture. The children love to look at photographs of themselves.

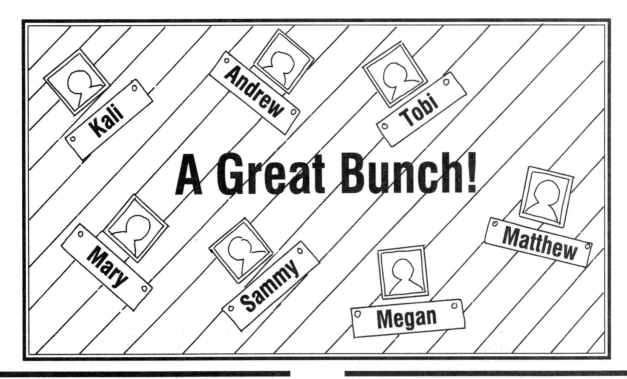

Math

This chapter is filled with play activities in which the children can be guided into discovering mathematics through four basic skills areas—numbers, measurement, sorting and classifying, and graphing.

The first area of study is numbers. Giving symbols a quantity, addition, subtraction, fractions, simple time and simple money concepts are all covered in this area. Children progress at different rates, and the activities build upon previously comprehended skills. Therefore, be alert to the difficulty level for the children in your particular class.

The second area of study is graphing. This area requires understanding from the other three areas of study. Graphing is a cumulative skill. The children graph to discover quantity, classification and measurement through the utilization of numbers. To captivate the children, graphing activities in this chapter require items such as jellybeans, gummy bears and photographs.

The third area of study is sorting and classifying. Here, concepts of color, shape, size, sequence, patterning and set building are covered. The activities utilize items from the children's environment and are play-oriented.

The fourth area of study is measurement involving the understanding of length, width, height and volume. The children are introduced to the measurements of liquids and solids. They are also given the opportunity to develop their vocabulary regarding variations in measurement (i.e. long, longer, longest and full, empty).

Candy Counting

Objective: To introduce the basic principles of addition

Materials: jellybeans, gumdrops, addition flash cards

Directions: On a table, draw three large circles in a row. Place an addition sign between the first two circles and an equal sign between the last two circles. At one end of the table, place a pile of jellybeans and a pile of gumdrops. Give each child in the class an addition flash card. Have the children take turns coming to the table and solving their addition problem. Use the correct number of gumdrops and jellybeans to represent the numbers in the equation. To solve the equation, have the children count all the candy on the table. The rest of the class should be their support group.

Sweet Addition

Objective: To reinforce addition skills

Materials: flannel board, cookies made of felt, an empty cookie bag, an addition and equal sign made of felt, addition flash cards

Directions:

1. Set up a flannel board as shown below.

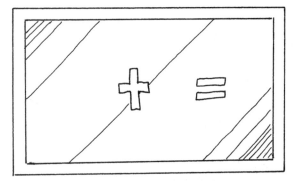

2. Fill an empty cookie bag with cookies made of felt.

3. Hold up an addition flash card and have the children solve the equation using the felt cookies.

 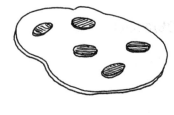

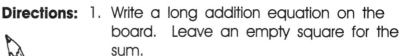

Buttons Up

Objective: To reinforce addition skills

Materials: buttons, glue, paper, pencils

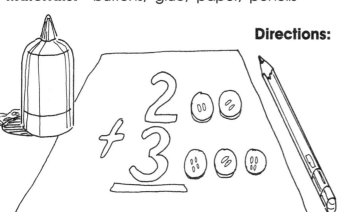

Directions:
1. Write a long addition equation on the board. Leave an empty square for the sum.

2. Have the children copy the equation on a piece of paper and glue an appropriate number of buttons to represent each number in the equation.

3. Have the children count the number of buttons on their page and write the number in the empty square.

• •

Cotton Ball Counting

Objective: To teach addition principles

Materials: tweezers, cotton balls, addition flash cards, an ice cube tray, large resealable plastic bag, paper, pencil

Directions: Place a large resealable bag full of the items mentioned above in a corner of the classroom. When children have some spare time, encourage them to try this activity.

1. Using tweezers, the child should place the correct number of cotton balls to represent the first number in the equation into the ice cube tray.

2. This is repeated for the second number in the equation.

3. To solve the equation, have the child count the total number of cotton balls in the tray. He/she should then write the equation and the answer on a piece of paper.

Extension: Blindfold a child and place cotton balls in his/her hand. Have the child guess how many are in his/her hand. Have the child count the cotton balls while blindfolded.

Number Puzzles

Objectives: To reinforce number recognition and to build problem solving skills through puzzling

Materials: Patterns below and on page 195, laminating paper, Xacto knife, corrugated cardboard, glue, resealable bags, markers/crayons

Directions: Make a copy and cut out the patterns below and on page 195. Have the children color them. Then, laminate the cutouts and glue them to corrugated cardboard. Use an Xacto knife to cut along the puzzle lines. Each puzzle should be stored in a resealable bag. Leave the activity in the math center for the children to assemble.

Number Puzzle Patterns

Number Puzzle Patterns

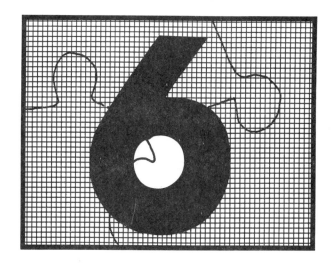

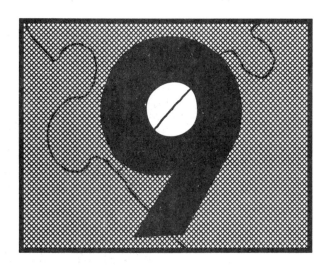

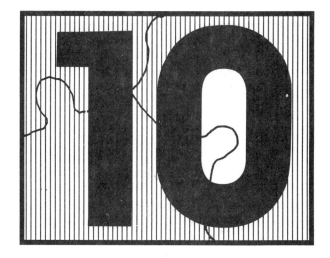

195

Simple Solutions

Objective: To introduce basic subtraction word problems

Directions: Choose volunteers to act out the math word problems below. Ask the children chosen to follow your directions carefully.

● Three boys were swimming in a pool. One boy's mom called him out of the pool to get some lunch. How many boys were left swimming in the pool?

● Five girls were skipping along when two bumped into each other and fell to the ground. How many girls were left skipping?

● Nine children were watching TV. It got very late, and four children fell asleep. How many children stayed awake?

● Seven children rode their bikes to school. Three children got flat tires. How many children will be able to ride their bikes home from school?

Subtraction Books

Objective: To enhance subtraction skills using concrete counting objects

Materials: ten 8 1/2" x 11" sheets of white paper per child, markers, stapler, posterboard, glue, crayons

Directions:

1. Give each child ten sheets of paper to label 1 through 10.

2. Have the children draw or glue the number of objects corresponding to the numbers on each page.

3. The students then staple the pages together in order.

4. Give the children subtraction problems and ask them to use their books to solve the equations. Using a piece of posterboard, have the children cover the number being subtracted.

Deduct From the Domino

Objective: To practice subtraction skills

Materials: paper, pencils, a package of dominoes

Directions: Give each child a sheet of paper and five dominoes. Have the children examine the dominoes they were given. On the paper, have the children write the largest number represented on one half of a domino. Below that number have the children write the other number represented on the same domino. Have the children subtract the small number from the large number and write their answer below the first two numbers. Have the children continue this process for the remaining dominoes.

Calorie Cutting

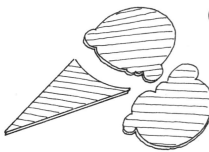

Objective: To simplify the subtraction concept

Materials: different colors of felt, flannel board, scissors, flash cards

Directions: Out of felt, cut an ice cream cone shape. Affix the cone to a flannel board. Cut ten different colored scoops of ice cream from felt. Let the students solve subtraction problems on flash cards removing ice cream scoops from the top of the cone.

Extension: For a special snack time, serve ice cream cones. Discuss how you subtracted from a full container. This activity could be used for addition and division as well.

Counting Books

Objective: To give tangible substance to number symbol

Materials: hole punch, metal rings for binding, posterboard rectangles, pumpkin seeds, glue, markers

Directions: Give each child ten posterboard cards labeled with the numbers 1 through 10. Have the children draw a large pumpkin on each card. The next day, distribute pumpkin seeds to each child. The children should glue the correct number of seeds to the pumpkin on each card. Punch holes in the top of each card and bind the ten cards together using metal rings.

Piece of Pizza Please

Objective: To introduce the concept of fractions

Materials: paper plates, construction paper, glue, scissors

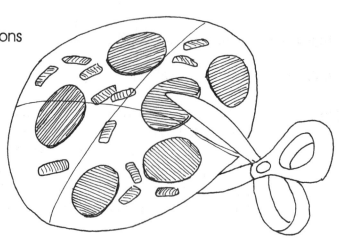

Directions: Give each child a paper plate and some construction paper. Have the children decorate their plates to look like their favorite type of pizza. When their pizzas are complete, have them decide how many people they would like to share their pizza with. Have the children cut their pizzas into the correct fractions. On the back of each slice of pizza, have the children write the fraction of the pizza it is.

Fraction Folding

Objective: To teach the concept of fractions

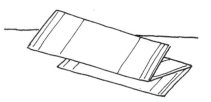

Materials: four 8 1/2" x 11" sheets of paper per child, crayons

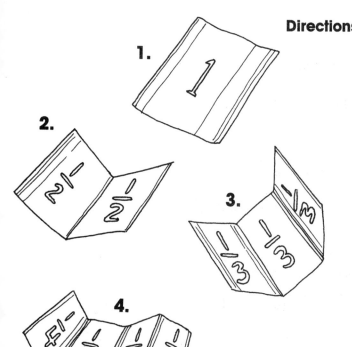

Directions: 1. Have each child color a single sheet of paper a solid color and write the number 1 in the center of the page. Discuss with the students how this is a whole sheet of paper.

2. Have students fold the next piece of paper in two equal parts and write 1/2 on each part. Students should color each part a different color.

3. Students then fold the third piece of paper into three equal parts and label each part with 1/3. Have them color each part a different color.

4. The fourth sheet of paper should now be folded into four equal parts and each part should be labeled with 1/4. Have the students color each part a different color.

Flannel Board Fractions

Objective: To teach the concept of fractions

Materials: flannel board, felt, marker, scissors, fraction flash cards

Directions: Out of felt, cut patterns of apples, oranges, pizzas, cookies, chocolate bars, cake and other edibles. Cut the items in different fractional parts. Be sure to mark the back of the item with the appropriate fraction. Place the pieces of each item next to each other on the flannel board. Hold up fraction flash cards and have the children take turns locating the edible on the felt board that is cut into the same number of pieces thus matching the fraction.

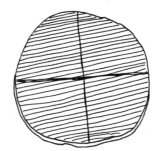
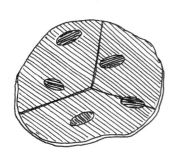

Parts Assembly

Objective: To reinforce fraction concepts

Materials: yarn, cardboard, large blunt needles, scissors, a hole punch, marker, ruler

Directions: 1.   Cut three 6" x 6" cardboard squares for each child.

2.   Cut each square into a different fraction (1/2, 1/3 and 1/4). Label each part of each square with the correct fraction.

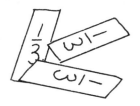

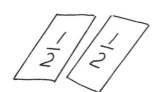

3.   Punch holes along the inner lines of each square's cut lines.

4.   Have the children sew the fractions together to form a whole square.

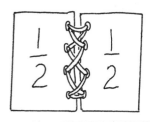

Apple Portions

Objective: To teach the concept of fractions

Materials: an apple, a knife, white paper, tempera paint, activity page below

Directions: In a group, cut an apple in half. Cut one of the halves in half again. Explain that there are four quarters in a whole apple and two halves in a whole. Using apple sections dipped in tempera paint, teach the children fraction concepts by having them match their own section of apple to the drawings below.

- -

Name_____

Using apple sections dipped in tempera paint, stamp your section of apple to the matching fraction pattern below

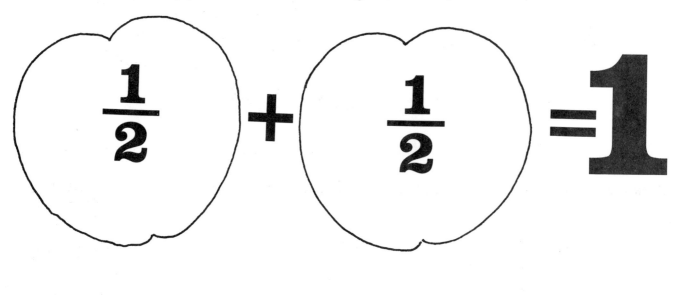

A Step In Time

Objective: To teach children to count by 5's in preparation for telling time

Materials: chalk, a large play area

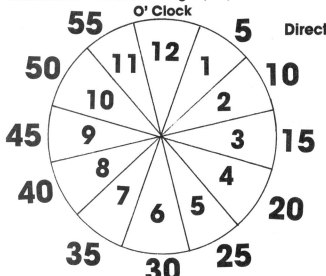

Directions: Draw a very large circle on an open playground space. Divide the circle into twelve equal parts. At the center of each part write a numeral. Begin with 0 and mark each point around the circle five digits higher each time (See illustration). Have the children practice counting by 5's as they hop from point to point. The remainder of the class should count with the jumper. When the jumper gets to 0 circle he/she must call out "Zero Clock" or "O' clock." Allow each person the opportunity to count around the circle.

The Floor Clock

Objective: To give the children an opportunity to learn telling time using a large visual aid

Materials: paint, paintbrushes, a large sheet, scissors, poster board

Directions: Paint a large circle on an old bed sheet. Place the numbers of the clock on the circle. In the center of the circle place a large solid color dot. Out of posterboard cut a large and small arrow for the hands of the clock. When introducing the tough concept of telling time, focus primarily on the hour and half hour times. Have the children walk around the clock and pretend to be the small hand while the large hand is pointing to the 12. At each digit, they should call out the time. Once this concept is being absorbed, place the large hand on the 6 and have the children walk around the clock again, calling out the time as they walk.

What Time Is It Tom/Tina?

Objective: To reinforce telling time skills

Materials: clock sheet from "The Floor Clock" activity, flash cards with times

Directions: Lay the clock sheet on a large open play area. Choose one player to be "Tom." "Tom" should stand on the dot in the center of the clock. "Tom" must pick a flash card and note the time written. Be certain to help those having difficulty reading time. The other children must call out, "What time is it Tom?" "Tom" must place the hands on the clock indicating the time on the flashcard. The other children must guess the time "Tom" indicated. The person who correctly guesses the time becomes the new "Tom" or "Tina."

The World's Largest Watch

Objective: To develop telling time skills

Materials: small paper plates, hole punch, tape, scissors, brads, markers construction paper, posterboard

Directions:

1. Give each child a paper plate. Have the children turn their paper plates up-side down. Using markers have them copy the digits of the clock.

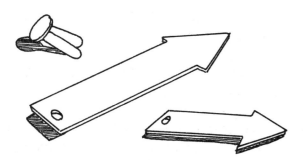

2. Show the children how to cut the hands of the clock out of posterboard and fasten them to the center of the plate using a hole punch and a brad.

3. Cut a strip from construction paper to form a band to wrap around each child's wrist. (Remember to cut it large enough to slip over the child's hand.) Glue the ends together and tape it to the bottom of the plate. Let the children "wear" their watches.

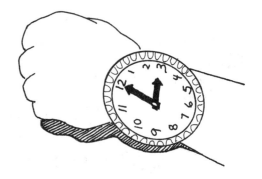

Count Your Pennies!

Objective: To teach coin value

Materials: clear tape, graph paper, quarter, dime, nickel, at least 41 pennies

Directions: Have the children gather around the front of the class. On a large sheet of graph paper, tape a penny. Discuss the value of a penny and tape one penny beside the first penny. Below the penny, tape a nickel to the graph paper. Discuss the value of a nickel with the children and tape five pennies beside the nickel. Below the nickel, tape a dime. Discuss the value of a dime and tape ten pennies beside the dime. Finally, tape a quarter below the dime and discuss the value of a quarter with the children. Tape twenty-five pennies beside the quarter.

Tub Toys for Purchase

Objective: To teach the value of money

Materials: a large empty tub filled with lots of play toys with price tags (The price tag should be labeled 5 cents, 10 cents, 25 cents or 1 cent), quarters, dimes, nickels, pennies

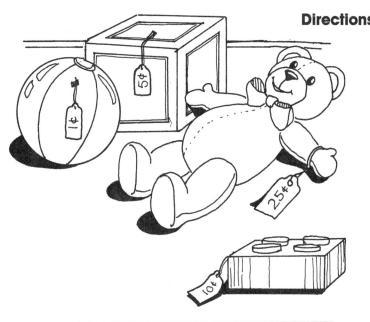

Directions:
1. Put price tags on all the objects going into the empty tub.

2. Give each child a dime, penny, nickel or quarter to spend at the tub.

3. Ask for one volunteer shopper at a time. Be sure to collect the money from the child each time. Eventually, choose one child to be the store clerk and collect the money.

4. Collect the toys at the end of the activity and allow children to play this game during their free time.

Coin Matching

Objective: To develop the concept of money

Materials: white drawing paper, coins, crayons

Directions: 1. Give each child a quarter, dime, nickel and penny.

2. Have the children place a coin under their paper. Using crayons, have them rub very hard over the coin's face. An imprint of the coin will be visible on the paper.

3. Have the children flip the coin over, place the paper over the coin and repeat the rubbing action with crayons. The reverse side of the coin should look quite different.

4. The children should repeat steps 2 and 3 for all four coins. Have the children take a crayon and join matching sides of each coin.

Role Play

Objective: To practice applying money value

Materials: empty grocery boxes and containers, play cash register, play grocery cart, coins

Directions: Set up a corner of the classroom as a grocery store. Allow the children the opportunity to role-play a store clerk and a merchant. Be sure to price the grocery items with price tags. Use real coins if possible.

Penny Pinching

Objective: To match quantity with number value

Materials: empty egg carton, 55 pennies, marker, small plastic bag

Directions: Cut an empty egg container so that there are only ten sections left in the carton. Label each section with a number from 1 to 10. Put 55 pennies in a small bag. Have the child place the correct number of pennies in each labeled section of the carton. The child can check his/her work by noting if all the pennies are used. Have the child count the pennies as they are removed from each section of the carton.

Currency Value

Objective: To review the value of currency

Materials: a copy of the activity sheet below for each child, quarter, dime, nickel, penny, pencils

Directions: Give each child a copy of the activity sheet below. Review the value of a dime, nickel, quarter and penny. Have the children fill in the missing quantities.

- -

Fill in the missing quantities. See example.

Gummy Bear Graph

Objective: To introduce graphing

Materials: one little bag of gummy bears per child, a sheet graph paper per child, a marking tool, crayons

Directions: Give each child a little bag of gummy bears and a piece of graph paper containing a diagram similar to the one below. Have the children record their gummy bear colors on their graph by coloring one square per bear. Have the children count and record the number of each color of gummy bear in the Totals column.

Gummy Bear Graph																Totals
yellow																
red																
orange																
green																
white																

Birthday Graphing

Objective: To develop graphing skills and remind each other of birth dates

Materials: a large sheet of graph paper, individual class photographs, tape, markers

Directions: Divide and label a large sheet of graph paper as shown on the diagram below. Have each child tape his/her photograph beneath the month in which he/she was born. After all the children have taped their pictures to the graph total the number of birthdays in each month. Hang the graph in the class as a reminder of the birthdays each month.

Jan.	Feb.	Mar.	Apr.	May	June	July	Aug.	Sept.	Oct.	Nov.	Dec.

Weather Graph

Objective: To develop graphing skills while paying attention to weather patterns

Materials: a large sheet of graph paper, markers

Directions: For one month, graph the weather each day. Label a graph as shown below. Each day, choose a volunteer to color a square below the day's dominant weather pattern. When the month is complete, decide which type of weather occurred most frequently, least frequently and which type of weather each child would like to see the next month. If the weather is graphed for several months, the weather between months can be compared.

Estimation Graph

Objective: To develop estimation and graphing skills

Materials: large, clear plastic jar, 10 to 15 large marbles, a large sheet of graph paper, marker, paper scraps

Directions: Fill a large, clear plastic jar with 10 to 15 large marbles. Give each child a chance to guess how many marbles are in the jar. Have each child write his/her guess on a small scrap of paper. Using a graph like the one below, check off each child's guess. What was the most common estimation? Open the jar and count how many marbles are in the jar. How many people on the graph guessed that number?

Marbles	1	2	3	4	5	6	7	8	9	10	11	12	13	14	15
Totals															

Have You Ever Ridden?

Objective: To graph different modes of transportation and their frequency of use

Materials: chart paper, adhesive stars, a marker

Directions: Discuss different modes of transportation with the children (i.e. cars, boats, planes, trains, buses, trolleys, tractors, taxis, trucks, etc.). On the left side of a piece of chart paper write the modes of transportation. Ask the children mode by mode, if they have ever ridden on the vehicle. Have each child that has ridden that form of transportation come to the chart and stick an adhesive star to that mode. Repeat this for each of the modes. When the graph is complete, have the children discuss on which mode the largest number of children have ridden. Then, discuss on which mode the least number of children have ridden.

Transportation Graph		
Boat		
Plane		
Train		
Trolley		
Bus		
Tractor		
Bicycle		
Taxi		
Motorcycle		

Play Time

Objective: To graph favorite play time activities

Materials: chart paper, small circles cut out of one color of construction paper, a marker, tape

Directions: Give each child a small construction paper circle. Write the following headings on a piece of chart paper: *skipping, swinging, playing tag, bouncing balls.* Tell the children that they are going to make a chart to discuss the most popular play time activity. Read the headings and have each child decide his/her favorite activity. Have each child tape his/her circle under the activity he/she most likes to play. Review the chart after all the children have placed their circles on the chart. Discuss which activity is the most and least popular.

Bouncing Balls	Skipping	Playing Tag	Swinging

All Sorts of Balloons

Objective: To develop graphing skills while sorting by properties

Materials: balloons of varying size shape and color, 3 large sheets of graph paper, markers

Directions: 1. Prepare three large sheets of graph paper as illustrated.

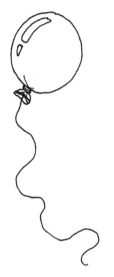

Color

		Totals
Orange		
Blue		
Red		
Yellow		
Black		
Green		

Shape

		Totals
Oval		
Round		
Oblong		

Size

		Totals
Small		
Medium		
Large		

2. Place a large pile of balloons varying in size, shape and color in the front of the group. Sort the balloons first by color. Have children volunteer to approach the pile of balloons and graph a balloon's color property. After all the balloons have been graphed by color, fill in the Totals column.

3. Repeat step 2 but sort and graph the balloons by size.

4. Repeat step 2 but sort and graph the balloons by shape.

Sorting Center Activities

To further stimulate and develop sorting skills, set up a center in your classroom. Allow the children the opportunity to explore new sorting properties in their free time. Some ideas for the center are listed below.

- mixed beans tray
- jelly bean jars
- rock collections
- fruit and vegetable baskets
- seeds tray
- soil samples
- leaves
- sea shells

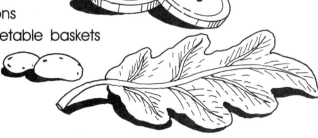

Shapes Patterning

Objective: To introduce patterning and to review basic geometric shapes

Materials: colored foil paper, white paper, scissors, glue

Directions: Cut many basic geometric shapes out of colored foil paper. Give each child a handful of the cut-out shapes along with a sheet of white paper. The paper should be divided into horizontal rows of six squares. (See illustration.) Have the children make patterns in each row by gluing the various shapes on their paper. Talk about each other's patterns when the children have completed their activity.

Patterning

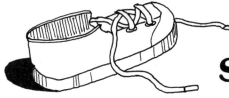

Shoe Patterning

Objective: To reinforce the concept of patterning

Materials: shoes, large floor space

Directions: Have each child remove his/her shoes. Place the shoes in a pile across from the children. Line the shoes in a pattern. Try a repeated pattern of a Velcro® shoe followed by a lace shoe. Try a light shoe followed by a dark shoe. Try a couple of small shoes followed by a large shoe. Try a sandal followed by a running shoe. Have the children guess the pattern being established. When the children appear to fully comprehend the patterning idea, allow them the chance to create their own pattern for the remainder of the class to guess.

Rubber Stamp Patterns

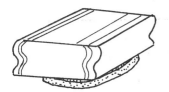

Objective: To teach the concept of patterning using rubber stamps

Materials: 3 to 4 different rubber stamps, ink pad, paper, a large sheet of graph paper

Directions: Using different rubber stamps on a large sheet of graph paper, make a pattern for the children to see. With the children, discuss why it is a pattern. Once the children seem to understand the pattern concept, start a pattern for a student volunteer to repeat. Eventually, let the children design their own patterns.

. . . .

Pattern Macaroni Jewelry

Objective: To reinforce patterning skills

Materials: macaroni, rubbing alcohol, an empty margarine dish, yarn, food coloring

Directions:

1. Fill an empty margarine dish with macaroni, a few drops of food coloring and a teaspoon of rubbing alcohol. Shake the container until the macaroni is the desired color.

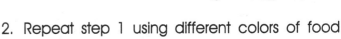

2. Repeat step 1 using different colors of food coloring.

3. Give each child a piece of yarn. Tie a knot at one end and let the children make a piece of jewelry by stringing the different colors of macaroni into a pattern.

Peg Board Shapes

Objective: To review basic geometric shapes

Materials: Styrofoam, 20 toothpicks per child, yarn, scissors

Directions:
1. Cut the Styrofoam into 6" squares.

2. At 1" intervals, push toothpicks into the Styrofoam. There should be five toothpicks in each of four rows.

3. Give each child a few strands of yarn. Demonstrate how to make different shapes by wrapping the yarn around the toothpicks.

Shape Books

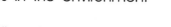

Objective: To look for geometric shapes in the environment

Materials: lightweight posterboard, small metal clip rings, crayons, hole punch, scissors

Directions:
1. Help the children cut five circle shapes out of lightweight posterboard per book. Then, they punch two small holes out of each circle and fasten the circles together with metal clip rings to make a circular book.

2. Help the children title the first page, "My Book of Circles." Have them draw a circular object on each page.

3. Have the children repeat the first two steps to make a book of triangles, squares, rectangles, pentagons, hexagons, etc.

4. Encourage the children to share their shape books together.

Sponge Shapes

Objective: To reinforce basic geometric shapes

Materials: household sponges cut in various geometric shapes, a different color of tempera paint for each sponge shape, 8 1/2" x 11" sheets of white drawing paper, black construction paper, glue

Directions: Give each child an 8 1/2" x 11" sheet of white paper. Have children use geometric shape sponges to paint their paper. Remind them to use one color of paint for each sponge. When the paint has dried, mount the paper onto a sheet of black construction paper. Laminate and let the children use them as place mats.

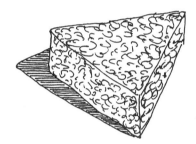 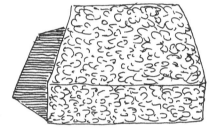 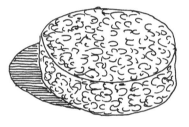

Shape Mobile

Objective: To introduce some of the more difficult geometric shapes

Materials: hole punch, posterboard, markers, regular clothes hangers, yarn

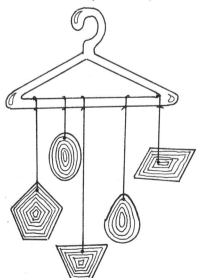

Directions: Introduce the children to the rhombus, pentagon, trapezoid, ellipse and oval shapes. Cut out each of the shapes (approximately three inches in diameter) from posterboard and give each child one of each shape. Using a marker, have each child draw the shape of their cutout directly on the cutout. (See diagram). They should repeat drawing the shape (getting smaller each time) inside the cutout, as many times as possible. This will create an optical illusion. Punch a hole in the top of each shape. Use yarn to hang the cutout shapes from a clothes hanger. Display them in the classroom.

The Geometric Shape Tree

Objective: To reinforce basic geometric shapes

Materials: artificial Christmas tree, glitter, glue, string, scissors, copies of the shapes cutouts below and on page 215, construction paper, stapler

Directions: Set up an artificial Christmas tree in the classroom. Tell the children that the tree in the classroom is a geometric shape tree and that they are going to be responsible for decorating it. Give each child a copy of the geometric shape cutouts. Have them glue the pages to sheets of construction paper. Next, the children should cut out each shape and decorate it using glue and glitter. Explain that when string is stapled to the top of each shape, it will become an ornament for the geometric shape tree. Let the children place their ornaments anywhere on the tree.

- -

Shape Cutouts

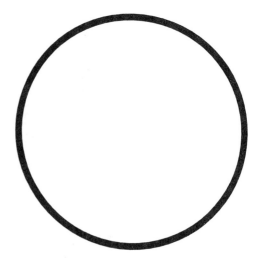

Shape Cutouts

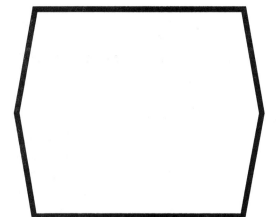

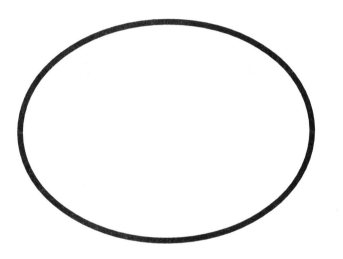

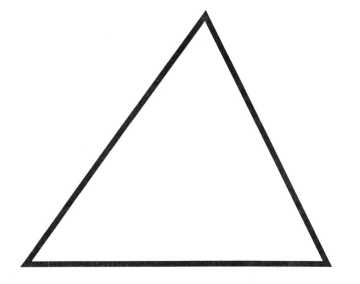

3-D Shape Match-Up

Objective: To match 3-D shapes with 2-D planes

Materials: soup can, baseball, ice cream cone, cereal box, dice, an enlarged copy of 3-D Match-Up below

Directions: Provide the children with the objects listed above so they can match them to the enlarged copy. Be sure to call the 3-D objects their appropriate names.

- -

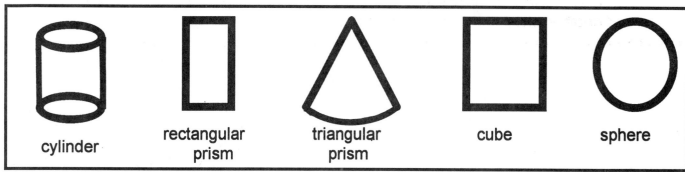

| cylinder | rectangular prism | triangular prism | cube | sphere |

3-D Match-Up

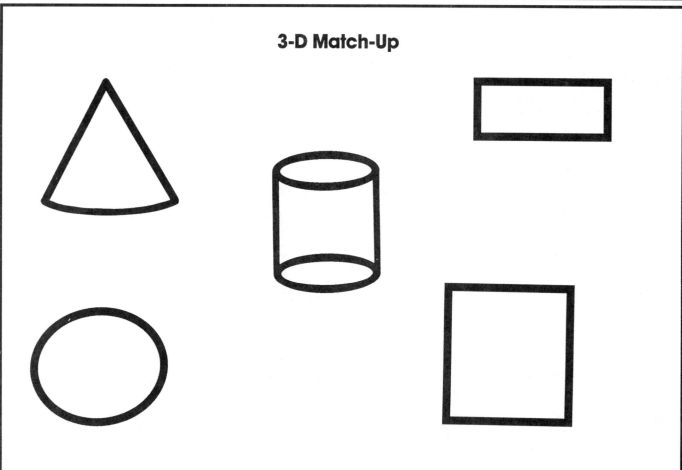

Left/Right Tag

Objective: To recall left and right concepts

Materials: yellow and red ribbon strips

Directions: Determine a boundary for a game of tag. Choose one person to be "It." Each child must tie a yellow ribbon to the left side of his/her body and a red ribbon to the right side of his/her body. The players must try to avoid being tagged by "It." "It" will begin the game by calling out "left" or "right". The players must respond by hopping on a left or right leg. "It" can switch the right and left theme at any time. "It" must also follow his/her call. "It" tries to tag another child who then becomes "It."

• •

The Sock Hop

Objective: To reinforce right and left concepts

Materials: masking tape, adhesive name tag labels, music and a music player, a large carpeted area

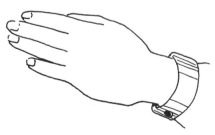

Directions: Have the children remove their shoes. Stick an adhesive label to the top of each child's foot. Write an "R" on the right foot label and an "L" on the left foot label. Be certain that the letters are facing the children. Use masking tape to form a very large circle on the floor. Start some music. Have the children begin hopping on their left feet outside of the circle. When the music stops, they must switch feet and begin hopping on their right feet inside the circle. Continue the cycle having the children alternate feet when the music stops.

• •

Hokey Pokey

Objective: To practice left/right skills

Materials: masking tape, a large carpeted area

Directions: Using masking tape, make a large circle on the floor. Have the children gather around the circle. Begin the "Hokey Pokey" but use the following left and right body parts: hand, elbow, shoulder, ear, hip, knee, and foot.

Decorative Rights and Lefts

Objective: To remind children of the concepts of right and left

Materials: white drawing paper, yarn, markers, construction paper scraps, glue, glitter, buttons, scissors

Directions: Have the children choose a partner. Each child should trace around his/her partner's feet and hands. After both partners have a tracing of their hands and feet, they should cut them out. Let the students use any scraps to decorate the feet and hand patterns. On the back of each hand and foot, help the children to write whether it is the right or left.

• •

Sequencing Numerals

Objective: To practice numerical order

Materials: potatoes, knife, tempera paint, a thick, black permanent marker, white paper, paper plates

Directions:

1. Cut five potatoes in half and, using a knife, carve a number from 1 to 10 on each potato.

2. With a marker, label the top of each potato with the number carved in its base.

3. Have the children dip the carved end of the number 1 potato into paint.

4. On white paper, have them make a print of each potato from 1 to 10 in the correct numerical order.

Extension: Using the potato stamps, have the children stamp their phone numbers on strips of posterboard.

Changing Objects

Objective: To order a picture by time sequence

Materials: posterboard, scissors, glue, copies of the illustrations below

Directions: Glue the illustrations onto posterboard. Cut out the illustrations along the dotted lines. Label the backs of the cards with the correct sequential order. Let the children shuffle and reorder the cards.

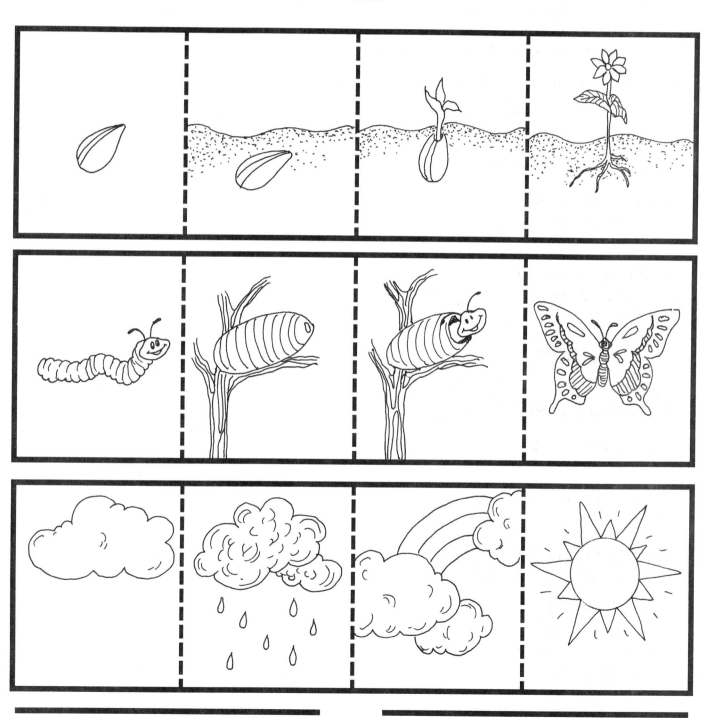

Counting Collection

Objective: To introduce sets

Materials: various classroom objects, large box, hula hoops

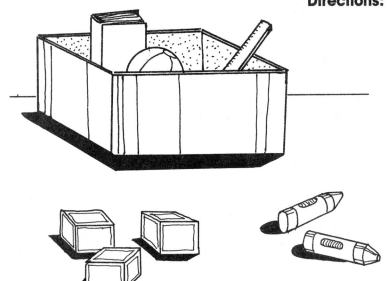

Directions: Have 5 children collect objects around the classroom. Instruct the chosen children to each select one type of object and collect five of each item. (Example: five crayons, five blocks, five Legos®, five rulers, five books.) Place all the objects in a large box and mix them up. Lay five hula hoops at the front of the class. Have volunteers pick objects out of the box and place them in a hula hoop. Similar objects should be placed in each hula hoop. Once all the objects have been sorted, count the number of objects in each hula hoop. Discuss with the children how each hula hoop represents a set of five.

Extension: Try introducing the children to sets of 2, 10, etc.

Bundling Bunches

Objectives: To reinforce sets and to introduce counting by 2's, 5's or 10's

Materials: chopsticks, rubber bands

Directions: Place a large pile of chopsticks on a table. Have a volunteer select ten chopsticks and wrap a rubber band around the bunch. Have another volunteer repeat the same activity. After five volunteers have bunched five bundles of chopsticks, talk about sets and counting by 10's. Then, repeat the activity bundling bunches of 2's and 5's.

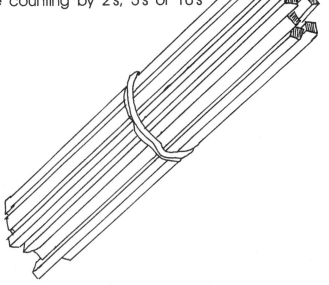

Odd/Even

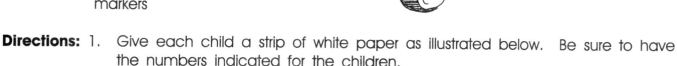

Objective: To extend set concepts to odd and even numbering

Materials: 24" x 4" strips of white paper, popcorn, glue, blue and red markers

Directions: 1. Give each child a strip of white paper as illustrated below. Be sure to have the numbers indicated for the children.

1	2	3	4	5	6	7	8	9	10

2. Under each number, have the child glue an equivalent number of popcorn.

1	2	3	4	5	6	7	8	9	10

3. Where possible, have the child circle the sets of two under each number.

1	2	3	4	5	6	7	8	9	10

4. Explain that all the popcorn will fit into a set if the number is even, while one popcorn will not fit into the set if the number is odd.

1	2	3	4	5	6	7	8	9	10
ODD	EVEN	ODD	EVEN	ODD	EVEN	ODD	EVEN	ODD	EVEN

5. The students should trace the odd numbers using a blue marker and the even numbers using a red marker.

Sorting Sets

Objective: To sort objects into sets and determine similarities

Materials: 2 hula hoops, round objects (i.e. marble, wheel, globe), red objects (i.e. red Lego®, red crayon, red car, red marker), red/round objects (i.e. apple, red ball)

Directions: Place two hula hoops on the floor. Place red objects in one hula hoop and round objects in another hula hoop. The objects that are both round and red should be placed in a separate category. Overlap the hula hoops and place those objects in the overlapped section.

Tying It Together

Objective: To place pictures in sequential order

Materials: hole punch, ribbon, posterboard, crayons, scissors

Directions: Give each child four pieces of 4" x 6" posterboard. Have the children color a picture of one season of the year on each card. Punch 2 holes on both sides of each card. Have the children arrange their cards in sequential order and tie them together using ribbon.

Extension: Have the students draw pictures of things that fall into sequential order other than seasons. Pass the cards already tied together around the classroom and have volunteers take turns telling a picture story in order of events illustrated.

Sorting Buttons

Objective: To divide buttons into various categories

Materials: buttons of all different shapes, sizes, colors, textures and number of button holes; markers; color crayons

Directions:

1. Place a large pile of buttons on each child's desk. Have the children divide their buttons into small, medium and large size buttons.

2. Have the children divide their buttons into various colors.

3. Have the children divide their buttons into similar shapes (square, round, oval, triangle).

4. Have the children divide their buttons into similar textures (smooth, rough, furry).

5. Have the children divide their buttons into groups of buttons that have the same number of holes.

Extension: As a group, graph the class findings.

Shell Sorting

Objective: To develop comparison skills

Materials: matching scallop shells of various sizes, shapes, colors

Directions: On paper plates, arrange seven scallop shells of various sizes, shapes and colors. Be certain to include one matching pair of scallops on each plate. Using a marker, have the children trace around the edge of each scallop on their plate. Finally, have each child color in the tracings of the matching scallop pair on his/her plate.

Big/Small

Objective: To make comparisons between large and small animals

Materials: drawing paper, crayons

Directions: Give each child a sheet of drawing paper. Demonstrate how to fold the paper in half. On one side of the paper, have the children draw a mouse. On the other side, have them draw a dinosaur. Help the children label each side with the appropriate title-"large" or "small." Then, ask the children to think of other animals that are large and small. Have the children add drawings of these animals onto their folded drawing paper.

Tallest/Shortest

Objective: To align the students from tallest to shortest

Directions: Discuss with the children how people come in all different shapes and sizes. One way to compare the children is to compare their height. Ask the children who they think is the tallest person in their classroom. Ask them who they think might be the shortest person. Then, align the remainder of the children in between. Be sensitive to the children's feelings if there are children who might be insecure about their size. Stress how all people are unique.

Patterning Bulletin Board

Bulletin Board

Objectives: To create an interactive bulletin board that teaches patterning and enhances the beauty of the classroom

Materials: adhesive Velcro®, black felt, yellow yarn, scissors, construction paper, laminating paper, stapler, bead shape patterns below and on page 226

Directions: Cover a bulletin board with black felt. Cut four strands of yarn slightly shorter than the width of the bulletin board being decorated. Staple the yarn to the bulletin board as shown below. Using the patterns below and on page 226, cut bead shapes out of construction paper. Laminate the shapes and affix a piece of Velcro® to the back of each one. Title the bulletin board, "Pattern Me Please." Stick the shapes in patterns along the yarn strands. Let the children arrange their own patterns. Change as frequently as desired.

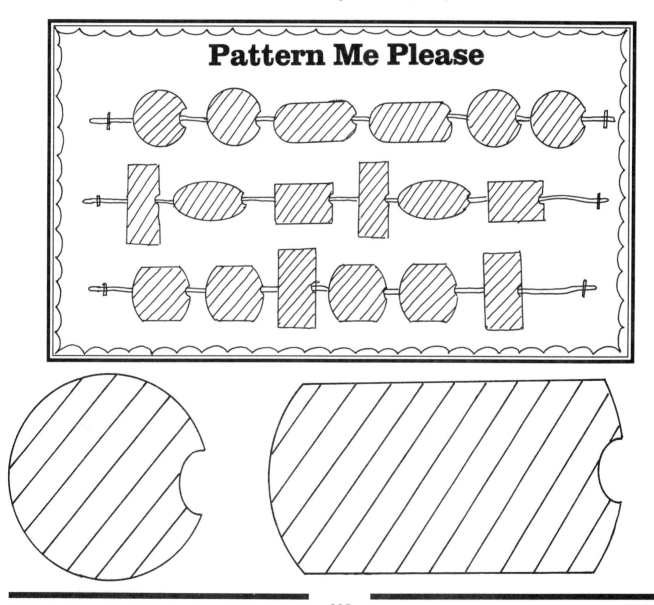

Bead Shape Patterns

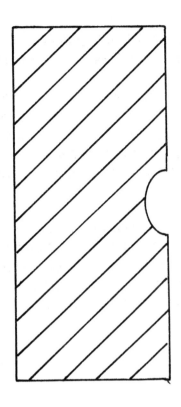

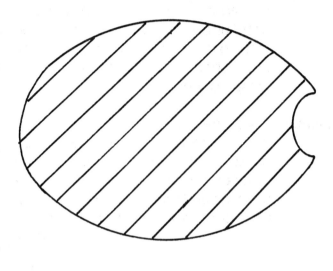

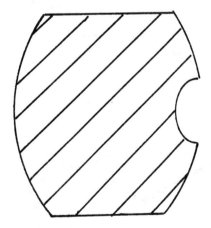

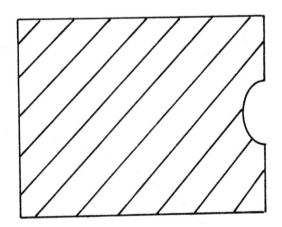

Fishing Fun

Objective: To match quantity with number symbol

Materials: magnet, marker, piece of string, yardstick, small glass bowl, child's wading pool, construction paper, stapler, contact paper, scissors, shark and fish patterns below

Assembly: Tie a piece of string to the end of a yardstick. Attach a magnet to the end of the string to create your fishing pole. Cut approximately 20 shark shapes out of construction paper. Write a number between 1 and 10 on each shark. Laminate the shark shapes using contact paper. Place a staple in the center of each shark. Cut tiny fish out of a different color construction paper. Laminate these as well.

Directions: Place the shark shapes in the child's wading pool. Choose a volunteer to try to catch a shark with the yardstick fishing pole. (The magnet will stick with the staple on the shark.) Have the child call the number on the shark he/she catches. Have the child pick an equal number of small fish (stored in a small glass bowl) to feed the shark. After returning his/her shark to the pool, the child may choose the next fisherman.

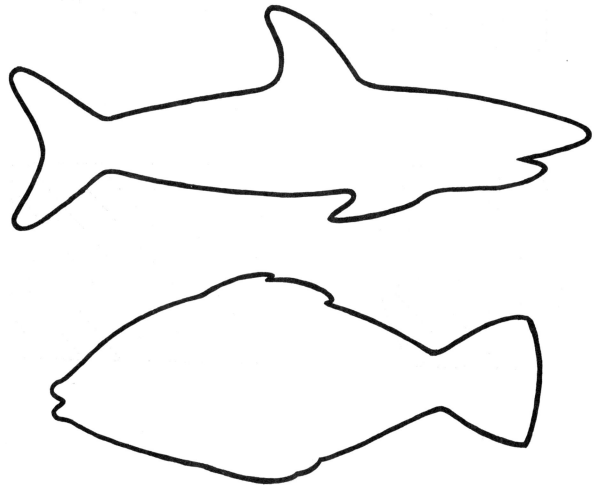

Clothesline Quantity

Objective: To develop the concept of quantity

Materials: articles of clothing, clothesline, clothespins

Directions: Hang a clothesline in the classroom. Attach many articles of clothing to the clothesline using clothespins. Be sure to have several clothing articles match. For example, have three socks, four shirts, two pants, five shoes and two ties. Discuss with the children how many of each article of clothing is hanging from the clothesline. Then, discuss which articles of clothing you have the most, least, and equal amounts of.

Liquid Measurements

Objective: To demonstrate that liquid can be measured

Materials: measuring cup, empty gallon milk jug, empty pint milk carton, one-cup plastic cup, pitcher of water, chart paper

Directions: This activity is best done outdoors or over a water table. Divide the class into small groups. At each table, set the items listed above. Ask the children to use their measuring cup to fill the empty gallon milk jug with water. Ask them how many full measuring cups of water it takes to fill a gallon milk jug. Chart the results together. Do the same activity but use the pint-size milk carton and then the plastic cup. Again, chart the results. Explain how liquid is being measured when they are pouring water into each container.

Less/More/Equal

Objective: To develop the understanding of quantity

Materials: 9 glasses of water, 9 clear plastic bowls of rice, 9 jars of jelly beans, 9 bundles of chopsticks, copies of the chart on page 229

Directions: Set up three stations in the classroom. At each station, have the children discuss the differences in quantities of the objects in the containers. At Station One, be sure to have two equal amounts of the same object in two of the three containers. At Station Two, have one container filled with an obviously larger number of objects in it than the other two containers at the station. At Station Three, have a container filled with an obviously lesser amount of objects in it than the other two containers at the station. Label each container at each station with either an a, b or c. Have the students use the chart on the next page to record their discoveries.

Less/More/Equal Chart

At each station, record your findings on the illustrations below. Draw the missing quantities and remember to give the items their correct title (a, b or c).

Station One

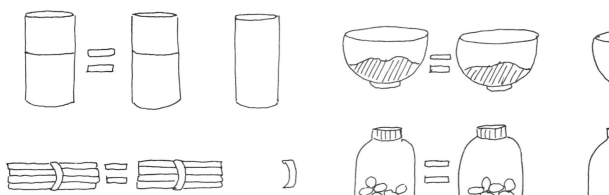

Station Two

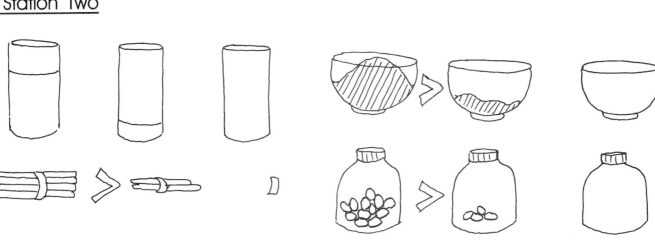

Station Three

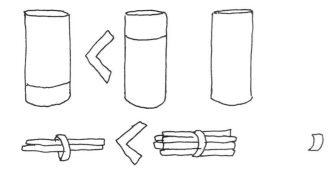
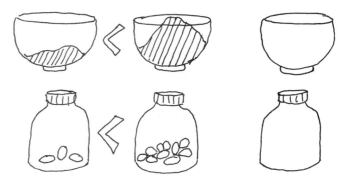

Measuring Concepts

Objective: To teach the concept of quantity by properties

Materials: 8 shallow boxes, straws of varying length, rocks of different sizes, apples of different sizes, pipe cleaners of varying length, crayons of varying length, green beans of varying length, balls of varying sizes, shells of varying sizes

Directions: Place the eight shallow boxes at the front of the class. Divide each box into three equal parts. Label the box parts as shown below. Place all the objects for sorting in a pile. Sort into the boxes as follows:

straws: sort by long, longer, longest
pipe cleaners: sort by long, longer, longest
green beans: sort by short, shorter, shortest
crayons: sort by short, shorter, shortest
balls: sort by big, bigger, biggest
apples: sort by big, bigger, biggest
shells: sort by small, smaller, smallest
rocks: sort by small, smaller, smallest

Big Foot

Objective: To measure height using a ruler in inches

Materials: ruler, pencils, drawing paper, scissors, glue, markers

Directions: Have each child trace an outline of his/her shoe. Instruct the children to cut along the tracing of their shoe. Have the children decorate their cutout with markers. Collect all the shoe prints and have the children help place them in sequence from largest to smallest, widest to thinnest, or shortest to longest. Have each child measure his/her foot cutout using a ruler. The students should write the length of their foot on the back of their cutout. Display shoe cutouts in a sequential order down a school hallway.

Teddy Bear Day

Objective: To teach matching quantity with number symbol

Materials: teddy bear for each child, number flash cards, large container of buttons

Directions: Instruct each child to bring a teddy bear from home. Give each child ten buttons. Hold up a flash card with a number between 1 and 10 drawn on it. Have the children place an equal amount of buttons on the chest of their bear. (This activity could be used for addition and subtraction purposes as the children develop their skills.)

Munchies Measurement

Objective: To apply the concepts of measurement to cooking

Materials: large mixing bowl, wooden spoon, raisins, nuts, dry cereal, coconut, dried bananas

Directions: In a large bowl, help the children measure and mix dry ingredients such as the ones listed below. Use a large wooden spoon to combine the ingredients. Serve the mixture for a special snack time.

1 Cup raisins
1 Cup nuts
1/2 Cup coconut
1 Cup dried cereal
1/4 Cup dried bananas

Math Jump

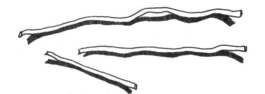

Objective: To measure objects of varying heights using strings as measuring tools

Materials: string, stapler, chart paper, 5 classroom objects of varying heights

Directions: Set a jumping course using five different objects. Be sure that all the children can jump over the objects. The objects should be of varying heights. Have children take turns jumping over the objects in the course. When everyone has completed the course, measure the height of the objects with a piece of string. Cut a length of string to match the length of the each object. Staple the strings to a piece of chart paper. Be sure to label each object under the string it matches. Discuss with the children the measurements discovered. Discuss the shortest and longest objects.

MATH

Measuring Concept Bulletin Board

Objectives: To reinforce measuring and to decorate the classroom

Materials: construction paper, scissors, patterns below and on pages 233-236, stapler, yarn, tape

Directions: Cover the bulletin board with a decorative paper. Use the patterns below and on pages 233-236 to make cutouts from construction paper. Cut three of the balloon pattern. Arrange the objects on the bulletin board in groups together. (See illustration below.) From the three balloon cutouts, staple stands of yarn of varying length. Tape the title, *Long, Longer* or *Longest* to the appropriate strand of yarn. This bulletin board display complements the Measuring Concepts activity on page 230.

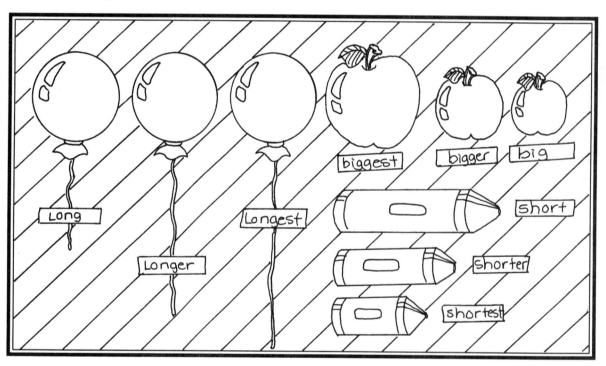

Short

Measuring Concept Patterns

233

Measuring Concept Patterns

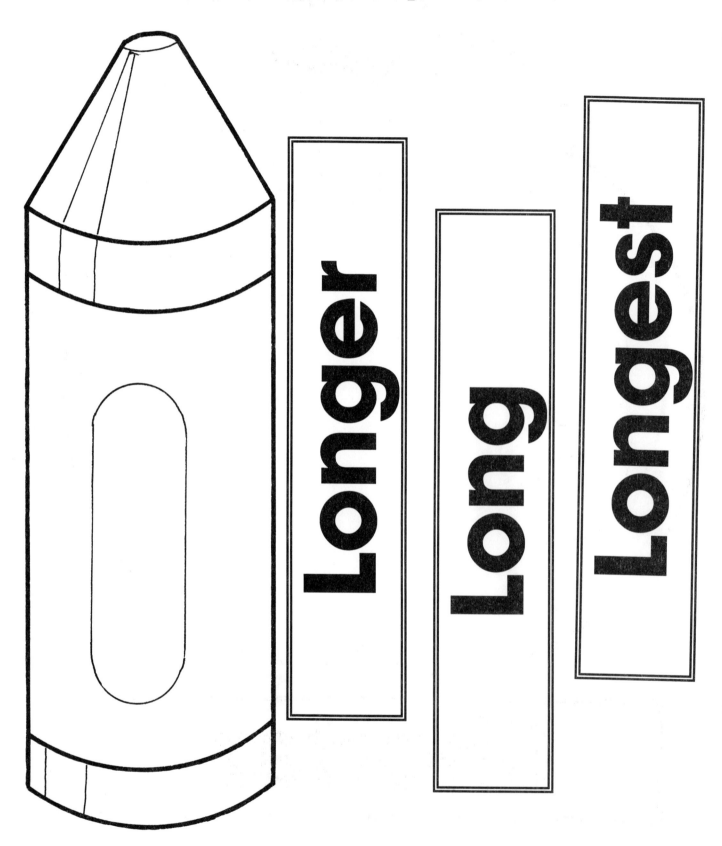

Measuring Concept Patterns

Shorter

Measuring Concept Patterns

Bigger

Shortest

Big

Biggest

Science

Through the activities in this chapter, it is hoped that the children will cultivate a positive attitude towards scientific study. Children are very good at observing things in their environment, but they often are curious and desire explanations. The hands-on experiences presented in this chapter include the following topics: weather, plants, animals, sun, moon, Earth, rocks, water, air, senses, magnetism, microscopic discoveries, energy movements and conservation. Through the exploration of these topics, it is hoped that the children will apply greater understanding to the environment in which they live.

Weather Calendar

			APRIL			
SUN	MON	TUE	WED	THUR	FRI	SAT
1	2	3	4	5	6	7
8	9	10	11	12	13	14
15	16	17	18	19	20	21
22	23	24	25	26	27	28
29	30					

Objective: To have children record weather patterns on a weather calendar

Materials: large sheet of posterboard, colored construction paper, scissors, tape, marker, weather symbol patterns below

Directions: Trace around the weather symbol patterns below on construction paper. On a large piece of posterboard draw a calendar like the one shown above. The squares on the calendar should each be two inches. Gather the children in a group. Discuss some weather words with the children (i.e. sunshine, rain, snow, wind, clouds, hail, lightning, thunder). For each word given, cut out one of the symbols from construction paper to represent it. Ask the children to describe the weather of the current day. Ask for a volunteer each day to tape the symbol representing the day's weather in the correct date on the calendar.

Weather Sounds

Objective: To recognize and classify various weather sounds

Materials: tape recorder, blank cassette

Directions: Plan this activity in advance. Tape various weather sounds at different times. When complete, play for the children. Ask the children to close their eyes and listen to the sounds. Ask them to call out the weather they hear.

• •

Hot/Cold Thermometer

Objective: To distinguish between hot and cold temperatures

Materials: posterboard, one-inch elastic, markers, tape, scissors

Directions:

1. Draw a large thermometer on a sheet of posterboard.

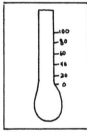

2. Cut a slit in the top and bottom of the the thermometer.

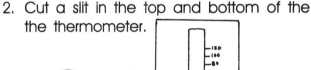

3. Cut a large strip of one-inch wide elastic and thread it through the thermometer as shown.

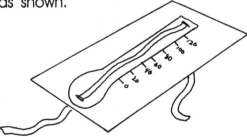

4. Tape the ends of the elastic together and color one side of the elastic red to represent the mercury.

5. Pull the elastic so that the red side is showing.

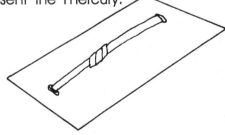

6. Each day, have the children pull the elastic to show more mercury for hot days and less mercury for cold days.

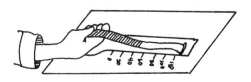

Rainbow Reflections

Objective: To demonstrate how a rainbow is created

Materials: small mirror, glass of water, sunshine

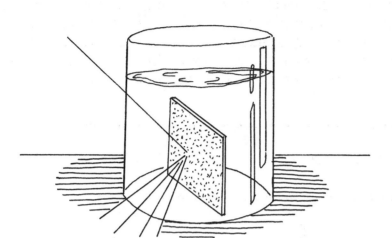

Directions: Place a small mirror in a clear glass of water. Place the glass in the window so that the sun will shine on the mirror. Rotate the glass until a rainbow is reflected against a wall. Have the children look for the colors of the rainbow. Explain that the sun is made up of these colors and when the sun shines through the raindrops or water, the colors are separated.

Extension: If a garden hose is available, take the children outside and spray a fine mist of water from the hose. Stand with your back to the sun. A rainbow will appear in the fine mist. Ask the children to explain what is happening. This might also be an appropriate time to sing a song such as "Mister Sun."

Weather Collage

Objective: To relate weather elements to activity opportunities

Materials: magazines, scissors, glue, markers, posterboard

Directions: Pick a weather type and have the children fill a posterboard with things that relate to that particular weather. For example, for a snowy day theme, the children might want to color pictures or cut out pictures of skiers, snow scenes, sledding children, warm clothes, fire - places, hot chocolate, etc. When the children have completed their collage, display it in the classroom. When the children are bored or do not know what to do on a particular weather day, have them refer back to their collage for ideas.

Weather Shoes

Objective: To match approriate footwear to weather elements

Materials: rubber boots, snow shoes, snow boots, sandals, tennis shoes, dress-up box, copies of the worksheet below, markers

Directions: Put all the types of footwear mentioned above in a dress-up box. Then, ask the children to dress in what they feel would be appropriate footwear for the weather you describe. Eventually, give each child a copy of the worksheet below. Have them draw the appropriate footwear under each weather element. Encourage the children to draw more than one type of footwear for each element.

- -

Draw the appropriate footwear for each weather element.

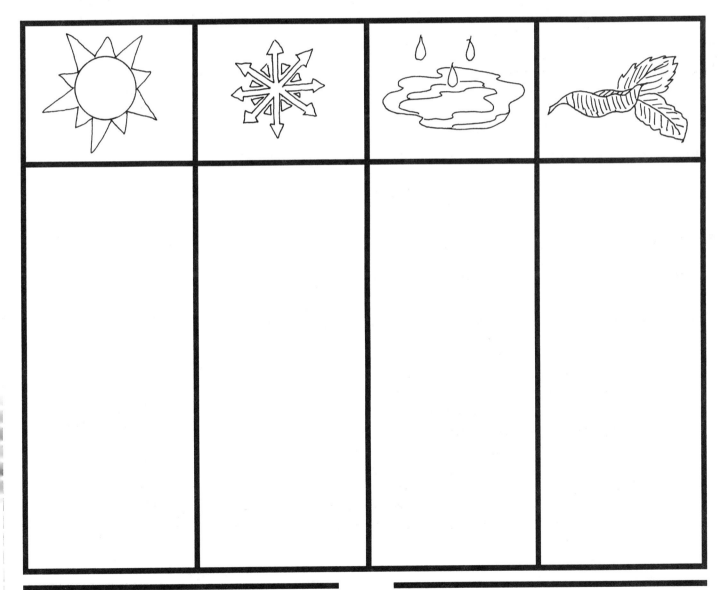

Worm World

Objective: To learn more about earthworms

Materials: (per 10 students) - 10 clear plastic cups, one gallon of chocolate ice cream, one package of chocolate sandwich cookies, a wooden mallet, 20 gummy worms, masking tape, markers, brown paper bag

Directions: Discuss earthworms with the children and their need for a moist, warm place to live underground. Discuss how they break down decaying matter in the soil and how their burrows allow air to enter the soil thus helping plants grow. Explain why people like to have the earthworms in their gardens. Follow the recipe below to make a living space for imaginary earthworms. While following the recipe, continue discussing the nature of earthworms.

1. Give each child a clear plastic cup. Have the children use a strip of masking tape and a marker to label their cup with their name.

2. Place a package of chocolate sandwich cookies in a brown paper bag. Have the children take turns crushing the cookies with a wooden mallet.

3. Pour a small amount of crushed cookie into each child's cup. Have the children place a scoop of chocolate ice cream onto the crushed cookie.

4. Pour a little crushed cookie over the ice cream layer and have the children put two gummy worms into their new home. Enjoy for a special snack!

Squirmy Worms

Objective: To make earthworms out of play dough

Materials: one cup salt, one cup flour, one tablespoon of powdered alum, water, mixing bowl

Directions: Mix the salt, flour and alum with enough water to give it the consistency of putty. Give each child a ball of the dough and have the children make earthworms by rolling the dough on a flat surface. During this activity, discuss attributes of earthworms.

Sensational Spiders

Objective: To make a spider out of egg cartons and pipe cleaners showing the unique attributes of spiders

Materials: several empty egg cartons, 8 pipe cleaners per child, paintbrushes, black paint, string, pictures of spiders

Directions: Read about spiders to the children. Discuss how they have eight legs and how they eat mosquitoes, flies and other insects. Place pictures of spiders around the classroom for the children to examine. Then, have the children make egg carton spiders following the steps below.

1. Give each child a single section of an empty carton with eight holes punched in his/her section.

2. Instruct the children to paint their egg carton section black to represent a spider's body.

3. When the paint is dry, have the students insert eight pipe cleaners into the eight holes of their spider's body section.

4. Help the children attach a string to the top of their spider's body. Hang the spiders around the classroom.

Extension: Let the children watch the video of *Charlotte's Web.*

Spider Webs

Objectives: To examine spider webs and to attempt to draw one

Materials: black construction paper, white chalk, plastic insects, glue, one copy of the web on page 244 (per child)

Directions: Discuss different kinds of spider webs with the children (e.g. sheet-web, tangled web, orb, etc.). Discuss the function of a spider's web. Place pictures of spider webs around the classroom for children to examine more closely. Have the children use white chalk on black construction paper to draw their own spider web. Have them glue plastic insects on it for added effect. Use the drawings on page 244 to help the children draw a web.

Spin Your Own Web

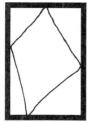 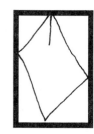 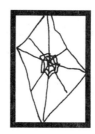  

For practice, use the drawings above to help you draw your own spider web in the space below. Then, try drawing your own spider web with white chalk on black construction paper.

Animal Body Coverings

Objective: To discover the many types of body coverings for animals

Materials: feathers, fur fabric (fur), sequins fabric (scales), shells, felt (skin), doll's hair (hair), six shoe boxes, pictures of many different animals, tape, scissors, magazines

Directions: Fill each of six shoe boxes, with one of the animal body coverings. Have the children cut out pictures of animals from magazines. Collect all the pictures. Gather the children in a circle. Let each child feel the body covering in each shoe box. Discuss how animals have different types of body coverings and how humans are covered with skin. Have the children feel their skin. Discuss which shoe box a picture of a human would belong in. Then, have the children tape the pictures of the animals to the correct body covering shoe box. Be sure to include some unusual animals such as snakes, turtles and fish.

• •

Egg Matching

Objective: To compare relative egg sizes to the animals that laid the eggs

Materials: a large sheet of chart paper, markers, pictures of egg-laying animals, tape

Directions: Ahead of time, draw a chart like the one shown. Discuss egg-laying animals with the children. Discuss how they can be very large like a dinosaur or very small like a hummingbird. Other animals to discuss could include snakes, hens, birds, ostriches, spiders, fish, etc. Discuss with the children how the size of an egg is usually relative to the size of the animal that laid it. With this in mind, have the children tape pictures of egg-laying animals on the chart based on relativity of size.

Extension: Bring some real eggs to school for the childen to view.

Caterpillar to Butterfly

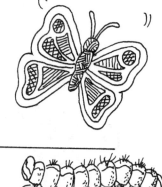

Objective: To show the transformation of a caterpillar to a butterfly

Materials: a large glass jar with a perforated metal lid, leaves, twig, dirt, drawing paper, crayons, caterpillar

Directions: Find a caterpillar to place in a glass jar with small holes poked in the lid. Provide the caterpillar with fresh leaves to eat each day. Also, provide it with a small twig and some dirt. Let the children watch what takes place over time. Eventually, the caterpillar will form a chrysalis (cocoon). Discuss what has happened to the caterpillar. Read the book, *The Very Hungry Caterpillar.* Have patience and eventually a butterfly will appear from the chrysalis. Take the jar outside and free the butterfly. Have the children record the transformation of the caterpillar to a butterfly on a sheet of drawing paper. Have the children fold the paper in three equal parts and fill each section with a step in the process. Help the children label each part with one of the following: caterpillar, chrysalis or butterfly.

Life Cycle of a Frog

Objective: To show the life cycle of a frog

Materials: crayons, stapler, three sheets of drawing paper per child, scissors, glue, copies of diagrams on page 247

Directions: Discuss the life cycle of a frog with the children. Discuss amphibians, the significance of a frog's tongue, and diet of thousands of insects each summer. Have the children fold three 8 1/2" x 11" sheets of drawing paper in half lengthwise. Staple the pages together along the folded edge. Have the children color the patterns on page 247 and cut them out. Have the students make a cover page for the book. Then, they glue the pictures of the frog's life cycle in order in the book. The children should use one page for each stage in the cycle. Have the children label the pages in the book as follows: eggs, tadpole, tadpole with hind legs, tadpole with front legs, frog.

Extension: See if you can get an aquarium to use to view the frog's life cycle before your own eyes. Pet stores can provide details about terrarium upkeep and the nurturing required in the process.

Life Cycle of a Frog Patterns

Eggs

Tadpole

Tadpole with front legs

Tadpole with hind legs

Frog

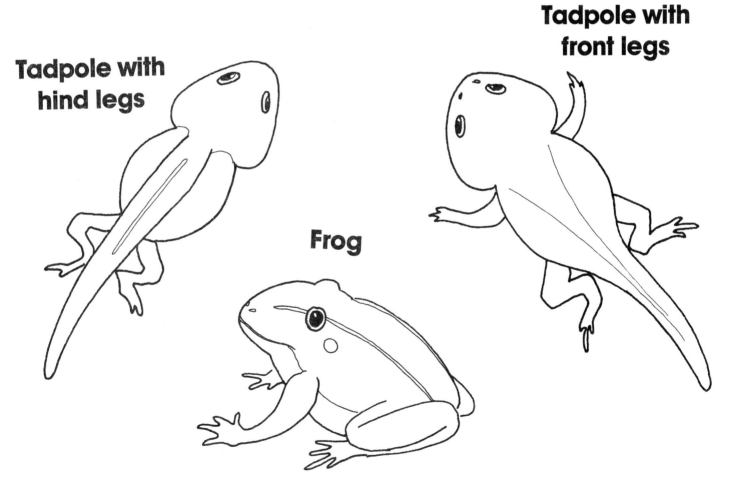

Animal Footprint Comparison

Objective: To differentiate between various animals' footprints

Materials: construction paper, scissors, tape, copies of the cutout patterns below and on page 249

Directions: Using construction paper, cut out the footprints below and on page 249. Tape the footprints around the classroom and have the children guess which animal each print belongs to. Compare the sizes of the footprints. Use size words and comparison words while discussing the footprints.

- -

Animal Footprint Patterns

Duck Print

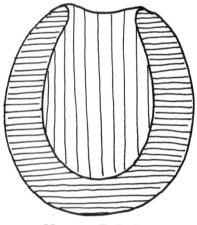

Horse Print

Cat Print

Dog Print

Animal Footprint Patterns

Rabbit Print

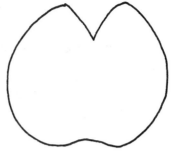

Pig Print

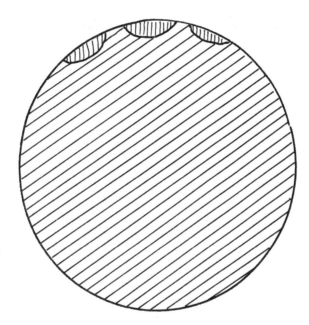

Elephant Print

Bird Print   **Squirrel Print**   **Mouse Print**

The Ants Go Marching

Objective: To investigate real ants

Materials: *The Ants Go Marching* by Berniece Freshet, an ant farm, marker, chart paper

Directions: Read the story, *The Ants Go Marching*. On chart paper, record facts the class has learned about ants. Discuss things like what they eat, where they live, and their social habits. Borrow an ant farm and add facts to your list as the children discover ant facts with their own eyes.

• •

Caring for Wild Animals

Objective: To observe and classify wild animals

Materials: chart paper, markers, popcorn, pine cones, peanut butter, birdseed, bread crumbs, empty milk cartons

Directions: Discuss with the children what types of food wild animals might eat. Talk about how they as a class might care for some of the local wildlife. Have the children scatter seeds, bread crumbs or popcorn around an area close to their classroom window. The children might also like to attract different types of birds by making hanging bird feeders. Some ideas for hanging feeders are as follows:

1. Cut windows in an empty milk carton and fill it with birdseed.

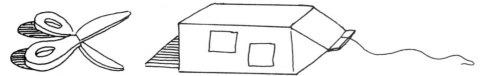

2. Hang up a pine cone stuffed with peanut butter and rolled in birdseed on a tree.

3. String long strands of popcorn and tie them from a tree.

On chart paper, have the children record what animals came and ate the food they left out. What food was most popular? What animal was most popular? Were animals afraid?

Pinwheel Magic

Objective: To study the movement of air

Materials: (per child) pinwheel pattern on page 252, straw, brad, scissors, tape

Directions: Give each child a copy of the pinwheel pattern on page 252. Discuss the nature of air. Talk about how it is invisible, how you can create it by blowing and how it moves things. Explain how a pinwheel works with air (by blowing or wind).

1. Have the children cut along the dotted lines.

2. Help the children put a brad through the center of the square and the tip of every other point on the square.

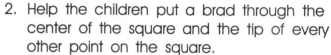

3. The children should tape the end of the brad to a straw.

4. Let the children try their pinwheels outside on a windy day.

Extension: Bring a windsock, kite and flag to school. On a windy day, demonstrate how each object works. Have the children explain why and how each object moves.

Pinwheel Pattern

Color the pinwheel pattern below. Cut along the dashed line to the center circle's edge. Put a brad through the center of the square and the tip of every other point. Attach the pinwheel back to a straw and give your pinwheel a try.

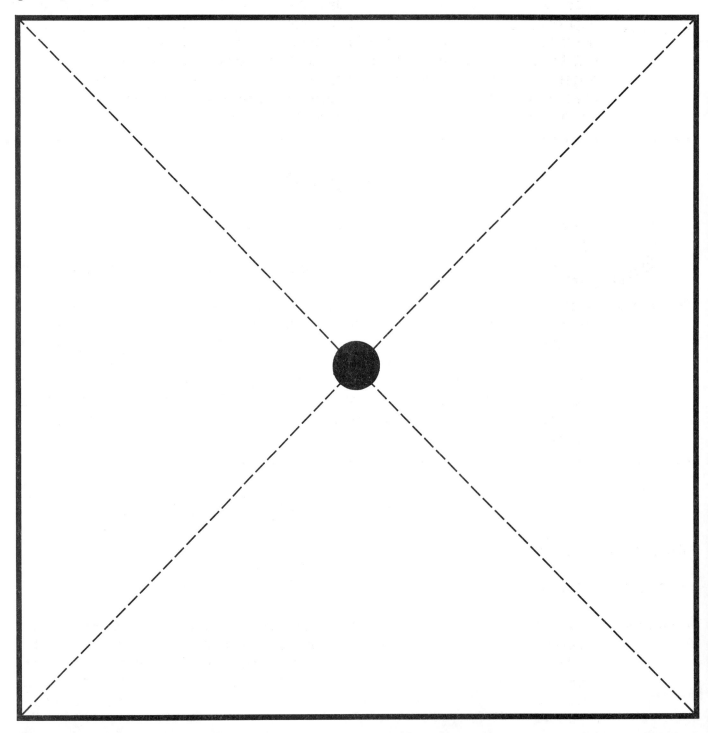

SCIENCE

Moving Air

Objective: To observe that air is movable

Materials: a plastic syringe for each child

Directions: Give each child a syringe. Let the children explore the syringe and discover its uses. After the children have handled the syringes, they will notice that they can trap and move air in them. Let the children blow air on each other's arms using the syringes. To reinforce the concept of air movement, have the children pull the syringe plunger back to the end of the barrel. Have them place a finger over the nozzle and try to push the plunger. They should discover that there is air trapped in the syringe because it is very hard to push the plunger to let the air out when a finger is blocking the nozzle.

Trapping Air

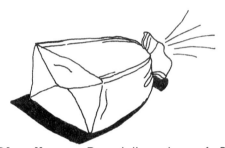

Objective: To observe the properties of air

Materials: plastic bag, *A Bag Full of Nothing* by Jay Williams

Directions: Read the story *A Bag Full of Nothing*. Hold up a flat plastic bag. Have the children examine it. When they have agreed that it is empty, bring the ends of the opening of the bag together and blow air into the bag. Seal the opening of the bag with your hand so that none of the air can escape from inside the bag. Have the children press gently on the bag. Ask about what is inside the bag. See if the children can agree that it is air. When they do agree, discuss the color, shape and other properties of air. Fill the same bag up with solid objects and do a comparison.

Filling Balloons

Objective: To discover the properties of air

Materials: balloons, hand pump

Directions: Show the children an inflated balloon. Discuss the characteristics of the inflated balloon. Then, fill a balloon with air using a hand pump. Discuss what is inside the balloon. Discover what happens when balloons are freed without tying the ends. Discuss what the stream of air from the deflating balloon or hand pump feels like. Talk about the children blowing air from their mouths and moving air from a fan.

Big Book of Everything for Kindergarten IF8652 253 ©Instructional Fair, Inc.

Wind-Driven Creatures

Objective: To observe the force of air

Materials: yarn, 18" x 14" sheets of thin posterboard, construction paper, crêpe paper streamers, markers, string, stapler, glue, one dowel per child

Directions: Follow the steps below to make a creative windsock. When completed, discuss the effect the force of air has on the windsocks.

1. Help the children form a cylinder using a sheet of posterboard. Staple the edges together.

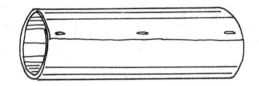

2. Have the children decorate their cylinder using the items listed above. Encourage them to make creative creatures.

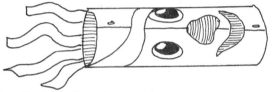

3. Each child should knot the ends of four, twelve-inch pieces of string. Staple the strings to the opening of the windsock.

4. Gather the four strings together and tie them to a thin dowel. Explore the effect of the force of air on the windsocks by letting the children run around outdoors with their creatures.

Whirly Copters

Objective: To observe the effect of air force

Materials: one 7 1/2" x 3/4" strip of paper and one paper clip per child

Directions: Follow the visual directions below and let the children make and fly their Whirly Copters outdoors. Discuss the effect the force of air has on their copters.

a.

b.

c.

d.

Water and Air Mixture

Objective: To examine air in water

Materials: plastic cup, a clear water basin filled with water

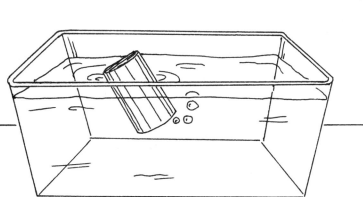

Directions: Have the children gather around a clear water basin to observe the experiment. Explain to the children that the plastic cup has air in and around it. Turn the cup over and place it straight into the water. Explain how there is air and water in the cup. To prove your point, tip the cup slightly while still submerged. An air bubble should rise to the surface. Let all the air out of the cup. Have the children guess when the cup has no air left in it. Let the children take turns trying the experiment.

Does It Float?

Objective: To compare floating and non-floating objects

Materials: a large clear water basin per group, crayon, rubber band, plastic spoon, metal spoon, paper clip, bottlecap, button, rock, cork, candle, eraser, small wooden block, aluminum foil ball, copies of the record sheet on page 256, markers

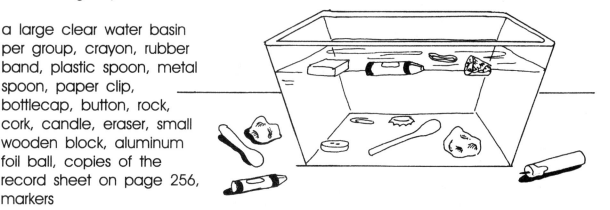

Directions: Divide the children into two or three groups. Fill a large clear water basin with water for each group. Provide the groups with the objects listed above. Give each child a copy of the record sheet on page 256. Ask the children to place one object at a time into the water basin to determine whether it is a floating or non-floating object. Then, each child should draw the results on the record sheet. If the object floated, it should be drawn on top of the water on the record sheet water basin. If the object did not float, it should be drawn on the bottom of the water basin record sheet.

Float/Sink Record Sheet

Record whether or not the objects floated by drawing them in the appropriate place in the water basin.

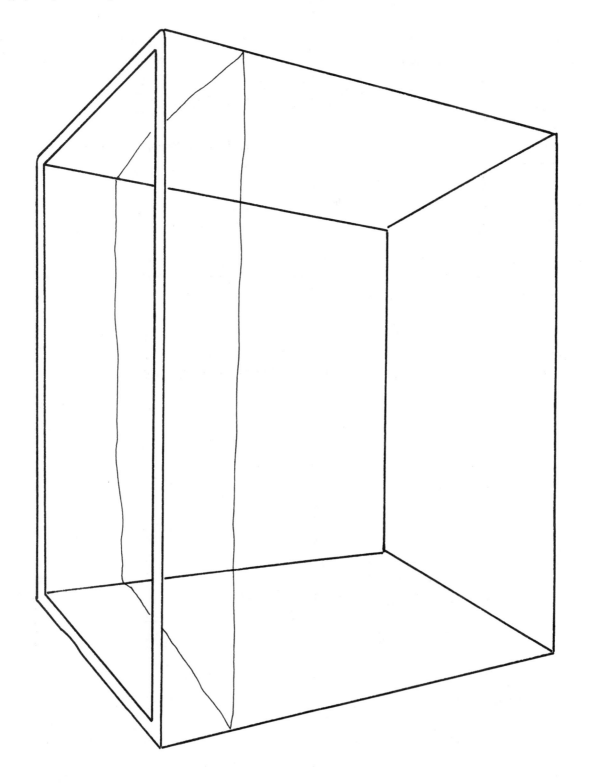

Solar Experiment

Objective: To prove that dark colors absorb heat from the sun and white colors reflect it

Materials: a dark T-shirt, a white T-shirt, one sheet of black construction paper, one sheet of white construction paper, tape

Directions: On a warm sunny day, tape a sheet of black construction paper and a sheet of white construction paper on a sidewalk. Let the sheets sit out in the sun for at least an hour. Have the children feel the two sheets. Ask why they think the black sheet is warmer than the white sheet. Explain that dark-colored items absorb the heat from the sun while the light-colored items reflect it. Do the experiment again but this time compare black and white T-shirts. Ask the children what type of clothing they would prefer to wear on a hot summer day and why they would make that choice. Ask about other areas where you might choose light or dark because of the heat-absorbing process (e.g. car seat covers, desert, beach towels, etc.).

Sunshine Prints

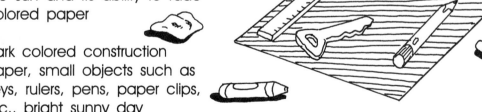

Objective: To examine the strength of the sun and its ability to fade colored paper

Materials: dark colored construction paper, small objects such as keys, rulers, pens, paper clips, etc., bright sunny day

Directions: Give each child a piece of dark colored construction paper. Have each child place his/her paper in direct sunlight. Have them place small objects like the ones mentioned above on top of their paper. Have them place the objects in a pleasing arrangement. By the end of the day, the papers will be faded, except the areas that were protected by the objects. Bring the papers indoors. Laminate them and let the children use them as place mats.

Moon Phases

Objective: To recognize the phases of the moon

Materials: black and white construction paper, scissors, tape, string, phases of the moon patterns below and on page 259, glue

Directions: Read *Goodnight Moon,* by Margaret Wise Brown. Cut out the phases of the moon below and on page 259. Give each child one copy of the patterns. Have the children observe the moon on a weekly basis. Have them report to the class what they see. With each new phase, hang a large pattern representing it from the ceiling. At each new phase, give each child a pattern of the occuring phase. The children should glue the phases in sequence on a piece of paper. When the entire cycle of phases is complete, help the children title each phase.

Extension: During the fall season, the moon often appears to be very large. It is given the name "Harvest Moon." Discuss why the moon appears to be on the horizon line and why it is so much larger in relationship to the objects on Earth.

- -

Moon Phase Patterns

New Moon

Waxing Cresent

Moon Phase Patterns

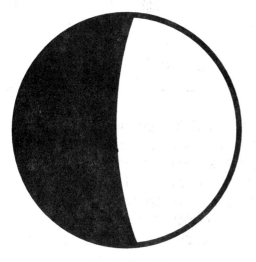

First Quarter

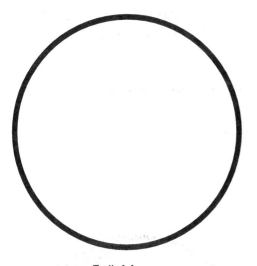

Full Moon

Last Quarter

Waxing Gibbous

Waning Gibbous

Waning Cresent

Daytime/Nighttime

Objectives: To demonstrate the rotation of the Earth and the effect the sun has on it

Materials: flashlight, darkroom, *Grandfather Twilight* by Barbara Berger

Directions: Read the story *Grandfather Twilight*. Discuss night and day concepts with the children. Ask what nighttime is and what daytime is. Ask what they see at each time. To demonstrate the concepts, choose a child to be the sun and give him/her a flashlight. Then, choose a child to be the Earth. Ask the "Earth" to turn around very slowly while the "sun" shines the flashlight on the "Earth." Explain that sunlight shines on the Earth as it turns. Explain that the area that is lit is daytime on the Earth and the area that is dark is nighttime on the Earth. Even though it is dark, explain to the children that the sun is still in the sky.

• •

Sunshine For Growth

Objective: To discover if plants need sunshine to grow

Materials: 4 plastic cups, potting soil, 8 bean seeds, paper plates, water

Directions:

1. Poke a drainage hole in the bottom of each plastic cup.

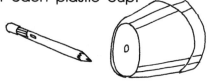

2. Fill the cups with potting soil and plant two bean seeds in each cup.

3. Water the plants daily.

4. Place two cups on a paper plate in a sunny spot.

5. Place two cups on a paper plate in a dark spot (e.g. a closet).

6. Continue watering all the cups.

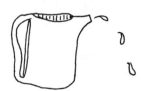

7. Help the children record what happened to the plants after eight days. Discuss the importance of light for plant growth. Explain how we, ourselves, need plants in order to grow. Therefore, we all need the sun.

Coloring Carnations

Objective: To demonstrate how plants absorb water for nourishment

Materials: 4 white carnations; red, blue and green food coloring; 4 clear glasses; water

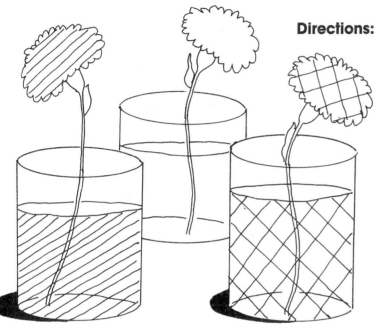

Directions: Fill four glasses with water. Place a carnation in each glass. Help the children add a different color of food coloring to three of the glasses. Place the glasses in the same location. Have the children observe the carnations throughout the day and the next morning. Ask the children what they observed. Explain to the children that a plant drinks water through its roots and stem. The water goes up into the plant kind of like a straw. Explain that the colored water went into the stem and leaves and changed the color of the flower. Ask the children why the white carnation in the glass without food coloring did not change its color.

Seed Sorting

Objective: To discover seeds in the foods we commonly eat

Materials: watermelon, green pepper, tomato, orange, apple, cantaloupe, pear, pumpkin, snow peas, potting soil, cup to plant in, water, paper, crayons, glue, knife

Directions: Gather the children in a group. Explain that many of the foods we eat have seeds in them. Cut the foods listed above in half so that the children can see the seeds inside them. Have each child collect a seed from each item. Have them wash and dry their seeds and glue them on a sheet of paper. Beside each seed, have the children draw the whole food from which the seed came. Plant a fast-growing seed (i.e. snow pea) from the collection. Observe the results.

Dancing Raisins

Objective: To experiment making objects move

Materials: raisins, seltzer water, large clear glass

Directions: Have the children gather in a group. Discuss how objects move. Ask the children if things can move if they do not have a motor. Then, fill a large glass with seltzer water. Place a few raisins in the water. The raisins will sink and then rise again because of the carbonation. Ask the children to describe what they observe.

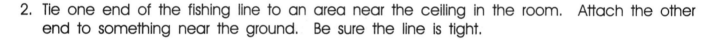

Propelling Balloons

Objective: To demonstrate non-motorized object movement

Materials: scissors, long oval balloon, plastic straw, 4 yards of monofilament fishing line, masking tape

Directions:

1. Cut a straw in half and slide it onto a 4-yard piece of fishing line.

2. Tie one end of the fishing line to an area near the ceiling in the room. Attach the other end to something near the ground. Be sure the line is tight.

3. Blow up a balloon but keep the end sealed with your fingers.

4. Tape the balloon to the straw on the fishing line. Be sure the rounded end of the balloon is heading towards the ceiling.

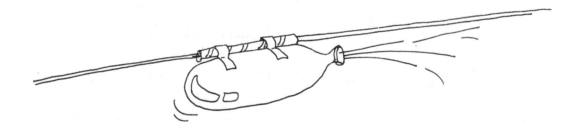

5. Slide the balloon towards the ground (not touching) and release the sealed end. Watch the balloon take off.

6. Discuss with the children why the balloon is moving.

Feel Boxes

Objective: To heighten awareness of the sense of touch

Materials: shoe box, scissors, stapler, tube sock, masking tape, cotton swabs, ball of yarn, rock, shell, button, eraser, coins, sponge

Directions: In the side of the shoe box, cut a hole large enough for a small hand to fit through. Cut off the toe section of an old tube sock. Staple the open toe end of the sock inside the hole of the box. Fill the box with the objects mentioned above and tape the box shut. Discuss with the children the sense of touch. Talk about the millions of tiny sensors we have on our bodies. Explain how we can figure out what an item is based on our sense of touch. Then, ask for volunteers to reach in the "Feely Box" through the sock and tell what they are feeling before they pull it out to see. Change the objects in the box often to keep the activity exciting.

- -

Touch Tray

Objective: To sharpen awareness of the touch organs

Materials: knitting needle, ice cube, cotton swab, cooked spaghetti noodles, pussy willows, leaves, fur, feather, fork, tray

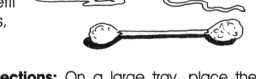

Directions: On a large tray, place the items mentioned above or use other objects. Have the children examine the objects closely. Have them describe how the objects feel. Explain that our hands have many tiny touch organs that are very close together. They sense hot/cold, soft/hard, smooth/rough, pain, etc. Leave the objects out on the tray for the children to explore during their free time.

Tasty Treats

Objective: To introduce four main tastes

Materials: lemon, lime, salted peanuts, oranges, small paper condiment cups (4 per child), knife

Directions: Give each child four paper condiment cups. Cut the lemon, orange and lime in tiny pieces. Fill each of the cups with a separate taste sensation. Use lemon to represent sour, lime to represent bitter, orange to represent sweet and peanuts to represent salty. After all the children have had their four cups filled, ask them to taste their foods. Discuss how the foods taste and what their favorite flavors were. Explain to the children that their tongues have taste buds on them that allow them to taste sweet, sour, bitter and salty. Most of the children will tell you they liked the sweet taste. For an additional treat, provide a hot chocolate drink for a snack. A large marshmallow on top makes a perfect addition to this tasty treat!

I Spy and I Hear

Objective: To identify items by their visual or auditory description

Materials: blindfolds, a dark pair of sunglasses

Directions: Explain to the children that their ears, eyes, nose and throat are connected. For example, when they cry, their noses will run, and if they get a cold, their ears can feel clogged. Tell them that the games they are going to play involve their ears and eyes. To play "I Hear," have the children blindfold themselves. Tell them that you want them to focus on the sounds they are hearing. Then, describe a sound in the environment. Call out "I hear with my ear a _____ " and make a sound relating to an object or animal. Have the children guess the sound. The child who guesses correctly gets to describe the next item while the rest of the children try to guess. To play "I Spy," choose an item to describe that you see. Call out, "I spy with my eye a _____." Whoever is describing the item should wear a pair of dark sunglasses so the children guessing do not know what the caller might be looking at. Descriptive clues about color, size and shape should be given for the items the children are spying with their eyes. Clues about the loudness, softness, pitch, distance away, etc. should be given for the items they are hearing with their ears.

Matching Smells

Objective: To match similar smells

Materials: bananas, coffee beans, potpourri, lemons, 8 paper cups with perforated lids,

Directions: Discuss the function of the nose. Explain to the students that there are tiny nerves inside the nose that pick up things in the air and send messages about them to the brain. Talk about things that smell good and things that do not. Then, play the following game. Prior to the lesson, prepare eight paper cups with perforated lids. Designate two cups for each of the items listed above. Choose a child to be the smell matcher. Ask the child to place similar smelling cups together using his/her nose as a guide.

Sequential Sounds

Objective: To order sounds by typical event sequence

Materials: tape recorder, blank cassette

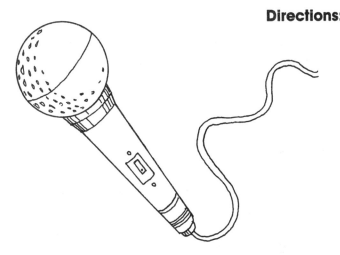

Directions: This activity takes some preparation before class. Tape various sounds that belong together but tape them out of order. For example, tape a car starting up, a car door shutting and a car driving by. Another example would be a train in motion down a track, a conductor yelling, "All aboard!" and the train blowing its horn. Be creative! When you play the sounds for the children, have them guess what the sounds are first. Then, have them tell which order the sounds should be in.

Magnifying Snowflakes

Objective: To examine snowflakes with a magnifying glass

Materials: black construction paper, a snowy day above 32°F, magnifying glasses, scissors, 8 1/2" x 11" sheets of white paper

Directions: If you live in a snowy climate, on a warm snowy day, take the children into the school yard to examine snowflakes more closely. Give each child a sheet of black construction paper and a magnifying glass. If the snowflakes are big enough, you may not even need the magnifying glass. Tell the children to let the snowflakes land on the construction paper. The flakes melt fast, so encourage the children to work as quickly as they can. Explain to the children that although all snowflakes have six sides, no two are identical. Encourage the children to find similar looking flakes. Later, when you are back inside the classroom, let the children make paper snowflakes following the directions below.

1. Fold an 8 1/2" x 8 1/2" sheet of paper four times as illustrated below.

a.   b.   c.   d.

2. Cut out designs along the edges of the folded paper.

3. Open up the snowflake. Hang the flakes from strings to decorate the classroom.

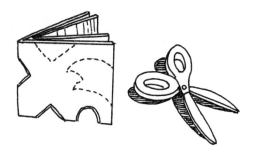 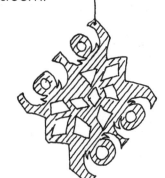

Exploring the Microscope

Objectives: To recognize that many objects have invisible parts and to explore the microscope

Materials: sand, pond water, leaf, strawberries, tree bark, microscope, slides

Directions: Obtain a microscope for this activity. Discuss how there are parts to objects that we cannot see with the unaided eye. Make slides of various items for microscopic examination. Have the children take turns looking through the microscope and describing what they see. Ask what the microscope did to the objects they looked at. Some ideas for slides include the following:

sand particles - are really little grains of rock
pond water - contains tiny little creatures in it
leaf - has tiny veins running through it
strawberry - (outer edge) has tiny hairs all over it
tree bark - has tiny creatures, dirt particles and plant growth on it

Magnify and Sort

Objective: To magnify shells to examine their properties

Materials: one magnifying glass per child, 5 scallop shells per child, one paper plate per child

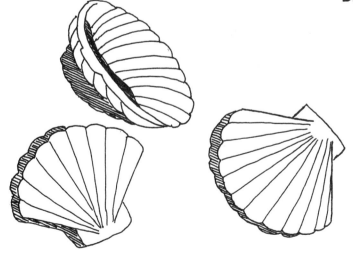

Directions: Give each child a paper plate, five scallop shells and a magnifying glass. Ask the children to examine their shells very closely using their magnifying glass. Ask them to consider things like color, shape and texture. Then, suggest that they look for two shells that are a perfect match or very much alike. Finally, ask the children to place their shells on their paper plates in order from largest to smallest or darkest to lightest. Check their work as you collect the shells.

Liquid and Solid Comparisons

Objective: To discriminate between liquids and solids

Materials: gelatin mix, ice cubes, ice cream, butter, kettle, metal spoon, mixing bowl, 4 clear plastic cups, large tray, water, crayons, scissors, drawing strips below, glue, 8 1/2" x 11" sheet of paper per child

Directions: Talk to the children about the difference between solids and liquids. Place a large tray on a table. Line four plastic cups along the top of the tray. Place an ice cube in the first cup. Discuss its properties as a solid. Then, place a scoop of ice cream in the second cup. Discuss the ice cream's properties as a solid. In a mixing bowl put a package of gelatin. Add hot water from a kettle. Place 1/2 cup of the mixture in the third cup on the tray. Discuss the liquid properties of the gelatin. Place a scoop of butter on a metal spoon. Hold the butter over the steam from the kettle. Have the children watch the melting process. Place the liquid butter in the fourth cup. Let the items on the tray remain untouched as you discuss what is taking place on the tray. Finally, discuss the significance of heat and cooling in the making of liquids and solids. What happens when a liquid is cooled? What happens when a solid is heated?

Give each child a copy of the drawing strips below. Have them color the page and cut along the dashed lines. Then, have the children glue the squares in each set onto a piece of paper in the correct sequence.

Bubble Fun

Objective: To experiment with water and air

Materials: wire coat hangers, water, Joy® dish soap, light corn syrup, shallow pan, large mixing bowl, measuring cup

Directions: Using a mixing bowl, have the children help make a great bubble mixture. To do this, combine six cups of water, two cups of liquid Joy® and three quarters of a cup of light corn syrup. Mix the ingredients well and let them sit for four hours before using. Pour the ingredients into a shallow pan when you are ready to use. Give each child a wire coat hanger. Help them shape a loop out of the hanger and bend back the sharp ends. (See picture below.) Have the children dip their wands into the shallow pan. Explain to the children the importance of moving the wand slowly in order to create a large bubble. Discuss the involvement of air and water in this process.

Inside a Bubble

Objective: To examine a bubble from the inside

Materials: glycerin, Dawn® dishwashing soap, old car tire, 2 hula hoops, large bucket, utility knife, water, measuring cup

Directions: Have the children make their bubble mix by combining the following ingredients in a large bucket.

    1 cup Dawn® dishwashing soap
    4 heaping teaspoons of glycerin
    1 gallon of water

Collect an old car tire and carefully cut it in half using a utility knife. (See diagram.) Pour an equal amount of the mixture into each tire half. Place a hula hoop in each tire half. Have the children take turns standing in the center of a tire half and gently pulling the hula hoop straight up. A bubble will enclose around them. Have the children lift the hula hoop above their heads if possible. Have the children describe what it is like being inside the bubble.

Magnetic or Not?

Objective: To explore magnetism

Materials: small keys, aluminum foil, metal paper clips, brads, pencil, cork, small wooden block, small nail, plastic pen cap, eraser, quarter, piece of yarn, horseshoe magnet, large wooden tray, copy of page 271 for each child

Directions: Place the items mentioned above on a large wooden tray. Have the children discover which items are attracted to the horseshoe magnet and which items are not. Give each child a copy of page 271 to record his/her findings. Discu what the items are made out of and why they think certain objects are attracted to the magnet. Let the children try any other objects and see if their findings are correct.

• •

Magnet Magic

Objective: To explore magnetism

Materials: horseshoe magnets, small circular magnets, small pompons, craft eyes, yarn, felt, glue, construction paper scraps, posterboard

Directions: Give each child a small circular magnet. Have the children turn their magnet into a creative creature. Provide the children with the items listed above to create their creatures. Tell the children that you will show them how to make their creatures move magically. When they are finished, have the children form a group. Choose two children to hold tightly to a piece of posterboard between them. Choose a child to move his/her creature by placing his/her creature on the top of the posterboard and holding a horseshoe magnet below the posterboard. Have the child drag the magnet along the bottom of the posterboard beneath the creature he/she made. Once the magnets have attracted, the child can move the creature around the posterboard magically.

Magnetic or Not?

Draw a line from the horseshoe magnet to the items it would attract.

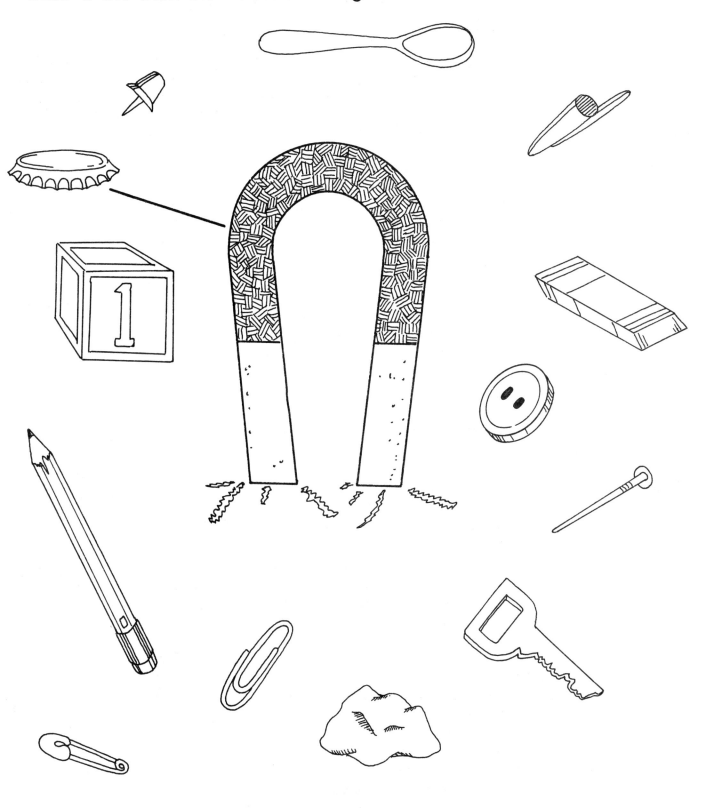

Plant a Tree!

Objective: To establish the importance of trees

Materials: lemons; paper towels; small plastic cups; damp, sandy soil; knife

Directions: Discuss the significance of trees in our world. Include the things trees give us like paper, fruit, nuts, lumber, shelter for animals and shade on hot days. Talk about the fact that trees use carbon dioxide which we exhale. Tell the children that we need to keep the world full of trees. On an average, each American uses seven trees a year. Tell the children that they are going to have a chance to grow their own tree. Follow the directions below to have the students germinate and plant a lemon tree.

1. Cut open a lemon and have the children locate the seeds. Explain how the seeds, if planted and cared for, could become a tree.

2. Have the children wash the seeds and place them in a sunny spot to dry for a day or two.

3. Then, have each child wrap his/her seeds in a damp paper towel and place them in a cool, dark place until they sprout.

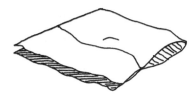

4. Sprinkle the paper towels with water every other day for two weeks.

5. After the roots have sprouted, have the children place the seedlings into small plastic cups filled with water.

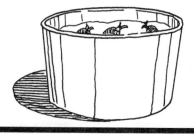

6. Transplant the four to five inch seedlings into sandy, damp soil.

Tree Seed Masterpieces

Objective: To relate seeds to the trees they came from

Materials: posterboard, glue, small, brown paper bag, tree seeds

Directions: Have the children go on a seed hunting expedition. Give each child a small, brown paper bag to put his/her seeds in. Have the children note the casings, pods, the flying apparatus, or the hard shells of the seeds. Discuss what trees the seeds came from. Finally, let the children design a masterpiece using their seeds. Give each child a piece of posterboard and some white glue. Have them make a design of their choice by gluing the seeds in place.

Investigating Tree Stumps

Objective: To discover the age of a tree

Materials: old tree stumps, magnifying glass, *The Giving Tree* by Shel Silverstein

Directions: Read *The Giving Tree* to the children. Discuss what happens to a tree as it ages. Take a magnifying glass on a nature hike (preferably in a wooded area). Have the children look for old tree stumps. Explain to the children that each year a tree grows, it adds a new ring of cells under its bark. These cells form channels that carry the nutrients to the tree. These cells also form a ring. Tell the children that each light and dark ring together represent one year's growth. See if the children can guess the age of a tree stump they find by counting the annual rings. Tell the children they can also tell what kind of spring the tree experienced each year by looking at the rings. A wide, light ring means that there was plenty of rain and sun for the tree to grow. If the ring is narrow it means the weather was harsh that spring. The dark ring is formed during the summer months. Ask the children how they thought the growing seasons of the trees they found were. Ask an assistant at a lumber yard if he/she has any scraps of old logs that indicate the tree's rings. Place the scraps in the science center for frequent viewing.

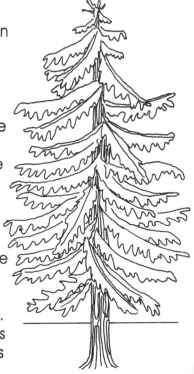

Plaster Fossils

Objective: To create a fossil out of plaster of Paris

Materials: jellybeans, dry noodles, plastic utensils, raisins, peanuts, plaster of Paris, large plastic container with a lid, non-stick cooking spray

Directions: Explain how people learn about things that happened millions of years ago by studying fossils. These people examine bones, rocks, metals, etc. Tell the children that they are going to be scientists making their own geological finds of fossils. To make an amusing fossil, follow the directions below.

1. Have the children spray a large plastic container with a lid with non-stick cooking spray and fill the container half full with plaster of Paris.

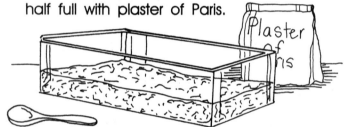

2. Collect items like jellybeans, dry noodles, raisins, peanuts and plastic utensils.

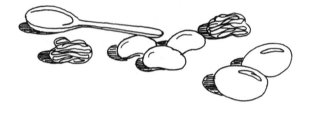

3. Put the collected items in the plaster of Paris and mix together.

4. The following day, remove the plaster of Paris from the container and break a section off for the children to examine.

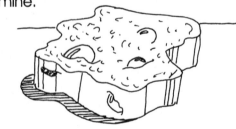

5. Break the plaster of Paris into more pieces and put them on a geological finds display. Let the children label the items in the plaster as items one might find on an expedition.

Fun With Fossils

Objective: To create fossils by making impressions of common objects

Materials: fast-drying clay, rolling pins, sticks, stones, shells, chicken bones

Directions: Discuss what prehistoric times were like. Read about dinosaurs and if possible, obtain some fossils to show the class. Tell the class that they are going to be making their own fossils. Give each child a ball of fast-drying clay. Have the children roll their clay into a 1/2" flat, circular shape. Then, have them press sticks, small rocks, shells or chicken bones in the clay. Some children might want to create a footprint of a prehistoric creature by stepping in their clay and adding details like claws or talons. Encourage them to be creative! Let the clay dry and establish a day to set up a museum for the other classes to view your archeological finds. You might want the children to title and date their fossils. Have fun!

Rock Gardens

Objective: To examine rocks closely

Materials: one clear plastic container per student, water, flashlight, magnifying glass, small brown paper bag per child

Directions: First, take the children on a nature hike and have them collect rocks with interesting colors, shapes and textures. Remind them to keep the rocks small. Have each child fill a small brown bag 1/4 full of stones. Back at school, have the children arrange their rocks in a pleasing fashion. Discuss patterns of formation, geometric shapes, stacking or any irregular patterns. Have the children place their rock pattern in the bottom of a clear plastic container. Have them add some water to their container. The stones' natural beauty will be enhanced. Have the children examine their rocks using a magnifying glass. Turn all the lights off and place a flashlight on each child's garden. This makes for another interesting effect.

Geological Art

Objective: To examine geological items closely

Materials: clear plastic cups with lids, various geological items (dirt, pine needles, leaves, small stones, sand, etc.)

Objective: Provide each child with a plastic cup and lid. Explain that they are going on an expedition to look for various geological items to put in their cups. Mention the items listed above to get the children thinking. On the nature hike, have the children fill their cups with layer after layer of different soils, rocks, sticks, leaves, etc. Discuss what happens to the items on the top layer of earth outdoors. Explain that their layers are an example of Earth's surface. The mixture of colors and layers creates a very pleasing display as well. Place the cups around the room and enjoy them for their aesthetic beauty.

Terrarium World

Objective: To build and care for a terrarium

Materials: an empty glass aquarium, pebbles, branches, moss, small plants that like shade, plastic cover, topsoil, a few rocks

Directions: Discuss the significance of caring for an ecological environment. Explain how a terrarium is a miniature environment. First, fill the bottom of the aquarium with a layer of pebbles. Cover the pebbles with a layer of topsoil about two inches thick. Next, add some branches, moss and shade-loving plants. Place a few rocks in the environment. You could also add a few small creatures and some worms. Cover the aquarium with a perforated sheet of plastic. Sprinkle the terrarium with water on a regular basis. Be careful not to over water it.

Hot Water Races

Objectives: To demonstrate the fastest way to boil water on the stove and to show an energy conservation method

Materials: 2 glass cooking pans equal in size, water, measuring cup, stove

Directions: Using a measuring cup, have the children fill two glass cooking pots with an equal amount of water. Turn the front two burners of a stove on at the same temperature setting. Cover one pot; leave the other uncovered. Place the pots on the burners at the same time. See which boils first. Ask the children to explain why the covered pot boiled first.

You're Not in the Dark!

Objective: To explore ways to conserve the energy that powers electrical lights

Materials: one plastic light switch plate (neutral color) per child, acrylic paints, paintbrushes

Directions: Begin by discussing the fact that the energy that powers electrical lights comes from the Earth. Have the children recall how often they flip on the light switch at home and forget to turn it off when they leave the room. Talk about ways to conserve the energy used on lights at the children's homes. Consider turning off the lights every time they leave a room, using daylight as long as possible, making sure the light bulbs are well dusted and reminding other members of the family about conservation. Using acrylic paints, have the children decorate a light switch plate to use in their homes to help remind the family about conserving energy. Help the children write conservation phrases on them.

Sand Sensations

Objective: To understand the properties of sand

Materials: sandpaper, stones, rock sugar, paper lunch bags

Directions: Discuss where sand on a beach or desert comes from. Your discussions should include the effects of wind and water on rock erosion. Give each child a piece of rock sugar and a paper lunch bag. Have the children place their rock sugar inside their bag and have them seal their bags tightly. Then, instruct the children to place their bags on the floor and crush the rock sugar with their feet. Have them examine the contents of their paper lunch bags. Discuss how the rock sugar has changed and compare how rock erodes to become sand. Then, have the children rub sandpaper over a stone to make a small pile of sand. Remember to discuss the amount of time the whole process of erosion takes.

Soil Searching

Objective: To examine the Earth's soil

Materials: fresh soil, large glass jar, water, magnifying glass, paper plates, drawing paper, crayons

Directions: Take a nature hike and collect some fresh soil. In the classroom, give each child a paper plate and a scoop of soil. With a magnifying glass, have each child examine his/her sample of soil. Have each child fold an 8 1/2" x 11" sheet of paper in half. On one side have the children draw what they see in their soil samples. Place a soil sample in a large glass jar filled with water. Cover and shake the jar. Then, let it stand overnight. Have the children record the results of the soil in the jar on the remaining side of the paper.

Flowing Rivers

Objective: To investigate the nature of water flow

Materials: dirt, water table, water, measuring cup

Directions: Discuss how a river moves. On a water table, pile up dirt into a small hill. Dig a valley at the base of the hill. Slowly, pour a cup of water on the hilltop. Some water will be absorbed and some will stream along the sides. Allow the children to pour a few cups of water. Discuss why the water chooses the path that it does.

Part Water

Objective: To investigate particles in river and ocean water

Materials: river water, ocean water, heat source, pan, glasses

Directions: Place a glass of river water and a glass of ocean water where the children can investigate them. Discuss how difficult it is to see particles in the water with our unaided eyes. Place some river water in a pan and heat it until nearly all the water boils away. Discuss the grey matter left in the pan. This is made out of salt and chalk. Then, boil a cup of ocean water. Ask the children if they might recall the taste of ocean water. Once all the water has boiled, a teaspoon of salt will be left. Have the children try to guess what might have caused this result.

Icy Waters

Objective: To recognize the change in the properties of water when different temperatures are introduced

Materials: ice cube trays, water, heat source, freezer, pan, measuring cups

Directions: Remove an ice cube tray from the freezer and place the ice into a small cooking pan. Let the children watch as the ice slowly melts. Pour the melted ice into a measuring cup. Have the children record how much liquid there is in the cup. Pour the liquid back into the ice cube tray and freeze again. Take another measurement once the ice has been melted a second time. Have the children hypothesize why this might be happenning.

Volcanic Eruptions

Objective: To assimilate the flow of lava

Materials: tall glass bottle, vinegar, baking soda, red food coloring, sand, funnel

Directions: Discuss what a volcano is. Explain what causes a volcano and its dangers. Explain what lava is. Have the children guess how the lava might flow in a volcano. Place a large pile of sand in the water table. In the center of the pile, place the tall glass bottle filled with two tablespoons of baking soda. Pile the sand up to the edge of the opening of the bottle. Add a few drops of red food coloring to the baking soda. Finally, add the vinegar to the bottle with the aid of a funnel. As the flow begins, remind the children to watch the path of the lava. Have the children guess why the lava chose the path it did.

Extension: Find a piece of hardened lava rock to show the class. Compare it to other rocks focussing primarily on weight and texture.

• •

The Modern Rock Museum

Objective: To identify various types of rocks

Materials: lava, sand, shells, bedrock, stones, fossels

Directions: Have the children bring various types of rock from home. Discuss what a rock is and why it has the characteristics that it does. Tell the children that they are going to make a rock museum for the rocks at school. Show the children how to label the rocks and place them on display.

• •

Under the Earth's Crust

Objective: To examine the earth's interior

Directions: See if construction workers are digging in your area and watch the hole they are digging grow. Maybe the construction worker will strike rock. Discuss the different levels and components of the Earth's crust.

Science Review Match

Objective: To match items

Materials: pencil, copies of the activity sheet below

Directions: Review the concept of matching with the children. Give each child a copy of the activity review sheet below. Instruct the child to match the first item in each row with an item that belongs together.

Name_____

Find a match for the first item in each row. Circle the match.

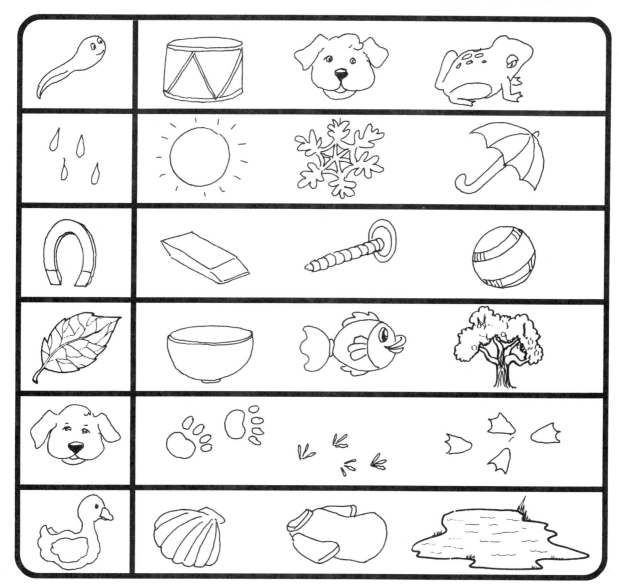

Animal Homes Bulletin Board

Objective: To create a bulletin board that teaches different animals and the homes they live in

Materials: patterns below and on page 283, stapler, yarn, construction paper and decorative paper

Directions: Cover a bulletin board with a decorative paper. Title the bulletin board "Home Sweet Home." Enlarge and copy the patterns below. Cut the patterns out of construction paper. Staple the animals and their homes anywhere on the bulletin board. With the children's help, staple a length of yarn between each animal and its home. Talk about other animals and their homes.

Animal Homes Patterns

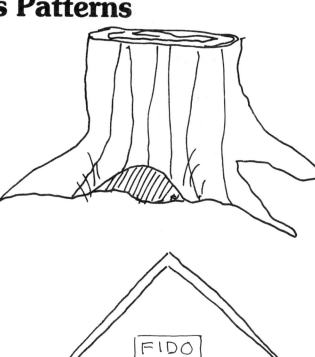

FIDO

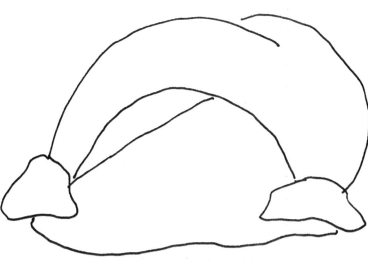

Animal Coverings Bulletin Board

Animal Coverings

Objectives: To serve as an animal coverings teaching aid and to decorate the classroom

Materials: animal patterns below and on page 285, fabric fur, a feather, skin-colored felt, sequins fabric, a shell, push pins, stapler, marker, yardstick, yarn

Directions: Cover a bulletin board with a solid color of paper. Divide the bulletin board into six columns using a marker and yardstick. Along the top of the columns, attach a feather, a piece of fabric fur, a square of skin-colored felt, some yarn, a square of sequins fabric and a shell. (See illustration above.) Have the children color the animal patterns and cut them out. Have the children help you determine the type of body covering each animal has and staple the animal in the correct column. This bulletin board display complements the Animal Coverings activity on page 245. Title the bulletin board "Animal Coverings." Label each column as shown above.

Animal Patterns

Social Studies

Social studies for kindergartners consists of learning about the environments in which they live and how they should live in these environments. The activities presented in this chapter deal with the children, the classroom environment, the family and the extended community.

The activities dealing with the children in this book help them discover things about themselves. They learn how to take care of themselves (personal hygiene), they learn about manners, and they learn about personal safety. Self-esteem is also a big emphasis in this chapter.

In the classroom environment, the children are encouraged to care about one another, share with each other and play fair. The activities teach the children to interact with and be kind to each other and to share cleaning responsibilities.

The family is also an area of importance in this chapter. Activities relating to this topic incorporate the building of communication between family members, encourage respect for family and encourage appreciation for the environment in which one lives.

The extended community of a child is the community in which he/she lives every day. Activities relating to community helpers, signs in the community, recycling and conserving to protect the environment and transportation in the community are also prominent in this chapter.

The main goals of this chapter are to teach children to cooperate and to get to know one another and to respect the environment.

All About My Family

Objective: To create a mini-book about family

Materials: construction paper, markers, crayons, stapler, copies of the page pattern below

Directions: Tell the children that you would like them to make a miniature book about their family. To do so, give each child enough copies of the page below so that each child has one page per family member plus one more. Tell the children to draw the members in their family - one per page. On the extra page, encourage the children to draw whatever they wish (e.g. a family activity, a pet, a special family event, etc.). The children should then fold the pages on the dotted lines, add a cover and staple them together.

Castle Living

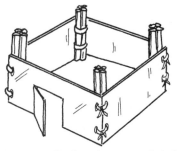

Objective: To create a child's fantasy home

Materials: carpet tubes, rope, a refrigerator box, scissors

Directions: Collect carpet tubes from a local carpet dealer. To make the corners for the castle, tie six four-foot long tubes together forming a large pillar. Stand the four corner pillars upright in a square formation. Cut up a refrigerator box to make the side walls for the castle. Cut a door out of the front wall. To attach the pillars to the walls, punch holes along the connecting edges of the walls. (See illustration.) Thread a rope from the back of the pillar to the front of the castle via the wall holes. Let the children decorate their home as they wish.

Home Sweet Home

Objective: To recognize different living environments

Materials: activity sheet below, crayons

Directions: Discuss the different kinds of homes people live in. Give each child a copy of the activity sheet below. Next to each type of home, ask the children to draw a picture of a person who might live there.

Next to each home, draw a picture of a person who might live there.

What's in a Name?

Objective: To build self-esteem

Materials: adhesive name tags, markers

Directions: Discuss with the children the significance of names. Discuss why parents choose the names they do. Some children might know the meaning of their names or the significance of the reason their name was chosen. Explain that names are sometimes hereditary, sometimes chosen for their meaning, sometimes chosen because of their relationship to someone else by the same name, etc. If the children do not know why they were given their particular name, have them ask their parents why they chose the name they did. Give the children a name tag and let them pick a wacky name for themselves for the day. There does not have to be any significance in their choice. Have the children wear their name tags throughout the day so that everyone can call them by their new names. Don't forget to pick a name for yourself!

Cover the Cough and Snuff the Sneeze

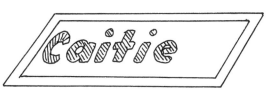

Objective: To develop good personal hygiene habits

Materials: tissues

Directions: Discuss personal hygiene with the children. During flu season, talk to the children about covering their mouths and noses when sneezing and coughing. Explain that this can be done using a tissue. Or, if none are available, tell the children to use their forearms to stop the spread of germs. Many people think that using their hand is effective. It is until they touch someone or something and spread the germs. Always promote frequent hand washing. Have the school nurse demonstrate effective hand washing.

289

Healthy Teeth

Objective: To reinforce dental health habits

Materials: *Dr. De Soto* by William Steig

Directions: Read the story *Dr. De Soto.* Have the children discuss what dental problem the sly fox had and what might have caused his bad toothache. Talk about the effect the following things have on teeth: eating too much sugar, brushing regularly, flossing regularly, drinking milk and eating vegetables, going to the dentist two times a year, biting on hard objects.

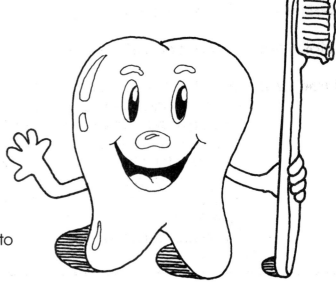

Extension: Have the school nurse come to your class and give a demonstration on brushing teeth properly. Encourage the children to talk to their parents about dental health.

No Baths?

Objective: To discuss personal hygiene

Materials: *Mortimer Mooner Stopped Taking a Bath!* by Frank B. Edwards and John Bianchi, chart paper, markers

Directions: As children acquire new self-help skills and independence, they also forget some important basic personal hygiene principles. As a reminder, read *Mortimer Mooner Stopped Taking a Bath!* In the story, Mortimer forgets to do a chore each day of the week. Have the children help you chart the things Mortimer forgot to do each day of the week. Discuss why it is important to put clean clothes on, clean your room, wash your hands, comb your hair, brush your teeth and take a bath.

Monday	
Tuesday	
Wednesday	
Thursday	
Friday	
Saturday	
Sunday	

Caring for Each Other

Objective: To learn to enjoy caring for others

Materials: *The Rainbow Fish* by Marcus Pfister

Directions: Read *The Rainbow Fish* by Marcus Pfister. Have the children reflect on the story. Ask what made the fish happy in the end and why the fish was so unhappy in the beginning. Talk about what it means to be beautiful on the inside as well as the outside. Have the children think of ways they could share themselves and care for others. Ask for volunteers to share their idea. Then, ask each child to turn to the person sitting behind him/her and give him/her an honest compliment. Ask them how it felt to give a compliment to someone. Then, have them think of someone they would like to care for. Tell the children to use the space below to write a note or draw a picture for someone they want to care for.

- -

Use the space below to write a note or draw a picture for someone you want to care for.

The Room Lived In By Pigs

Objective: To promote personal cleanliness

Materials: *Jillian Jiggs*, by Phoebe Gilman, *Just a Mess*, by Mercer Mayer, copies of the chart below

Directions: Have the children talk about how clean or messy they keep their rooms. Ask them how their parents feel about the cleanliness of their rooms. Ask who picks up the children's toys, games, clothes, etc. Ask the children if they think that they could be more helpful at home. Read *Just a Mess* and *Jillian Jiggs*. Talk about the problems and solutions given in each story. Tell the children that you have decided to give them a chance to prove that they can be helpful. Give each child a copy of the graph below. At the end of one week, ask the children to return their graphs. Have a reward planned for those members who participated.

- -

Participation Project

Dear Parent(s),
Please help your child keep a record of the activities that he/she participated in this week.

Activity	Sun.	Mon.	Tues.	Wed.	Thurs.	Fri.	Sat.
made the bed							
put clothes away							
brought dishes to counter							
fed family pet							

Please sign and return this to school with your child. Thank you for your participation too!
Signed _____

Manners, Manners, Everywhere

Objective: To reinforce manners in different areas

Directions: Discuss the following situations in which manners are needed. Have the children interact with you on these manners. Eventually, do role-playing to see if the children are fully comprehending the material.

1. Answering the phone:

☎ Remember to answer the phone saying, "Hello, _____ (insert child's name) speaking."
☎ Remember to ask, "May I ask who is calling please?"
☎ If the person being requested is not there, ask if you can take a message.
☎ Remember to never give your address to a stranger or volunteer who is home with you. Get an adult to help you if the person on the phone is asking improper questions.

2. At the dinner table:

☺ Remember to keep your mouth closed while chewing.
☺ Use your silverware for eating, not your hands.
☺ Remember to use "please" and "thank you" when asking for food to be passed.

3. In the classroom:

☺ Raise your hand if you want to speak or ask a question.
☺ Listen when someone speaks.
☺ Clean up after yourself.

4. When giving or receiving gifts:

☺ Remember to write a thank you note for every gift you receive.
☺ Pick a gift that the person receiving would like, not necessarily a gift you would like.

5. Standing in line:

☺ Remember to not push.
☺ Remember to go to the end of the line and wait your turn.
☺ Remember to say "excuse me" if you bump someone.

Feelings

Objective: To dicuss the realm of human emotions

Materials: *Feelings* by Joanne Brisson Murphy, hand-held mirrors

Directions: Read *Feelings* by Joanne Brisson Murphy. Discuss what causes people to feel different emotions. Have the children draw different emotions on the circles below. Provide hand-held mirrors for the children. Have them express an emotion into the mirror and look at the lines in their face. Ask them to consider the differences in their eyes and mouth during different expressions.

- -

Expressions

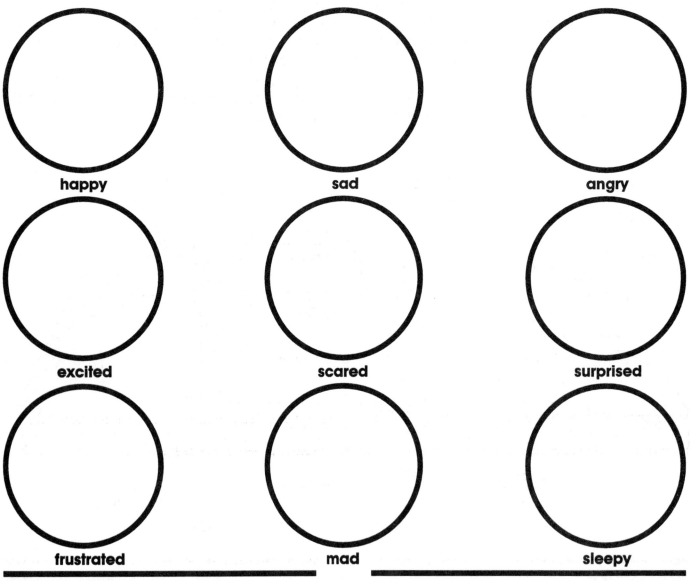

happy   sad   angry

excited   scared   surprised

frustrated   mad   sleepy

Neighborhood Diorama

Objective: To build a neighborhood diorama including buildings and people

Materials: small milk cartons, oatmeal cartons, shoe boxes, craft sticks, toothpicks, scissors, paint, paintbrushes, glue, large Styrofoam sheet, green felt, gray construction paper, craft moss, markers

Directions: Discuss what a community entails. Let the children name the types of buildings they know and the kinds of community helpers that live and work in the buildings. Tell the children that they are going to make a diorama (miniature model) of a community. Ask them to bring in small empty boxes that could be used for buildings in the diorama. Cover a large table with a thin sheet of Styrofoam. Cover the Styrofoam with a sheet of green felt. Cut strips of gray construction paper which the children can glue together to form roads. To make trees and bushes, use craft moss glued to craft sticks. Let the children plant the bushes and trees by poking them into the Styrofoam. Let the children begin constructing buildings out of their boxes. Help them title the buildings once they are painted. Remember to include a fire station, police department, library, grocery store, school, hospital, bank, etc. Have the children place the buildings in the diorama. Next, have the children make community helpers out of craft sticks glued together. Once they have colored them, let the children place the community helpers near the buildings in which they work or play. Let the children play with the display during their freetime.

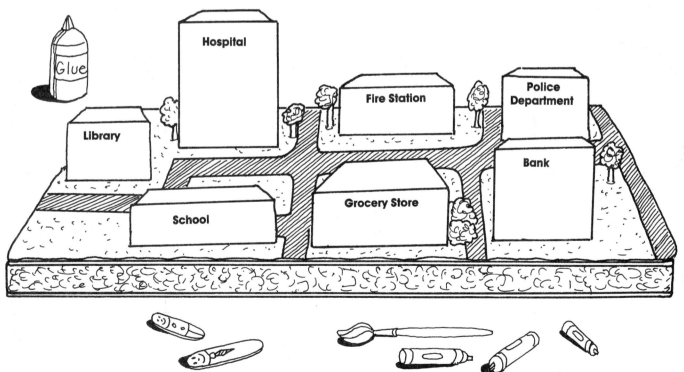

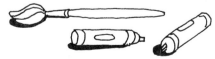

Nature in Our Neighborhood

Objective: To find and label different leaves of trees in the neighborhood

Materials: leaf guide below, a leaf guide book, tape, 3" x 12" strips of posterboard, markers, petroleum jelly

Directions: Take the children for a walk through the neighborhood. Have them specifically look for leaves. They should collect and bring their leaves back to class with them. Give each student a copy of the bottom half of this page and have the children use it as a guide to identify their leaves. If the children cannot find their leaves on the leaf guide below, help them to try and find them in the leaf guide book. Next, they should tape and label their leaves to a strip of posterboard. Let the children cover the leaves with petroleum jelly for longer preservation.

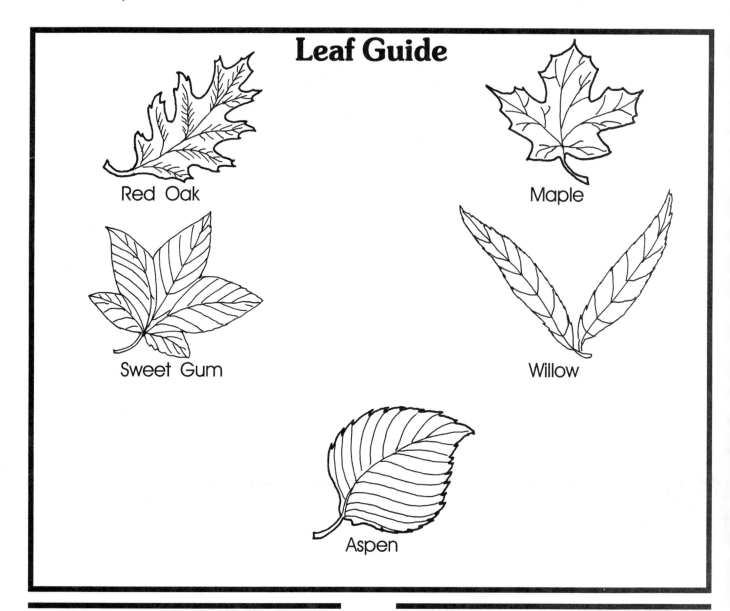

Leaf Guide

Red Oak

Maple

Sweet Gum

Willow

Aspen

Emergency Numbers

Objectives: To teach the children the emergency numbers they need to know and the proper use of them

Materials: worksheet below, markers

Directions: Discuss what an emergency number is. It it likely that all the children are familiar with 911. Talk about the only times to use this number and why. Tell the children that the other emergency number they must know is their home phone number. Discuss when and why this number is so important. It is also advisable to know a parent's work number. Give each child a copy of the telephone below. Have them fill in the emergency numbers they need. Encourage the parents to help their child memorize their address and the emergency phone numbers discussed.

Emergency Numbers

Fill in the emergency numbers below and hang it next to your phone.

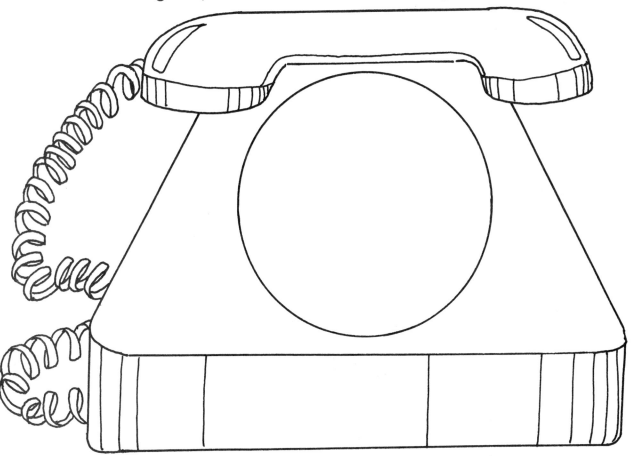

Community Helpers

Objective: To recognize the people in the community by what they do

Materials: paper doll pattern on page 299, scissors, newsprint, glue, markers, string, pictures of community helpers

Directions: Discuss what community helpers are and how they affect our lives. Show the children pictures of community helpers. Include firefighters, police officers, nurses, doctors, musicians, construction workers, bakers, dancers, garbage collectors, teachers and farmers. Ask the children to share what their parents might do for the community. Give each child two paper doll patterns. Explain how one pattern will be the front of the community helper and one side the back of the community helper. Have the children decide on a favorite community helper and draw in the details using markers. Have the children cut out the patterns. Have the children tear newsprint into small pieces. Next they lay their community helper marker side down. Tell them to place some torn newsprint on top of the cutout and help the children run a bead of glue around the edge of the cutout. Put the two uncolored sides of the cutout together. Pinch around the edges of the cutout and let dry for a few minutes. Tape a string to the top of the cutout and hang the community helpers around the room. Follow the visual directions below.

1.

2.

3.

4.

5.

6.

Community Helper Patterns

Color the front and back of a favorite community helper. Cut along the dashed line.

Communicating in Sign

Objective: To learn to communicate with others using American Sign Language

Directions: Using the chart below, teach the children some basic American Sign Language. Explain to the children that this is a language for the deaf community.
Tell them that when you are unable to speak or hear, sign language is a way to communicate.

Night

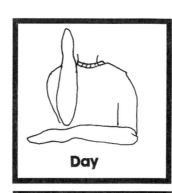

Day

Boy

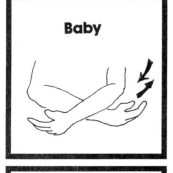

Baby

Sun

Children

Girl

I love You

Play

Friend

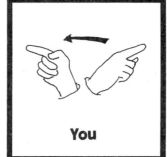

You

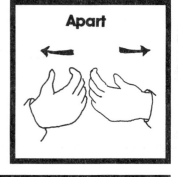

Apart

Pick a Park!

Objective: To care for the community by picking up trash in a local park

Materials: large paper trash bags, copies of the award below, extra adult supervision

Directions: Tell the children that they are going to be taking charge for creating a "litter-free zone." Give each child a paper bag to use to collect trash. Tell the children to be garbage detectives and look under benches, around trees and bushes, in fenced areas, etc. Place the paper bags of garbage in nearby receptacles. When you return to the school, discuss the job the children completed and give each participant a certificate for his/her efforts in caring for the environment.

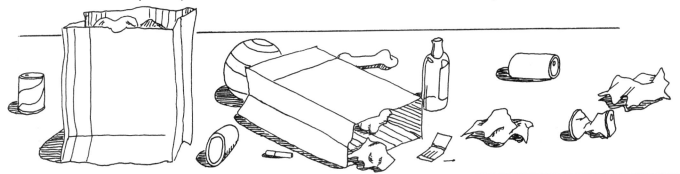

COMMUNITY HELPER AWARD
This is to certify
that

on _____
(Date)

_____
(Name of Participant)

**took responsibility and cared for the community
by making it a litter-free zone!**

Air Pollution Problems

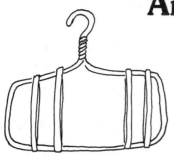

Objectives: To make the children aware of pollution problems and promote care and concern for the environment

Materials: 8 natural rubber bands, 2 wire clothes hangers, plastic bag

Directions: Tell the children that they are going to be experimenting with the pollution in the air. Follow the steps below to complete the experiment.

1. Bend two clothes hangers and stretch four rubber bands over the hanger.

2. Hook one hanger up in the shade outdoors. Place the other in a plastic bag and put it in a drawer.

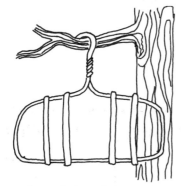

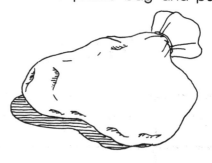

3. Seven days later, have the children examine the rubber bands on the hanger outside.

4. Compare the rubber bands that were outdoors to the rubber bands that were indoors.

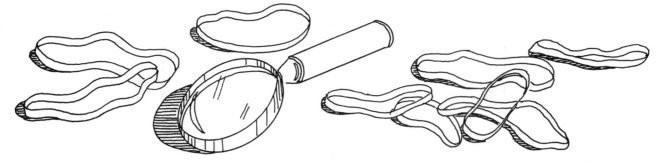

Discovery: Depending on where you live, the results will be different. The children living in smoggy areas will notice very quickly that the rubber bands left outdoors became cracked, and eventually they would break. Those children living in a clean air environment will notice that it takes much longer than a week to crack the rubber bands.

Solutions: Explain to the children that even though it is very difficult to see pollution, we know it is in our air and that it is our responsibility to take care of the Earth. Talk about ways to clean the air. Include ideas like car-pooling, using different products, saving trees, etc.

Transportation Systems

Objective: To determine whether a mode of transportation operates on ground, underground, above ground or on water

Materials: magazines, scissors, glue, chart paper, markers

Directions: Prepare a chart resembling the one below. Talk about different modes of transportation and categorize them into on ground, underground, above ground and on water. Have the children cut out pictures of the different modes of transportation from magazines. Have them glue the modes under the correct category on the chart. Have them draw additional modes of transportation on the chart if they can think of modes that were not cut out.

Transportation Chart

On Ground	Underground	Above Ground	On Water

Extension: If possible, arrange for a local field trip to explore the modes of transportation around the school. Depending on where your school is located, you could take a trip by bus, train, subway, streetcar, boat or monorail. Call your Chamber of Commerce for more information about the public transit forms of transportation near your school.

Vehicle Safety

Objective: To reinforce vehicle safety

Materials: grocery size box per child, 4 paper bowls per child, paint, string, scissors, street signs, brads, tempera paint, large paintbrushes

Directions: Ask each child to bring a grocery size box from home. Tell the children they are going to be making their own vehicle and practicing safety rules. Follow the directions below to make the vehicle.

1. Remove all the flaps from the box and have each child paint his/her box frame.

2. Attach two bowls onto two opposite sides of the box. Use a brad to attach the bottom of the bowls to the box.

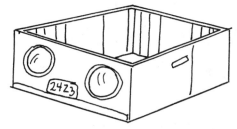

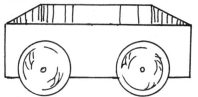

3. Using scissors, help the children poke a hole on opposite sides of the box. Knot a string through the holes as illustrated. This will be the harness to carry the vehicle.

4. Have the children try their vehicles.

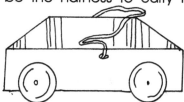

Place some street signs around the classroom. Before moving their vehicles, have the children buckle their imaginary seat belts while singing, *Buckle Your Seat Belt* to the tune of "Fréres Jacques."

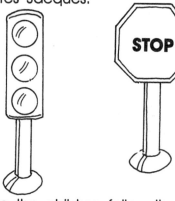

Buckle your seat belt,
Buckle your seat belt,
In your car,
In your car,
We care for your safety,
We care for your safety,
Please take care,
Please take care.

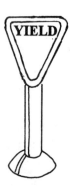

Have the children follow the leader around the room stopping at stop signs, yield signs, crosswalks and streetlights. Tell the children to pretend that children and animals are crossing the street in front of them. Ask the children to solve other problems along the route. Have the children park their vehicles and return to group time for further discussion of safety rules.

The Bus Ride

Objective: To imagine being on a bus with animal friends

Materials: Bill Martin Jr.'s *The Bus Ride*, an empty refrigerator box, chairs, paint, paintbrushes, markers, tongue depressors, scissors, paper plates, knife

Directions: Obtain an empty refrigerator box and transform it into a bus. Paint it yellow and cut a door in the side. Add bus features like headlights, license plates, a black strip along the side, etc. Set chairs behind the box so that the children can "sit" in the "bus."

Read Bill Martin Jr.'s story, *The Bus Ride*, and have the children make masks of the characters in the story. A mask can be made from a paper plate with a tongue depressor handle. The children should add features using various scraps from art supplies. Then, read the story again and have the children wear their masks to act out the story as you read it.

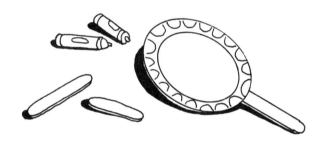

If I Could, I Would Be...

Objective: To imagine what it would be like to be a certain vehicle

Materials: drawing paper, chalk, hair spray

Directions: Have the children describe what type of vehicle they would be if they could be a vehicle. Ask them to think about where they would travel (air, road, sand, water, grass). Have them think of a name for themselves and how many travelers they could seat. Let the children illustrate their vehicles using chalk on drawing paper. Write their descriptions on their drawings. Spray the pages with hair spray to keep the chalk from smearing.

Farmyard Friends

Objective: To visit a farm in the spring and see all the new animals

Materials: proper dress, snacks for the animals and children, first aid kit, permission slips, extra adult supervision, copies of activity page 307

Directions: To locate a farm near your school, check the yellow pages under farms or contact your local 4-H Club. Call your local establishment and tell them that you would like to bring a group of children to visit their farm in the spring. Most farmers are excited about showing the new animals to people. Have the children get permission slips filled out before the trip. Prepare the children for the visit by singing songs and reading books about animals. Remind the children to wear jeans and rubber boots and soft shirts for the animals to rub against. Also, encourage the children to bring along a snack for the animals as well as themselves. Apples, carrots and granola are great snacks to feed the animals. Remind the children to ask the farmer which animals they may hold and feed and which they should not.

Once at the farm, have the children compare the softness of the lambs' coats to their mothers' coat. They could also feel how soft the baby ducks are. Have the children guess the age of the young animals. Ask the farmer to check their answers. Talk about the names of the baby animals versus the adult animals (e.g. calf vs. cow, colt/foal vs. horse, kid vs. goat).

Back at school, have the children fill out activity page 307. Encourage the children to show their parents their work and to tell them all about the animal babies they saw on their trip to the farm.

Baby Farm Animal Worksheet

Match the baby animal to its mother.

Goat

Lamb

Kid

Hen

Calf

Horse

Colt/Foal

Pig

Chick

Cow

Piglet

Sheep

Treasure Map

Objective: To teach the children introductory mapping skills

Materials: drawing paper, markers

Directions: Give the children drawing paper and have them design their own treasure map. Tell them to include things like mountain ranges, rivers, bridges, canyons, trees, etc. Have the children indicate, using arrows, exactly how to get to the hidden treasure. Tell them to be creative! (Note: You could draw a treasure map on the board together so that the children know exactly what to do.)

Which Way Boss?

> You may take three steps to the right!

Objective: To develop direction senses

Materials: large playing field

Directions: Choose one child to be the "Boss." The "Boss" should stand in one spot while providing navigation to the remainder of the class. The "Boss" must give a destination to the class. The class must call out, "Which way Boss?" before making any move towards the destination. The "Boss" may call out any set of directions and the class must follow them (e.g. "You may take three steps to your left!" or "You may run straight ahead for three seconds!"). The first child to reach the destination while following the correct set of directions is the winner and may assume the "Boss" position for the next round.

Map Reading Egg Hunt

Objective: To develop map reading skills

Materials: maps, plastic eggs

Directions: Before class, hide several plastic eggs around the school playground or classroom. Draw several maps to indicate the location of the eggs. Divide the class into small groups and give each group a map to follow. See which group can find its egg first.

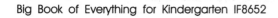

The Full Pollution Circle

Objective: To promote keeping our environment clean

Materials: celery stalk, food coloring, water, plastic cup

Directions: Talk to the children about pollution, how water gets polluted and where the pollution goes. Explain how we pollute ourselves when we eat plants and animals who have been nourishing themselves with polluted water from the ground. To demonstrate how this all takes place, put a celery stalk (bottom end cut off) into a cup with water. Place a few drops of food coloring into the water. Explain to the children how the food coloring is like pollution. Watch as the celery turns colors within a few hours. Talk to the children about ways to prevent water pollution.

School Compost

Objective: To promote keeping the environment clean

Materials: apple core, lettuce, Styrofoam cup, plastic bag, shovel, garbage can

Directions: Define the word "biodegradable" for the children. Discuss what things are and what things are not biodegradable. Explain that all biodegrable products break down and go back to the Earth. With the school's permission, find a spot in the back of the school yard where it is okay to dig a few holes. Dig four holes. Bury an apple core, piece of lettuce, Styrofoam cup and plastic bag. Cover the holes with dirt. Mark the spots where the items are burried. Wait a month and dig the items up. Have the children explain where the apple and lettuce went. Discuss why buying things that are packaged in biodegradable wrappings is better for the environment. If the school will okay it, have a separate garbage can in the classroom designated to contain only biodegradable waste. Start a school compost if city and state regulations allow it.

Extension: Consider contacting *The Natural Resources Defense Council* for environmental preservation activities to participate in. This particular group is starting a kid's environmental organization. Contact The Natural Resources Defense Council at 40 West 20th Street, New York, NY 10011.

Paper Making Magic

Objective: To promote recycling of classroom products

Materials: newspaper, blender, water, 3" deep square pan, window screen that fits inside of the square pan, measuring cup, flat piece of plywood the size of the newspaper, crayons

Directions: Talk to the children about recycling. Discuss how much paper is being used in schools every day. Think about how many trees are needed for the production of paper. Tell the children that they can recycle their own paper by following the directions below.

Have the children tear two and one half sheets of newspaper into tiny pieces. Then, have them place the pieces into the blender. Let them cover the blender once they have added five cups of water. Switch the blender on for a few seconds or until the paper has turned to pulp. Let one child place one inch of water and a screen on the bottom of the square pan. Then, have a child spread one cup of the blended pulp over the screen. Have a child lift the screen and let the water drain. Spread a newspaper sheet open. Place the screen with the pulp into the newspaper. Carefully flip the newspaper section over so that the screen is on the *top* of the pulp. Place the plywood on the top of the newspaper. Open the newspaper and take out the screen leaving the paper open. Let the pulp dry for at least twenty-four hours. When it is completely dry, carefully peel it off the newspaper. Give the children their recycled paper to draw on! See the visual directions below for extra help.

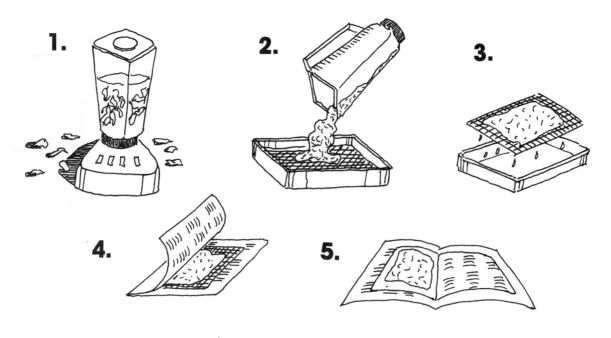

1.
2.
3.
4.
5.

Helpful or Hurtful?

Objective: To review environmental preservation idea

Materials: one copy of the activity sheet below per child, pencil

Directions: Review the ways that people can help protect the environment. Give each child a copy of the activity sheet below. Instruct the children to circle the items that are helpful to the environment. Discuss the activity sheet answers together.

• •

Things that Help the Environment

Circle the items that protect the environment. Color the picture.

Social Studies Review Match

Objective: To match items

Materials: pencil, copies of the activity sheet below

Directions: Review the concept of matching with the children. Give each child a copy of the activity review sheet below. Instruct the child to match the first item in each row with an item that belongs together.

- -

Name_____

Find a match for the first item in each row. Circle the match.

Baby, Have You Changed!
Bulletin Board

Objective: To recognize growth and development

Materials: baby photographs of each child, baby flannel fabric, stapler, push pins, *The Berenstain Bears' New Baby* by Stan and Jan Berenstain

Directions: Instruct each child to bring a baby photo of themselves to school. Be certain to put each child's name on the back of the photograph he/she brought to school. Cover a bulletin board with baby flannel fabric. Pin all the baby pictures to the bulletin board and have the children guess who the babies are. Read *The Berenstain Bears' New Baby* by Stan and Jan Berenstain. Discuss how babies lift their heads, then they learn to roll, sit up, crawl, walk and run. They learn this all in about one year. Talk about jealousy of new babies in the house. Discuss the roles of a big brother or sister. Title the bulletin board, "Look How We Have Grown!"

City/Country Bulletin Board

Objectives: To enhance the environment and reinforce differences between city and country life

Materials: construction paper, your own drawing of a city and country landscape on butcher paper, stapler, yarn, scissors, patterns below and on page 315, markers, chalk or paint for murals

Directions: Cover a bulletin board with a solid color of paper. Cover the top third of the bulletin board with a mural of a country landscape drawn on butcher paper. Cover the bottom third of the bulletin board with a mural of a city landscape drawn on butcher paper. Cut out the patterns below and on page 315. Color them and staple them to the middle section of the bulletin board. Have the children tell you which patterns belong in the city and which belong in the country. Staple a strand of yarn from the cutout to the landscape to which it belongs.

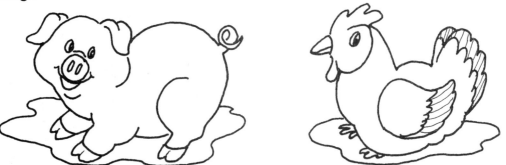

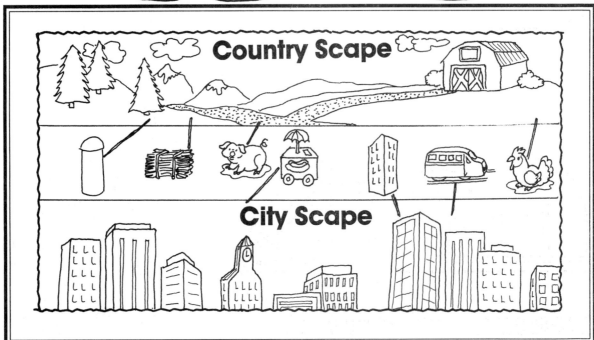

City/Country Patterns

Pet Projects Bulletin Board

Objective: To reinforce responsibility for pets

Materials: photographs of the children's pets, patterns on page 317, construction paper, scissors, stapler, decorative paper

Directions: Have the children bring pictures of their pets or pets they would like to have. Have each child introduce his/her pet to the class. Talk about what it means to care for the pets in our community. Be sure to cover feeding, exercising, loving and playing with pets. Cover a bulletin board with a decorative paper. Staple construction paper squares to various points on the bulletin board. Tape a photograph of a child's pet on each construction paper square. Write the pet's name on the construction paper above the photograph. Title the bulletin board, "Caring for Our Pets." Around the border of the bulletin board, cut out and staple colored copies of the patterns below and on page 317.

SOCIAL STUDIES

Pet Project Patterns

Share the Work Bulletin Board

Objectives: To provide the children with information regarding their personal responsibilities and to brighten up the classroom

Materials: 4 letter envelopes, colorful wrapping paper, push pins, construction paper, posterboard, markers, stapler, index cards

Directions: Cut two-inch strips of posterboard and write a child's name on each strip. Cover a third of the bulletin board with colorful wrapping paper. The remaining two-thirds of the bulletin board can be covered in the paper color of your choice. Pin four envelopes in a row going down the wrapping paper portion of the bulletin board. Staple four, one-inch strips of construction paper to the other side of the bulletin board. Staple the strips as shown below but remember to keep the staples close to the bottom of the strip to create a holder for the posterboard name tags. Tell the children that when they see their name on the bulletin board, they must check the envelope beside their name for the classroom job they must do for the week. Have index cards with classroom jobs printed on them stuffed into the envelopes. Remember to leave the names of the children displayed for a week at a time.

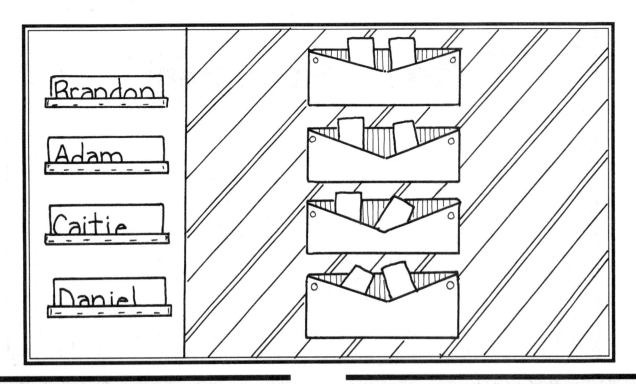

Setting the Table Bulletin Board

Objectives: To reinforce table manners and etiquette while creating an eye-pleasing environment

Materials: construction paper, scissors, colorful fabric, patterns below and on page 320, stapler

Directions: Enlarge the patterns below and on page 320 on construction paper and cut them out. Cover a bulletin board with a solid color paper. Title the bulletin board, "Proper Placement." Cut a large place mat shape out of fabric. Staple the place mat to the center of the bulletin board. Staple the eating utensils, plate, napkin, glass and cup in the proper placement as illustrated below.

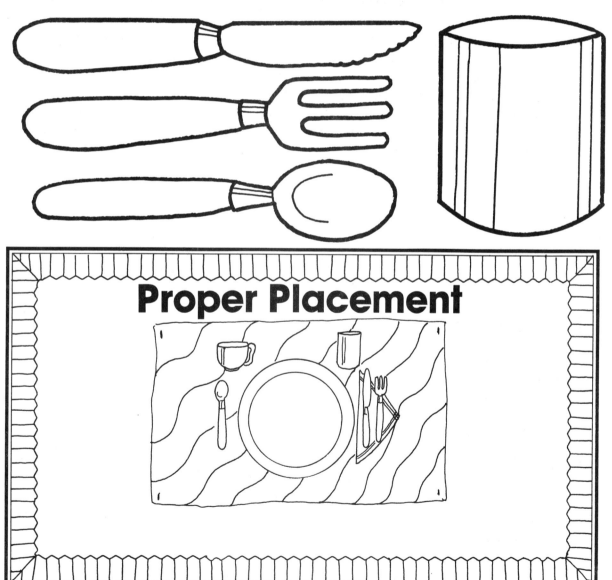

Proper Placement

Table Setting Patterns